CURes, HOORs AND FLOATING VOTeRs

THe MAURice HickeY DiARies

VOLUMe II

PAT SHORTT started in comedy when he left art college. With Jon Kenny he created D'Unbelievables, Ireland's most popular comedy duo. Together they performed their unique and critically-acclaimed brand of comedy in theatres all over Ireland, the UK and the US as well as various countries across Europe. As a solo artist Pat's one-man shows, including 'Pat Shortt Live' and 'You Won't Get Away With That Here', were very popular and his work hailed as 'comic genius' by *The Irish Times*.

An actor of note, Pat has appeared in many plays and films, most recently in the lead role of Josie in the movie *Garage*, directed by Lenny Abrahamson and written by Mark O'Halloran, which was awarded the CICAE Art and Essai Cinema Prize at the Cannes Film Festival. In recognition of his work in *Garage*, Pat was awarded an IFTA at the 5th Annual Irish Film & Television Awards, Best Actor in a Lead Role Film 2008. He also took the award for best actor at the prestigious Monte Carlo comedy film festival in Monaco. An Post issued a series of four stamps paying homage to the creativity of films recently produced in Ireland; Pat features on an 82c denomination stamp in his role in *Garage*. An accomplished musician also, Pat has recorded with many bands and toured extensively in the US with The Saw Doctors. In 2006 he scored a big hit in Ireland with the song 'The Jumbo Breakfast Roll' under the guise of showband singer Dicksie Walsh. Pat's television credits include Tom in *Father Ted* (Channel 4), and Bobby in *The Fitz* (BBC). Pat can currently be seen in the popular television show *Killinascully*. This successful series features Pat in a variety of roles, and was created by him for RTÉ. The first volume of the Maurice Hickey Diaries, *I Will in Me Politics*, is also published by The O'Brien Press.

JIM O'BRIEN is a freelance writer based in Rosenallis, County Laois. He has worked with Pat Shortt on both volumes of the Maurice Hickey Diaries: *I Will in Me Politics* and *Cures, Hoors & Floating Voters*. Jim was formerly a journalist with the *Irish Farmer's Journal*. He and Pat have known each other since college days and have collaborated on a number of ventures including the first series of *Killinascully* and scripts for Pat's stage shows.

CURes, HOORs AND FLOATING VOTeRs

THe MAURice HickeY DiaRies

VOLUMe II

PAt SHORTT

THE O'BRIEN PRESS
DUBLIN

First published in this form in 2008 by The O'Brien Press Ltd,
12 Terenure Road East, Rathgar, Dublin 6, Ireland.
Tel: +353 1 4923333; Fax: +353 1 4922777
E-mail: books@obrien.ie
Website: www.obrien.ie

Cures, Hoors and Floating Voters is based on columns which
have appeared weekly in the *Irish Farmer's Journal* under the
authorship of Councillor Maurice Hickey.

ISBN: 978-1-84717-117-7

Text written in consultation with Jim O'Brien 2008.

British Library Cataloguing-in-Publication Data
Shortt, Pat
Cures, hoors and floating voters. - (The Maurice Hickey diaries ; v. 2)
1. City council members - Fiction 2. Diary fiction
3. Humorous stories
I. Title II. O'Brien, Jim
823.9'2[F]

Front cover photograph and internal photographs of Councillor Maurice Hickey ©
Great Graphics, Cork.

1 2 3 4 5 6 7 8 9 10
08 09 10 11 12 13

Printed and bound in the UK by CPI Group.

CONTENTS

I'M AT IT AGAIN

The second book is always difficult, especially for authors like myself whose first work was such a masterpiece. The Mother says the challenge for me is to make the second effort even worse than the first.

When she heard I was writin' a follow-up to *I Will in Me Politics* she threatened to sue if I as much as mentioned her in an unfavourable light. 'Well,' says I, 'if I can't mention you "warts and all" I won't mention you at all.' The prospect of bein' written out changed her tune completely; she knows well that bein' ignored is even worse than bein' gutted. She agreed to let me write what I wanted as long as she gets to see it before it's published. I gave in, but told her if she wants to make any changes she'll have to take it up directly with the publisher. The poor man doesn't know what he's in for.

Others in the locality have been as excited about the prospect of my return to print as a bunch of young bulls waitin' to have their male prowess squeezed into oblivion. Certain friends, neighbours and colleagues have barely spoken to me since the first book hit the shelves while it has taken others months to thaw out. I'm afraid there could be a return to a general freeze if they read this latest offerin'.

When my publisher asked me to put pen to paper again, he suggested that I send him 'an outline of the theme, structure and focus of the book'; he might as well have asked me to describe Einstein's theory of relativity. I told him that, like my life, the book will have as much theme, structure and focus as the last frantic moments of a headless chicken; from one page to the next you never know what's goin' to happen. And that's the story of my life; every day I get up I have no idea what the day will bring, I'd probably stay in bed if I did.

This second book deals with my everyday life as county councillor, dutiful son, confirmed bachelor and regular at my local licensed premises, it also covers what my friend and driver, Manus, describes as 'a most significant and eventful period' in my life – my election to the office of Mayor, or Chairman of the County Council. This was a great honour for me and the Mother and I couldn't believe my luck the day it happened. It added a whole new concept to my career in public life – the concept of work. I had to turn up at everythin' I promised to turn up at, I had to be presentable, sober and on time. The effort to do that much was enough to kill me.

When the news of my attainment of high office reached Killdicken there was a mixed reaction. My kitchen cabinet comprisin' Messrs Cantwell, Cantillon, Quirke and Tom Walshe the publican were slow out of the congratulations traps, but were fierce quick to occupy the commentary box. Pa Cantillon said I'd need a brain transplant to cope with the demands of the office, while Tom Cantwell suggested I need a brain implant since there is little evidence of any grey matter in the space between my ears. Pa Quirke, the postman grunted his congratulations and wondered if I could put a word in with the engineerin' section about a job for his civil engineer son. Tom Walshe wanted me to do somethin' about the scourge of random breath testin' on the Borrisnangoul Road.

The only one to say 'Well done, Maurice,' was Lilly Mac at the Post Office who told me she was very happy for my Mother's sake. 'At least the poor woman won't have to worry about you for the next few months,' she declared, 'you'll have to stay out of trouble as long as you have that chain of office around your neck.' With encouragement like that I couldn't go wrong.

Earlier I mentioned my friend and driver Manus. Manus is a new addition to my world, he's a son of a cousin of the Mother's and he came to give her a hand with the drivin' when I got the Mayor's job. He's a college boy who was useful for the bit of speech writin' and a great help when writin' the book. More about him later.

While my mayorality dominates the book, my dealin's with political rivals includin' that miserable lime-green hoor, Percy Pipplemoth Davis, and the 'Blueshirt Bombshell', Moll Gleeson, also feature prominently. Of course my ongoin' love-hate relationship with Breda Quinn (Superquinn) rumbles on like an ulcer that flares up regularly.

As for the title, *Cures, Hoors and Floating Voters* I think it perfectly sums up the expectations and preoccupations of an Irish county councillor. This unique political animal is expected to cure all things from potholes to piles, he has to deal with every awkward hoor that God ever put into skin and is constantly preoccupied with capturin' that most rare, valuable and elusive specimen of political prey, the floatin' voter.

A MOTHER'S LOVE IS A ...

Recently I decided to make a few soundin's about runnin' for the Dáil. I suppose most councillors have notions of becomin' a TD and hittin' the big time. In some cases this is what you might call genuine ambition but in others it could only be described as bullock's notions. As for myself, a huge amount of people have been advisin' me lately that I should think about havin' a go at Leinster House. I'd be tellin' ye lies if I said I'm not interested. You see, I'm becomin' fierce popular, no matter where I go people know me even though I don't know them or the sky over them.

A few months ago, Superquinn and myself talked about my national prospects. After a long night's discussion she concluded I should make a run for it, 'Sure why wouldn't you: aren't you as good a gobshite as any of them.' Not what one would call a ringin' endorsement!

Before things went any further I decided I'd have to broach the subject with the Mother. On Friday night after the *Late Late* I took the opportunity to tell her I was thinkin' about the big time. Typical of an Irish mother, her response could be interpreted in many ways: 'Well, if that's what you want to do,' says she, 'I suppose that's what you want to do.' It's the kind of thing a mother says when you tell her you've decided to walk backwards to the North Pole wearin' nothin' but swimmin' togs. I knew that wasn't the end of it.

The followin' mornin' I hadn't the top off my egg when she cleared her throat in preparation for an official announcement. 'I've been thinkin' about this TD thing,' she began, 'and I'm not too sure about it. First of all, there's the expense. You know what it costs to get yourself into the Council; to get into the Dáil you could multiply that by ten. Then there's transport. At the moment I'm cartin' you from pillar to post and, aside from the occasional excursion to Borrisnangoul, Shronefodda or Teerawadra, we only travel between Clonmel, Killdicken, Glengooley and Honetyne. I might be in the process of changin' the car but I have no notion of drivin' anythin' bigger than the one I have. You most certainly won't find me on the road to Dublin on a regular basis.'

She straightened herself in the chair for her closin' remarks. 'Finally,' says she, 'when considerin' your run for national politics I'm reminded of your capacity for makin' a total eejit of yourself. 'Tis bad enough to pick up the *Weekly Eyeopener* in fear and trepidation as to what they might be writin' about you and the gobshitery you got up to locally. 'Tis nearly as bad to turn on the radio and hear Willy De Wig Ryan makin' an ape out of you, but the prospect of findin' you plastered all over the national papers and on RTE day in and day out would be too much for me. You won't get any support from me unless I get guarantees that you'll keep your feet firmly on the ground and out of your mouth; that you'll stay away from the high stool and stop actin' like an overgrown adolescent, and you'll do somethin' about your appearance. Without these, you can count me out of your campaign.' Before I could open my mouth she grabbed her bag and left for Mass.

I sat for a while and pondered her words. She didn't exactly deliver what you'd call an upbeat assessment of my political career or its prospects. In terms of a school report it registered even lower than 'could do better'. 'Twas more like 'couldn't do much worse.'

There's no one like a mother to put you in your place. With the wind taken out of my political balloon I opened my notebook and turned my attention to the issues on the ground: potholes, pollution and plannin'. Leinster House will have to wait.

DEAF EARS

I'm gettin' worried about the planet. There's no doubt but we're doin' fierce damage. It seems the ice at the North Pole is meltin', the water levels are risin' and the whole place is gettin' hotter by the minute. I've been readin' a bit in the papers about it and I must say there is cause for concern.

In the council chamber, Percy Pipplemoth Davis takes all the limelight when it comes to lookin' after the earth and I'm half afraid to support the hoor in case he uses it against me. The one forum where it is possible to freely raise the topic is in my local: the Tom Walshe School of Advanced Philosophy and Unadulterated Scutter.

I don't know if you've put much thought into the patterns of pub conversation, but I have. I suppose if the thing has a pattern it is this: risin' levels of alcohol lead to a parallel rise in the levels of nonsense. Generally, conversations in licensed premises begin with remarks about the weather or the traffic. These introductory observations are followed by attempts to draw down a serious topic for the evening. Some attempts will flounder particularly if no one knows anythin' about the subject, although if a lot of drink has been taken ignorance is no barrier to in-depth discussion. What's an even greater conversation killer is when someone in the company knows too much about a particular thing. The fear that he'll bore the backside off everybody means the subject is carefully avoided.

Anyway, I was in Walshe's establishment for a couple of pints the other night and after much talk about the weather and prices I decided 'twas time to introduce my chosen topic for the evenin'. 'By God, lads,' says I, 'I think the planet is fecked entirely. We'll be flooded, roasted and frozen out of existence within a few generations.' My remarks were greeted with dead silence. I went for a re-launch, 'I was watchin' the telly the other

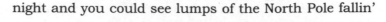

night and you could see lumps of the North Pole fallin' into the sea and poor misfortunes of polar bears fallin' along with them. An expert warned if we don't do somethin' soon 'twill be too late.' 'Too late for what?' asked Quirke, 'Sure polar bears are great swimmers. Do you want us to send them life jackets or something?'

'Listen, Maurice,' says Cantillon, 'What you're talkin' about is change. Things are changin' all the time. A few years ago the corncrake was disappearin', this year 'tis the polar bear next year 'twill be the one-eyed, three-legged Albanian cuckoo. There's always somethin' in danger of disappearin' off the face of the earth. The only thing that remains constant is the fact that there's always a prophet of doom to tell us we're all fecked.'

'True for you,' says Quirke. 'You've only to look around here and see that things are always disappearin'. Take the Cleary's of Budnanossal. There's not one of them left. There was three Cleary houses in that townland and there isn't a Cleary to be seen there now.' 'What happened them at all?' asked Tom Walshe. 'Ah sure,' says Cantillon, 'Auld Moss Cleary and Mag had no family and they left the place to her people, the Ryans of Shronefodda. They planted it. Then there was the Clipper Clearys. They built a new house in Cloontarva, the next townland. Finally there was Christy Cleary who drank two farms and ended up in the County Home. If I'm not mistaken, much of the proceeds from the sale of the two farms ended up in the till behind this particular counter.' An awkward silence descended on the company. A sudden fit of whistlin' and glass washin' came over Tom Walshe as he tried to cover his discomfort at the emergence of this last piece of hidden history.

Tom Cantwell, somewhat the worse for wear, broke the silence, 'So, lads,' says he, 'we've established that Walshe's porter was partly responsible for the disappearance of the Clearys, but the question remains: who is to blame for the disappearance of the polar bears?'

A COSTLY CURE

They say the cure can be worse than the complaint; never a truer word was spoken. I was lookin' forward to a few days' craic at the Ploughin' when I found myself smothered with a cold. My head felt as if 'twas packed with wet silage and the nose nearly melted off my face. All I wanted to do was crawl into the scratcher and hould on to my hot water bottle. I was prayin' I'd recover before the Ploughin'.

The common cold is a hoor of a thing and impossible to get rid of. I spent two days beside the fire dosin' myself with hot whiskey, lemon and pepper, honey and lemon and pepper, honey and lemon and pepper and cloves, honey and lemon and pepper and cloves and whiskey. I might as well have been drinkin' ditch water.

After nearly a week of confinement I ventured out as far as Pa Quirke's, just to get away from the house. As soon as he laid eyes on me Pa knew I wasn't a hundred per cent. 'Cripes, Maurice,' says he, 'if you don't do somethin' with that cold we'll be sendin' for Tinky Ryan and the measurin' tape.' 'Leave me alone,' says I, 'I've tried everythin' bar the guillotine to sort out this blasted thing. I'm fed up of it.' 'Sit down there,' says Quirke, 'I have the cure for you.' He went into the parlour and after rummagin' around for about five minutes he came back with a bottle of water. 'Don't tell me you're goin' to sprinkle me with Holy Water,' says I. 'No;' says he, 'this stuff is administered through the mouth.'

He put the kettle on and made me a tumbler of hot poteen laced with lemon and seasoned with a lump of crushed garlic. I had never tasted the likes of it in my life. It travelled through my innards like an active volcano; I was sure 'twas goin' to blow my head off. However, after the first sup it got easier, with each mouthful I felt better and by the time I got to the end of the first tumbler I was on the mend. When the second tumbler was inside my shirt I was fit to do a day's work. By the time I had made my way through the third dose, not only was I ready to go to the Ploughin', you could have tackled me up and I'd have done a bit of ploughin' myself.

At that stage Quirke made tay and walked me home. I fell straight into the scratcher, ready to sleep the sleep of the just – but there was no sleep to be had. No sooner had the head hit the pillow than the volcano erupted and the room began to spin. 'Twas spinnin' so fast I had to hang on to the headboard in case I'd be thrown off.

After much effort I managed to stop the rotation of the bed by keepin' one eye closed and the other open. I eventually went off to sleep but I'd have been better off stayin' awake. I had a dream that would frighten a ghost. I dreamt I was cyclin' down the Borrisnangoul Road when a big white-head bull jumped over the ditch and made for me. I turned the bike around and took off like a rocket in the opposite direction with the bull snortin' at my back wheel. I was pedallin' like a hoor when the chain came off, wrapped itself around my leg and the next thing I was fired up into the air. I landed with a crash and woke to find myself on the bedroom floor with my ankle caught between the headboard and the mattress. The pain was only ferocious.

The mother had to send for Quirke to dislodge me and I ended up in the hospital in Clonmel. I'll be at no Ploughin' match this year, I'm sittin' here with my ankle in the air and it as big as a bucket. I should be thankful for small mercies: my cold is cured.

A CLOSE ENCOUNTER WITH THE LAW

They say the idle mind is the divil's workshop. Since I tumbled out of the bed after dreamin' of bein' chased by a bull I've been confined to the house with a sprained ankle. To be honest, given that things are quiet on the political front it wasn't a bad time to be trapped indoors. By Wednesday I was bored of the whole thing and needed a break. I phoned Cantillon who arrived on the tractor to take me for a pint. After much gruntin' and groanin' I managed to get up into the cab and we took off for Walshe's with nothin' on our minds but drink and divilment.

We weren't halfway down the village when who appeared from behind the pier of Lenihan's gate but the new young guard and him with the hand up. As soon as we came to a halt he proceeded to walk around the tractor examinin' it as if 'twas a flyin' saucer. This fresh faced young guard fancies himself in a big way. He sports a tan that'd be the envy of Albert Reynolds and when he's not on duty he decks himself out in flashy leathers and rides around on a massive motorbike. They tell me he wears more perfume than an air hostess.

'Where do you display the tax and insurance on this thing?' he asked Cantillon who pointed to the top left hand corner of the cab. 'How do you expect me to get up there?' snapped the guard. 'I don't expect you to get up anywhere,' replied Cantillon. 'In fact, I have no expectations of you, high or low. However, if you want to read the details on my tax and insurance disks you'd better start climbin'.' By the time the guard had mounted the arms of the front loader and read all he wanted to read his yella jacket was covered in a mixture of grease, oil and cowshite.

Everythin' was in order with the paperwork but, far from bein' pleased, the guard seemed fairly upset that he had nothin' to show for his efforts. He was about to wave us on when he had a brainwave. 'Why is your passenger not wearing a seatbelt?' he asked a crusty faced Cantillon. 'I only require my passengers to wear restraints when I'm in danger of breakin' the sound barrier,' came the sharp reply.

'I'm afraid,' declared the guard, 'your passenger will have to dismount and you can continue without him. Count yourself lucky you don't have a few penalty points to take home with you.'

'Aren't you the busy little man, now,' says Cantillon. 'I'd say there isn't a criminal in the three counties that isn't shiverin' in his boots knowin' you're on the beat. They'll be comin' out with their hands up when they hear you pulled a half crippled man off a tractor to prevent carnage on the roads. By the time you're finished, 'tis a shortage of criminals we'll have.'

'No more of your guff,' barked the guard, 'Get that man off the tractor and be on your way.' 'You'll have to help me,' says I, pointin' to my bandaged ankle. I got myself to the door of the cab and the guard put up his hands to help me down. I fell into his arms and he carried me to the side of the street. As he grunted under my tonnage the divilment got the better of me. With my arms around his neck I looked into his eyes and asked, 'Do you come here often?' No answer. 'Do you like the band?' No answer. 'Will you stay on?' With that he fired me in over Lenihan's hedge and nearly made scutter of my other ankle.

The idle mind is indeed the divil's workshop. I'm lucky not to be charged with makin' indecent proposals to a guard in the course of his duty. Not even Bertie at his best would get away with that.

TEARS OF A CLOWN

I sometimes think the man and woman in the street and in the haggard have come to regard politics as a spectator sport, even a blood sport. Political matters are discussed in the pub only when the crowd want to have a go at me and rise a good laugh. I lost my temper with them the other night:

'If I wanted to be a clown,' says I, 'I'd have joined the circus.'

'Sure, isn't that exactly what you did,' shouted Cantwell.

There was another big 'yo-ho' so I finished my pint

and went home. I was fierce disillusioned. I've spent so much of my life goin' from one meaningless meetin' to another 'tis a wonder I'm not in a permanent coma. I've myself beaten into a fool bein' nice to every gobdaw that darkens my door. I have muscles on my right hand that are fit to burst from salutin' and shakin' hands and there's no thanks for it. You have no idea what a politician's life is like: everythin' you do from the time you get up till you go back to bed is political. Where you do your shoppin', where you get your haircut, where you eat the lunch, where you take a drink, who you salute and whose funeral you go to: 'tis all fair game for public comment.

Funerals are the worst of all: people are very touchy about the politician turnin' up to the family obsequies and particularly touchy about what part of the proceedin's you turn up to. If you go to the removal and not to the mass and burial they'll never forget you for it.

I remember when the Stumper Foley in Cossatrasna died I was at a conference in Mullingar. By the time the Mother got in touch with me the removal was over. I was up at cockcrow the followin' mornin' and between buses, trains and taxis I eventually got to the graveyard as the coffin was bein' lowered. In my considered opinion, I played a blinder.

That was until I canvassed Foleys durin' the last local elections. I found out fairly lively I didn't do as well as I thought. I was met at the gate by the Stumper's widow, Chrissy, and she spittin' fire at eighty-five years of age.

'Hickey,' says she, 'where do you think you're goin' with your beggin' bowl?'

'Well, Chrissy,' says I, with my hand out, 'How have you been keepin' since himself passed away?'

'Put that greasy hand back into your auld pocket, there'll be no-one touchin' that yoke in this house,' she barked.

'Why so because?' I asked, and me flummoxed.

'You know feckin' well why,' she answered, 'Stumper always voted for you and your father before you and his father before him. 'Twas some token of appreciation when the only few seconds you could manage to spare for his funeral was an appearance in the graveyard after the man was buried. You might as well have sent one of your feckin' auld posters and stuck it on to the cemetery gate.'

As hard as I tried to explain that I had got there as fast as I could, there was no talkin' to the woman.

'Go way outta that with your auld fibs,' she shouted, 'Ye're all the same. Of course when it came to Minnie Ryan's funeral you were at the wake, the removal, the funeral mass, the burial and the feed afterwards. You nearly got in to the feckin' coffin beside her.'

'Ha,' she continued, 'we all know what matters around here. Once you have the bit of land and the few notions 'tis easy to turn a politician's head. Between funerals and tribunals there's feck-all else to ye, and ye can't even get the funerals right.'

A target of abuse and a source of amusement: that's the lot of the politician. I think I'll join the circus: at least there I'll get paid when people fire things at me for the laugh.

A PITCH BATTLE

Things were too quiet. I was in the Post Office on Tuesday mornin' and 'twas as if everyone in the queue was asleep. When I got to the counter a half conscious Lilly Mac suggested that Killdicken should be renamed 'Snoozy Hollow.'

'Long may it stay that way,' I answered.

'What we need,' says Lilly, 'is a "no" campaign. Communities are at nothin' in this country unless they are objectin' to somethin'. It's the only way to create a bit of excitement.'

I nodded and left, thinkin' no more of Lilly's ramblin's. Most places on the planet would love to have it as quiet and cushy as we have it in Killdicken. However, we hadn't long to wait for things to get lively.

Over the summer people have been givin' out yards about the local GAA grounds. The place is in a ferocious bad condition. For dressin' rooms there's a converted cowshed, the pitch has more humps and hollows than a herd of camels and the goalposts would make the leanin' Tower of Pisa look straight.

In fact, them goalposts have come in very handy in tight matches. Many a ball driven in by visitin' teams would be headed for a certain score until the local umpire would lean against the posts and straighten them. Forwards were always baffled as to how they had so many near misses when playin' in Killdicken.

Anyway, it looks as if the movin' goalposts are to be consigned to history. A subcommittee of the club has drawn up a development plan for the Killdicken GAA grounds.

Club secretary, Brian Cahill, presented the finished plan at a public meetin' Thursday night and it looked mighty: new dressin' rooms, a small stand and a pitch that will be drained, ploughed, levelled and reseeded.

In response, I myself made a fine speech. I went back through the generations to the time when the Invader stopped our young men from playin' their national games and even stopped the priests toggin' out to say mass. I finished at the present day and the great opportunity we now see before us.

Everythin' was grand until Micksie Dunne, Chairman of the Club, got to his feet. 'Ladies and gentlemen,' he began, 'I don't know about ye, but this feckin' Celtic Tiger has made poodles of our young men. We must remember that what made us, what made the people before us and what made our games was hardship. God be with the days when we'd cycle forty miles in the drivin' rain to play a match. And when we got to the pitch was there a dressin' room? No! We togged out beside the nearest hedge with the briars tearin' the arses off us. We were proud to do it.'

Micksie was in full flight, 'When it came to the jerseys were they washed and ironed? No they'd be in a canvas bag in the back of the Lepper Condon's van and they'd be handed out in exactly the same condition they were in when the final whistle blew at the end of the last match. If the Lepper's greyhound had slept on the bag, the jerseys might have a bit of heat in them and a smell to frighten the enemy.'

The chairman wasn't finished: 'When we took to the pitch we weren't worried about humps and hollows because when a fella went up for the ball there was no sweeter sound than the crack of his ankle as he came down on a bit of rough ground. Would he give up? No! He'd play on till the foot was hangin' off.'

'I'm tellin' ye here tonight that ye're destroyin the hardship that made us and destroyin' the heart of our games. This very minute I'm launchin' a campaign of objection to this development. 'Twill happen over my dead body. I'll face the Lord God Almighty before I let ye do this.'

With that, Micksie and about five others walked out of the meetin'. The followin' mornin' we woke to a Killdicken plastered with posters announcin' our very own 'No' campaign. We've arrived in twenty-first century Ireland.

The kind of trouble caused by disputes like this is not good for anyone, least of all the local politician. As the crisis deepens I'm findin' myself stuck in no-man's land while the parish is more divided than it was durin' the Civil War.

At a big meetin' of the club the other night things broke out into open conflict. Despite Micksie's objections the new development plan was passed by a decent majority and a decision was made to apply for plannin' permission. He was furious, 'Ye crowd of auld cissies, yerselves and yere showers,' he shouted, 'Can't them young fellas wash in the river like we all did? "tis a massage parlour they'll want next, and gallons of baby oil for their fat backsides.'

Micksie vowed to stop the development at every stage. An Extraordinary General Meeting was called to discuss a motion of no confidence in him. Well, in the lead up to the EGM the whole parish was postered like there was an election on. Committee members and club members were gettin' phone calls in the middle of the night tellin' them what way to vote. Slogans were painted all over the place callin' on people to support 'Micksie: the man's man'.

The night of the meetin' came and there was such a crowd in the hall, people were hangin' out of the ceilin'. Sergeant Miller had the squad car from Clonmel on stand-by in case of trouble.

Micksie made a mighty speech extollin' the virtues of hardship, pain, discomfort and agony. He got a big cheer from the kind of people who treasure their bit of misery.

'I'm not frightened by the low down attempts of people in this club to silence me,' he declared, 'Remember, I'm the democratically elected chairman. They're tryin' to do to me what the Saxon strangers did to this country down through the years when they tried to take away all that was dear to us. They took our native language, our land and our national games, games that were made to be played by real men, not by cissies who want showers.'

There was a big 'yo ho' from the great unwashed.

'I will not be pushed out of my Chairmanship,' he shouted, 'I will not be pushed out of this club by namby-pambies. Even if ye sack me, I will not go.'

Calmly and collectedly the secretary, Brian Cahill presented the other side of the argument, even though he had to survive a constant rumble of grunts and snorts.

I was beginnin' to feel safe and anonymous in the middle of the crowd when one of Micksie's supporters demanded to hear from 'our local councillor'. As the only public representative to show up I found myself on the spot.

I was between the divil and the deep blue sea, with supporters on both sides of the divide. Anyway I got up, put on my funeral face and opened my mouth, 'It saddens me to see friends and neighbours so divided, people who have been close for generations, men who fought together on that pitch for the honour of the parish and the glory of the club. I know how Micksie feels about our traditions and I also see the value in movin' with the times. I think we should take our time with these decisions and get a mediator, someone like Canon McGrath.'

I was attacked by both sides.

'Get off the fence, Hickey,' shouted someone, 'before you get blisters on your backside.'

'Are you for me or agin me?' demanded Micksie. Turnin' to the crowd he shouted, 'Don't mind Hickey, he's only a double-dealer. I demand a vote now, get it over with.'

Micksie lost the confidence vote and refused to resign. He declared he was formin' a new club and was carried out of the hall, shoulder high. Those remainin' elected Brian Cahill as chairman and proceeded to put the development in motion.

As I left the hall both sides ignored me as if I was a bit of dirt. The middle ground is a lonely auld place.

HEAVEN OR HELL

It's November, the dead month. I had an hour to spare the other day so I went to the graveyard to get a head start at prayin' for those who have gone to the shadows.

As I walked among the gravestones I took to wonderin' about some of the characters I knew in this life and what they might be doin' in the next. But, do you know somethin'? I found it fierce hard to picture what the next world might be like, especially when it came to heaven. I had an easier job with hell.

For instance, the usual picture we have of heaven is of people dressed in white flutterin' around like pigeons over a cabbage patch. I can't imagine some of the fellas I knew flutterin' around in white dresses. For instance, my good auld friend, Dixie Ryan, spent most of his life in black boots, navy trousers and a navy gabardine coat. Even when Superquinn married him she couldn't get him out of these garments.

The vision of Dixie rigged out in a class of a weddin' dress with a pair of white wings on his back is more than I can imagine. Somehow, I can see him as a crow with a fag hangin' out of the corner of his beak and him flyin' around lookin' for another crow to go for a pint with. If Dixie Ryan is flutterin' around the place in white wings then, as far as he's concerned, he's in hell.

I passed the grave of Maggie Delaney and the thought of Maggie in wings is enough to make a fella faint. Maggie was 22 stone if she was a pound. St Peter would have needed to hand out a fair pair of them to lift Maggie; 'twould take the wingspan of a jumbo jet and a good long runway before she'd manage to be airborne. Anyway, the last thing Maggie would want is to spend eternity flyin' around with nothin' to do. She farmed all her life and liked nothin' better than tendin' to her stock. She had the finest herd of limousins in Tipperary and reared enough geese and turkeys to feed half the country.

If I was to give St Peter advice about Maggie, I'd tell him to give her a thousand acres of well-stocked land. She'd happily spend eternity flyin' from one end to the other countin' cattle, pluckin' turkeys, cuttin' weeds, and spreadin' fertiliser. If she was handed a pair of white wings and told she had nothin' to do but fly around and scratch herself, she'd be better off in the establishment run by the red bucko with hooves and horns.

As I passed the grave of Minnie Hennessy I got to thinkin' that there was a woman who'd love the white dress and the pair of wings. In fact she'd pester St Peter till he presented her with a harp to complete the ensemble. Minnie was born with enough notions to keep two bridge clubs goin'. She came from a long line of people who thought the Hennessys were a step above buttermilk. Every time there was a job done in the church a sign would appear under the finished product askin' the world to pray for 'The Hennessy Family of Gortnahuckrisha, whose generosity made this possible'. Cantwell said that if ever the Canon got around to puttin' toilets in the church there'd be a sign askin' us to pray for the Hennessys, 'Whose generosity put this bowl under your bottom'.

There's no doubt but one man's paradise is another man's perdition. As I walked home I started day-dreamin' about what 'twould be like to be St Peter and have the job of decidin' people's heaven and hell.

I imagined openin' the pearly gates and findin' Michael O'Leary pacin' up and down in his plaid shirt and he demandin' his place in paradise. I thought how his face would light up when I told him he'd be spendin' eternity in the company of a charmin' and intelligent woman. Imagine the head of him when he found himself in the bath with Mary O'Rourke.

GLOBAL VERSUS LOCAL

I'm fed up to the back teeth with this talk of an election. By the time pollin' day comes around I'd say a lot of people won't bother their heads to go out and vote – or maybe they'll vote in their droves just to shut us all up.

Anyway, believe it or not I'm still thinkin' of takin' a run at the big time myself. I've a feelin' in my water that the tide will run right for independents next time round. I reckon I could be another Joe Higgins. Imagine me standin' up in the Dáil and the country hangin' on my every word – it could happen.

I've been practisin' my parliamentary performance in front of the wardrobe mirror. Every mornin' I give speeches to the nation on the disgraceful state of the health services, the condition of rural schools and the plethora of potholes on country roads. There's no doubt but given half a chance I think I'd be mighty.

One mornin' last week I was in the throes of a major address on the Iraq war and the Yanks at Shannon when the Mother barged in: 'President Putin phoned,' says she, 'he's wonderin' if you'll have a chance to sort out Chechnya some time today. I told him you hadn't eaten the breakfast yet, but you had to sort out Kashmir and the Middle East first. Come down to the kitchen, you looderamawn. Terry Clancy is waitin' to know if you have any news on the retention for his cowhouse.'

I was anxious to meet Terry, there's at least ten number ones for the takin' in his family. He's in trouble with the council for buildin' a small cow-house without plannin' permission on an out-farm in Borrisnangoul. The cows are in danger of bein' evicted. Why he'd need to get plannin' in that isolated spot I'll never know. The only creatures likely to be affected by his construction, aside from the cows, are the odd fox and the occasional transatlantic goose. Anyway, the pen-pushers in county hall are very upset and want the cow-house knocked.

The Mother made tay for Terry and told him I wouldn't be long, I was on the phone to Kofi Annan. She presumed he was only interested in his cow-house, but she was wide of the mark.

If I may digress: the most unlikely people have an interest in things far beyond their own four bones. Sometimes politicians underestimate the electorate. We're inclined to think voters only care about the bread and butter issues, but they can be fairly concerned about marmalade and jam as well.

When I appeared in the kitchen Terry laughed as he apologised for interruptin' my conversation with 'Kofi'. He told me I could get back to global issues once we had his problem sorted out. I took down all the details and assured him that there would be no problem gettin' retention for the cow-house.

To my surprise once we were finished with his business he launched into a dissertation on world affairs. He told me he was fierce worried about Darfur and if he could lay hands on Kofi Annan he'd give him a piece of his mind. He went on to talk at length about pollution in China, the Indian economic miracle, the collapse of fish stocks and the meltin' of the ice caps ... and I thought he came to talk about his cow-house.

As he was leavin' I walked him to the gate, takin' the opportunity to tell him I was thinkin' of havin' a run at a Dáil seat – what did he think?

'You're askin' the wrong man for advice on that sort of thing, Maurice,' says he, 'I haven't the slightest bit of interest in parish pump politics.'

25

I stood at the gate with my mouth open as he went off on his tractor with his head full of international affairs while I was left to deal with the important things, like his cow-house.

THE WHEELS ON THE BUS GO ...

Have you ever come across the Rural Transport Initiative? It's a local scheme to provide transport for people who don't have a way of gettin' around. They use the school buses while the children are at school.

We have our own version of the scheme around here servin' Glengooley, Killdicken and Honetyne. Officially 'tis called the 'Glenkilhone Rural Transport Service', but to the locals 'tis known as the 'Pothole Express'. It goes from door to door on Wednesdays and Fridays and takes mainly older people to Clonmel to do a bit of shoppin', get their hair done and have the dinner.

I had occasion to use the service myself last week. The Mother was gone to Kilkenny and I was stuck for a lift to Clonmel. While I was in the Post Office on Friday mornin' I asked Postmistress, Lilly Mac if she knew anyone goin' to town.

'Why don't you take the Pothole Express', says she, 'or are you too grand for it?'

'Begod', says I, 'I never thought of that.'

'Stand outside the door and 'twill be along in ten minutes,' says she before she blew my ears off shoutin' 'Next!' at Tim Danagher who's as deaf as a stone.

I went outside and joined five or six local senior citizens as they waited for the bus. Mary Dillon and Lizzie Candon gave me an awful slaggin'.

'Don't try to use the free travel pass, Maurice', warned Lizzie, 'or we'll have to set up a tribunal.'

'I suppose,' mused Mary Dillon through her nose, 'Seein' we're carryin' an elected representative, we could say we're travellin' in a state vehicle.'

Along came the bus, one of Hogan's minibuses driven by Dick himself. He had a great welcome for me.

'If it isn't Councillor Hickey. Are you on a tour of inspection or something?'

'No, Dick,' says I, 'I'm a rural dweller who needs a lift to town. How much do I owe you?'

'The princely sum of €4.00 will do fine. Unless you got free travel pass in a brown envelope,' he remarked.

On the way to town, we went up and down every lane and boreen in the county. Dick was fantastic, at some houses he pulled up and blew the horn, some people were waitin' at crossroads and in other places he went into the house and linked his passengers out. He had a word for everyone.

'Did you remember to turn off the gas today, Mag?' He asked a woman we picked up in Shronefodda.

'I did,' she replied, 'and I hope your auld gas is turned off or we'll be openin' the windows in case we're found smothered.'

We stopped in Cossatrasna to pick up Bridie Nealon. As she got on Dick enquired if her dog came back.

'He did,' she answered, ''Twas romance took him. He's like the rest of ye men: there's only two things trouble him, his belly and his undercarriage. Talkin' about bellies, I see we have Councillor Hickey on board today. Are you carryin' him to test the springs?'

She then addressed me, 'Welcome on board The Pothole Express, Councillor. By the time we get to Clonmel you'll see why it got its name. We're nearly de-boned from havin' the life shook out of us on these feckin' roads.'

The crack was only mighty. On the way home Dick was in no rush since the schools were closed for a half-day. We made umpteen pit stops and by the time we got to Killdicken we were sore from singin'. Along the way I gave Dick a hand with the passengers; while he got them off the bus I retrieved their shoppin' from the boot.

When we got to our stop I was sweatin'. Mary Dillon took pity on me and handed me a hanky.

'This bus is new life to me,' says she, 'I spend the weekend rememberin' every detail of the Friday trip and I spend the week lookin' forward to the next journey.'

'By the way,' she continued, 'Lose some of that belly or the only rural transport you'll need is Tinky Ryan's hearse.'

THERE'S NO BIZ LIKE SHOWBIZ

There's murder in the parish. Preparation for the annual performance by the Killdicken Musical Society is causin' the usual trauma. 'Tis like world war feckin' three. The Society has been goin' since Adam was a boy and, true to form, the shenanigans off stage are far more entertainin' than anythin' appearin' in front of the curtain. Accordin' to Cantwell, 'when they're not fightin' like bantams they're at the other thing.'

For years Moll Gleeson insisted on bein' the leadin' lady. She fancied herself as a cross between Julie Andrews and Maria Callas: in my opinion the cross was more a mixture of Miss Piggy and Meatloaf. Year in and year out she bullied her way into the limelight. She was Cinderella, Annie Get Your Gun, Evita, Mary Magdalen and a very substantial Maria in *The Sound of Music*.

However, she came a cropper when she attempted to play the genie in *Aladdin and the Lamp*. The genie was expected to be light-footed and athletic but, despite her greatest efforts, Moll proved totally incapable of risin' to the challenge in either department.

Timmy Reidy was playin' Aladdin. Now Timmy is a wiry little snipe of a man who disappeared into insignificance beside Moll. Every time Moll appeared as the genie she was to twirl round three times, bow and declare, 'Master Aladdin, your wish is my command.' 'Twasn't as easy as that. The twirlin' didn't suit Moll who inevitably got a reelin' in her head and ended up in a heap on the stage. They were afraid she might twirl into the pit and flatten the band.

The end of Moll's stage career came in the pub one night after a particularly difficult rehearsal durin' which she lost her balance and fell on poor Timmy. She broke three of his ribs and while he was carted off to casualty in Clonmel the rest of the cast adjourned to the pub. As luck would have it, Pa Cantillon was there and feelin' no pain. On his way back from a call of nature he threw his arms around Moll, 'So Moll,' says he, 'you're Aladdin's genie. I hear they've had to send to Harland and Wolff for the lamp.'

Moll stormed out of the pub and didn't darken the door of the Musical Society for years, until this year. She did a course in art and stagecraft in the Tipperary Institute and since it finished she thinks Broadway would be too small for her. Anyway she offered her services to the Musical Society and they were so glad the cold war was over they took her on.

This year they're attemptin' *Les Miserables*: I dreaded havin' to sit through it. At the best of times it's a maudlin auld yoke, but in the hands of the Killdicken Musical Society it promised to turn the parish hall into a torture chamber.

Anyway, Moll designed the set with a mock up of the cathedral of Notre Dame as the centrepiece. She built it in her own backyard with the help of a few youngfellas from the Macra who are fierce handy with welders.

When they tried to take the thing to the parish hall they all but created a regional emergency. They put it up on a flat bed trailer and in the journey between Moll's house and the parish hall it pulled down telephone wires, knocked out the ESB and caused the first major traffic jam in Killdicken history.

At the hall there was another problem. The only way to get the cathedral into the buildin' was by takin' off a section of the roof or takin' the Cathedral apart. Moll refused to take the thing apart and the Community Council refused to let anyone tamper with the roof. There was a stand off that lasted three days.

The County Council resolved the matter when it removed the cathedral to the dump and sent a bill for €5,000 to the secretary of the Musical Society who forwarded it straight to Moll. The Society is in disarray, Moll has retreated to Lanzarote and thankfully *Les Miserables* has been abandoned.

HARES AND HOUNDS

Council meetin's can be the strangest affairs. They can move between the heights of common sense and the depths of tomfoolery. Our meetin' last week hit both ends of that scale.

In five minutes we passed motions that kick-started drainage works, sewerage works and renovations. We were like shoppers in a supermarket fillin' our trolleys as fast as we could to be home for the milkin'.

We flew through the agenda till we came to the part where Councillors propose votes of congratulations and condolences. Up to a few years ago these used to take up most of the meetin's. There'd be councillors congratulatin' Micky and Mary Mullins 'on the birth of their fourth son and we hope they'll keep goin' till they have the daughter.'

Fellas whose bull won first prize at the parish fair or whose daughter just graduated from college would be praised to the heights for their great achievements. Eventually things got completely out of hand and people would be proposin' votes of congratulations to horses, hounds and fightin' cocks.

Votes of condolence were even worse. Councillors spent hours eulogisin' their local dead to the point where there was little time for anythin' else. The worst part of the condolence list was the mutterin' that went on once the name of the deceased was mentioned. Councillors would lean over to one another and begin to trace the seed breed and generation of the person in question. The chatterin' would be particularly loud if 'twas a funeral some of them had missed.

'Jesus, Mary and Joseph,' a councillor would gasp, 'why didn't some one tell me Johnny Mangan was dead? I never even knew he was sick. Cripes, sure I knew him well and all belongin' to him.'

'Who'll get that place now, sure himself and Bridie hadn't chick nor child?' another would ask.

'Ah, the Neenans of Borris will get the whole lot. Sure the Mangans and Neenans are first cousins.'

Each vote of condolence would lead to a full discussion on the deceased and their extended families. A council meetin' mightn't finish till midnight with most of it taken up with graveside orations. Eventually, standin' orders were brought in restrictin' votes of condolence and congratulations to five of each per council meetin'. Proposals for such votes got on the agenda on a first-come-first-served basis with fifteen minutes allocated for the whole lot.

In the main, this proposal worked, but on occasion matters got out of hand. This week was one of those occasions. Fianna Fáil Councillor, Peter Cleary proposed a vote of congratulations to a local mare, Jolly Josie, who won a major international horsey trophy recently. He spoke at length about this animal as if she was after winnin' a feckin' Olympic gold medal. He lost the run of himself entirely and proposed a civic reception for her and her owner. There was uproar. It turned party political. The Fine Gaelers accused the Cleary of bein' typical Fianna Fáil, wastin' money on horses while people were lyin' on hospital trolleys up and down the country. The FFers drove the blueshirts mad tellin' them they knew nothin' about celebratin' because they knew nothin' about winnin'.

Things were dyin' down when Percy Pipplemoth Davis entered the fray. He enquired as to the kind of event Jolly Josie won. When he was informed the mare was a fox huntin' champion he lost his environmental rag and went nuclear.

'Over my dead body will this council be associated with providing a civic reception to celebrate and honour savagery,' he thundered.

At that, all sides turned on Pipplemoth. By the time the Chairman brought the place to order and adjourned the meetin' Percy was like a fox cornered by a pack of hounds.

We reconvened and concluded our business in peace. When I got home the Mother asked me how the meetin' went. 'Well,' says I, 'We spent five minutes spendin' millions and an hour and a half fightin' over a horse.'

FISCAL WRECKTITUDE

Wouldn't you miss the budget days of old, the days of the hairshirt and hardship. The day itself always fell early in the year when we were just about recoverin' from the Christmas. I suppose 'twas a kind of stick to beat us into line and make us straighten ourselves after the madness of the season of goodwill. I remember one particular budget fell on Ash Wednesday. Minister for Finance of the time, Bertie Ahern, arrived in the Dáil with a briefcase full of bad news and the ashes of four fireplaces daubed on to his forehead.

In the boom times, budget day became a cross between Christmas Eve and a rich aunt comin' home from America. You'd imagine the Minister for Finance spent the night before fillin' the boot of the Mercedes with €50 notes and took off the followin' mornin' with the boot open and money blowin' in all directions.

'Tis true to say that there's no penance left in the world. There was a time when the country was run by people who behaved like half starved monks, today, 'tis as if the country has been taken over by the little sisters of perpetual indulgence. The hardship is gone out of everything, even budget day, mortal sins are a thing of the past and the only sin of the flesh is obesity.

I can't see the climbin' of Croagh Patrick lastin' much longer, they'll build a cable car to the top or they'll provide helicopter flights to spare people the effort. At the rate we're goin, Lough Derg will become a fishin' resort with gourmet food, massage parlours and saunas.

We're gettin' as soft as putty and the government isn't helpin' one bit. But let me warn them, as soon as the first puff of chill wind blows, the pampered children of the nation will turn on them and throw them out of office. In the hands of a hungry electorate the ballot box is a severe and merciless weapon. On the other hand, bein' thrown out might suit the government fine. They'll be as happy as pigs in scutter to retire to the opposition benches after they have cleaned the cupboard bare. From the comfort and safety of the shoutin' benches they'll be able to fire insults by the bucketful at the poor misfortunes in power who have nothin' to spend and five years to spend it.

Ye know that I'm half thinkin' of havin' a run for the Dáil the next time round. Well, if the economists and the pundits are to be believed, there couldn't be a worse time to be anywhere near the levers of power. I'd be far better off on a high stool pontificatin' to the few auld faithfuls at the bar.

Anyway we survived budget day and I'm afraid I left the pub early convinced that Cowen had bought the people, the election, and any hope of a change. Maybe I should set up a branch of Independent FF? I could be the Jackie Healy-Rae of South Tipp? All I'd need is a bit of a greasy wig and a tartan capeen. I could get anythin' I want for the locals if I had the government by the short and curlies.

I better start thinkin' of my manifesto, how's about these few things for a start:

A return of the plastic bag

A complete reversal of the smokin' ban

Rural buses to be put on at night and weekends for those who like the few pints

Full drivin' licenses granted to anyone over forty who has no license but is willin' to drive slow

Children's allowance to be paid directly to the child from the time they reach eighteen until both parents are dead

Free A.I. service or a full bull grant for any farmer with less than fifty acres

Viagra on the medical card for married men over eighty-five (whose wives are still alive).

I think I'll have to run, if I wait till next time there mightn't be any money left to implement my policies.

I Shoulda Watched Out ...

I'm a grown man and I still miss Santy somethin' terrible. I remember as a youngfella the thrill of wakin' up and seein' the present at the end of the bed. To this day I can feel the shiver runnin' down my spine as I touched the parcel thinkin' the last person to touch it was Santy himself.

In some ways, I'm glad he doesn't come to me anymore because these modern toys are a total mystery to me. If he landed a Playstation or an MP3 at the end of the bed I'd have trouble openin' the box. Even Meccano was beyond me.

I remember one time Santy brought me this massive Meccano set. The Father took it out and spent all Christmas day buildin' a huge crane. He enjoyed it more than me, all I did was hand him the tools while he worked away till 'twas finished. I got fed up and took to watchin' Willy Wonka's Chocolate Factory.

Later that night Patsy Devereaux and his wife, Nora came to visit. They were distant cousins and as wearisome a pair as you ever met. While the parents entertained the visitors, boredom gave me renewed interest in the crane the Father built. 'Twas a handy yoke, with a spool of thread and a hook that lifted things up and down by the twistin' of a handle. I began to spin the crane around lettin' the hook fly out as far as it could and reelin' it in like a fishin' rod.

Things were goin' grand till I swung it right across the room where it got caught in the back of Patsy's head. I spooled in as hard as I could and nearly fainted when I saw part of the head comin' away with the hook. I was sorta relieved when I realised what had come unstuck from Patsy's head was in fact a hairpiece. But things went from bad to disaster. As the hairpiece flew through the air, Fido, our terrier, jumped up, grabbed it in his mouth and retreated under the dresser with what he thought was dessert. By the time I got it off him the wig looked like a dead rat.

I was sure I was goin' to be killed till I looked and saw that the Mother and Father and were bent in two tryin' to hold back the laugh. A very bald Patsy and a very frosty Nora left the house in high dudgeon and didn't darken the door again till the Father was on his deathbed.

Anyway, back to Santy, the one thing I loved gettin' was Lego. In fact up to very recently I kept a box of it under the stairs. Sometimes, when there was no one around, I'd take it out along with a bag of cowboys and Indians. I'd build myself the grandest fort you ever saw surrounded by yelpin' Indians and defended by cowboys who sounded like John Wayne. There was nothin' like it; 'twas as good as a holiday to me.

One day last week I had the house to myself when the song 'Santa Claus is Comin' to Town' came on the radio. I got a longin' for my Lego so I pulled out the box, opened the bag of cowboys and Indians and prepared for a mighty scrap. The Indians were gettin' the upper hand as I placed Chief Geronimo on top of a cushion and shouted, 'You are surrounded, Palefaces, surrender.'

From behind me a deep voice growled, 'The hell we will.'

I looked round and there stood Pa Quirke, the postman, and he smirkin' from ear to ear.

'Hickey,' says he, 'you're a big auld babba.'

He was gone before I had a chance to explain myself.

That night I went to Tom Walshe's for a pint. As soon as I parked myself at the counter I knew Quirke had been tellin' tales. Tom shouted from behind the bar:

'HOW, Big Chief Mikki Hikki! You come in peace – me give you good firewater.'

Happy Christmas to children of all ages.

THERE'S A LOT IN A NAME

On Christmas night the Mother and myself went to Pa Quirke's for a game of cards and a drink. In the course of the night Pa's wife May was full of questions about people from the parish, who they were related to, who married who and where people emigrated to.

'By God, May,' says the Mother, 'You have more questions than a barrister at a tribunal.'

'Oh,' says Pa, 'You see, my Missus is doin' a diploma in local history at the Tipperary Institute. She's workin' on a thesis on the Parish of Killdicken from 1857 to 2007. In future I'll be referrin' to her as "My wife, the professor".'

'Fair dues, May,' says I. 'But what's an intelligent woman like you doin' with an amadawn like Quirke?'

'Ah now, even amadawns have their uses,' replied Pa, 'I'm her chief research assistant. Who better to gather up bits and pieces of local history but your local postman?'

'Have you much done?' asked the Mother, 'I've a lot of information gathered,' answered May. 'I should get most of it finished in the early part of the New Year. When it's printed I'll sell it to people in the parish and beyond.'

'I suppose you'll have an official launch,' I remarked.

'Indeed I will, Maurice,' she responded, 'and you'll get an invitation.'

'And who might you be thinkin' of gettin' to launch it?' I enquired

'Oh now, that's a six-mark question, Maurice,' says she, 'Your colleague Percy Pipplemoth Davis has been very helpful and said he might be able to get me a publishin' grant from the Heritage Council.'

I nearly choked on my Mikado biscuit at the thought of my sworn political enemy usin' the wife of one of my best friends for political advantage. I must have gone pale at the gills because May immediately assured me she was only jokin'. It's amazin' how personally you take the political thing after a while.

Anyway, she showed us the information she had gathered and we spent till four in the mornin' goin' through old photographs, old documents and letters. 'Twas like a journey through time.

One of the amazin' things May has discovered is the importance of nicknames. She says they contain as much information as DNA, whatever that is.

Here's an example of some local nicknames she came across.

There's the 'Blue-arse Ryans' from Cossatrasna. The great grandfather, auld Murty went off to the South Pole with Shackleton. Seemingly he fell asleep while on watch one night and his backside froze to whatever he was sittin' on. He could never warm it again. Every house he went into he'd head straight for the fire, lift the tail of his coat and spend his night roastin' what was left of his own South Pole.

Then there was the 'Spatter Casey' who was as mean as ditchwater. The back mudguard of his bike broke off and he wouldn't pay to have it repaired. Durin' the winter you'd see him comin' for miles with a spray of water flyin' high into the air. He always had a line of spatters goin' down the middle of his back from the exposed wheel.

There's no doubt but people had a cruel sense of humour when it came to nicknames. I asked May about a family my father used to talk about, the 'Mice McCarthy's' from Crookdeedy and she laughed.

'I have a photograph of them here,' she said, 'The father, the mother and their two teenage sons before the lot of them emigrated in 1936.'

You'd have to laugh if you saw the photograph: the father and the two sons were about six foot six and built like haystacks. The mother wasn't far behind.

'Now,' says May, 'can't you see why they were called the Mice McCarthys?'

The Mother told us about a fella called 'the Yank Hannigan'. He left for America in June 1948, got as far as Cobh, got drunk and fell asleep. When he woke, the boat was gone so he came back home and never went beyond Clonmel after that. He never lost his American accent either.

SINGIN' THE BLUES

Have you ever had a visit from the black dog? I suppose in musical terms a visit from that particular animal is called 'the blues', in the pub they might call it bein' down in the dumps.

Without fail, every year as soon as the last bit of turkey is eaten a cousin of the black dog appears at my back door. My get-up-and-go seems to desert me when the last of the Christmas decorations is taken down and I lose the appetite for doin' anythin'. The Mother says I have that problem all year round, it only gets worse in January.

In fairness, I draw a lot of the trouble on myself. As soon as December is a smell away I put everythin' on the long finger with the promise, 'I'll tackle that after Christmas.' When Christmas is over the long finger turns around and pokes me in the eye, mornin', noon and night.

A combination of the bare cupboard and the long finger brings on the black dog and no matter what I do he won't go away.

It gets so bad I sometimes go to the brink of resignin' my seat and lookin' for a job that doesn't involve facin' the public. I bet you find that hard to believe but 'tis the truth. I sort of seize up like a clapped out engine and it takes a fierce belt of a hammer to get me started again.

The Mother sees the signs comin' as soon as New Year's Day is halfway over. She can't get me out of bed, there's no talk out of me and I leave the mobile phone in the drawer.

Last year, after I got over my fit of the doldrums she swore she wouldn't let it happen again. Sure enough, last Monday morning, New Year's Day, even the fry couldn't tempt me out of the bed. I put my head under the blankets and wished the world would go away. By Wednesday the Mother had enough of my mopin' and told me I'd better get out of the scratcher as she

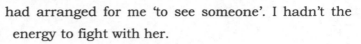

had arranged for me 'to see someone'. I hadn't the energy to fight with her.

As soon as I finished the boiled egg we took off in the direction of Clonmel and pulled up at a fine house on the outskirts of the town. 'Here we are,' announced the Mother, 'you're goin' to see Dr. Heaney and if you listen to him it might spare me a month of your mopin'. Now, in with you, I'll be back in an hour.' With that kind of motherly encouragement how could I resist?

Dr Heaney met me at the door, a nice man with clear skin and the finest mane of white hair you ever saw. 'This man has minded himself,' I thought as he showed me to his consultin' room. He took my coat and got me to lie down on a couch while he parked himself beside me in a very comfortable lookin' swivel chair.

He began proceedin's by askin' me to describe myself and talk about the kind of things that make me happy and the kinds of things that make me sad. That's all I remember. I woke an hour later to the sound of the Doctor snorin'. Both of us had slept through the whole session. The doorbell rang; 'twas the Mother. The good doctor shuddered and woke up.

'Ah Maurice, how good, how very good. I do hope you feel better. That will be €75 and I'll see you at the same time next week.'

I handed over the cash in stunned silence and left. When I sat into the car I turned to the Mother and asked, 'Why didn't you tell me that man is a prostitute?'

'Who? Dr Heaney? In the name of God,' she gasped, 'Have you gone mad entirely. That man is not a prostitute.'

'Well, he just charged me €75 for sleepin' with him.'

Havin' to part with so much for so little brought me to my senses fairly lively.

THE PRICE OF POWER

It started with a bang. The decorations weren't back on top of the wardrobe when the season of goodwill evaporated like steam from a sweatin' horse. I was in County Hall the day the holidays finished and who passed in with a spring in his step but the bould Percy Pipplemoth Davis.

Everybody was congratulatin' him and he was noddin' and smilin' like Mary Robinson on a good day. 'Is it gettin' married you are, Percy?' I enquired and me burstin' for news. 'Indeed not, Maurice,' the auld bladder-puss replied, 'Like your good self, I value my freedom too much. I won €10,000 in the local lotto. It sets me up beautifully to run a most effective campaign in the general election. I'll hardly need to touch my SSIA.'

He had such a smug auld face on him I was sorely tempted to give him a kick in the SSIA. Some hoors have all the luck. There he is, hardly a wet week in politics and he's runnin' for the senior championship with money to burn.

I was in the pub that evenin', moanin' and groanin' to my kitchen cabinet, Messrs Quirke, Cantwell, Cantillon and the Ceann Comhairle, Tom Walshe. 'Tis a risky business complainin' to them fellas, they'd turn on you as quick as they'd comfort you. Anyway, whether 'twas the remnants of the season of goodwill or genuine nature, they gave me the listenin' ear.

'You poor auld divil, Maurice,' says Tom Walshe, 'after all your years of service 'tis awful to see a Johnny-come-lately like Pipplemoth sweep your political future away with his ill-gotten fortune.'

'You wouldn't mind,' says Cantwell, 'if he won it dacent on the horses, on the dogs or at poker, but to win it in the feckin' local lotto: that's the lowest of the low.'

'It could be worse,' says Cantillon, 'he could've won it on *Winnin' Streak*. My missus is always buyin' them feckin' scratch cards. I've her warned if she ever gets the call to go on with Mooney she won't have me wavin' placards at the nation and brayin' like an ass. I'll go with her on condition I can wear a balaclava for the entire programme.'

'Erra, I don't know what all the moanin' is about,' says Quirke, 'Sure, Maurice, you have no notion of runnin' for the Dáil. Let Pipplemoth off and give him all the support in the world because if he's elected he won't be contestin' the next local elections. You'll have a clear run at it.'

'True for you,' says Tom Walshe. 'If he has money to burn let him burn it to hell. Suppose he wins, then he's out of the picture for the locals, and if he loses he won't have the price of a poster when he has to defend his council seat in 2009.'

'I'll say one thing,' chimed in Cantwell, 'If I was an advisor to Pipplemoth do you know what I'd tell him?'

'Do we have to answer that immediately or can we phone a friend?' asked Quirke

'What little brains you once had have been fried to a cinder from gapin' at television,' responded Cantwell. 'As I was sayin', if I was in Pipplemoth's inner circle I wouldn't let him spend one cent of that €10,000 on posters. I'd make him invest the lot in plastic surgery. If you remember, he had a beard durin' the local elections and he looked some way presentable. Since he shaved it off he looks like the back end of a plucked pheasant. Dustin the Turkey would look better on a poster than him.'

'Begod Maurice, you must be feelin' better now,' says the Ceann Comhairle, 'There's nothin' to sooth the wounded heart like a concerted verbal assault on one's enemies. People in Ballymena pay good money every Sunday to hear Paisley do that and you're gettin' it for free.'

'One last thing,' says he, 'as a result of this conversation, if I was you I'd get two presents for Pipplemoth: a copy of the guide to successful elections and a very good razor.'

VAN-ITY

Jealousy is an awful thing and I have a bad dose of it. You'll remember last week I was talkin' about Percy Pipplemoth Davis and how he won the parish lotto. That was bad enough, but when he told me he was goin' to spend it on gettin' himself elected to the Dáil I got fierce down in the dumps. As you know I haven't yet made up my mind whether I'll run myself and I'm ragin' that auld Pipplemoth got in the race ahead of me.

I've spent the week mopin' around the place, talkin' to myself and mutterin'. The Mother told me 'twas time for me to do the business or get off the pot. Well, on Tuesday mornin' I found myself in very urgent need of a pot. As she dropped me off in the car park at County Hall I was blinded by the sight of a luminous green Hiace van emblazoned with huge yella sunflowers on either side. Starin' out at me from the middle of the sunflowers in all his ugliness was the face of one Percy Pipplemoth feckin' Davis. The picture was bad enough, but the slogan was even worse. Along the length of the van, in letters made up with daisies was written: 'Who will save us? Vote for Davis.' What a dose of sickenin' scutter.

I nearly lost my reason. Would you believe it, I found myself lookin' around the ground for a rock to throw at the bloody auld van. I pulled myself together, went in to the council buildin's and got my few jobs done. I must have had a face like a bull on me because as I passed through reception on my way out Liz Cahill, one of the women on the desk enquired as to who ate my bun.

'Did you see that feckin' van in the car-park?' I demanded, 'Tis enough to give a fella fourteen kinds of the runs. Who in their right mind will vote for a clown like Pipplemoth?'

'Well,' says Liz, 'Any man who's into flowers does it for me. If Councillor

Pipplemoth appears on the ballot paper with a bunch of daisies and sunflowers, then he has my Number 1.'

'For God's sake,' says I, 'is the world gone mad entirely? That man is a total gobdaw. Can you imagine his wagon parked in the grounds of Leinster House? South Tipp will be the laughin' stock of the country.'

'Well, Councillor Maurice,' says Liz, 'If you don't want Councillor Davis to succeed could I suggest the only way to stop him is to enter the race yourself.'

'You know somethin',' says I, 'You could be right.'

'Just remember,' says Liz, 'If you want my Number 1, Councillor Davis is ahead in the flower power stakes.'

'Now Liz,' says I, 'there are certain things I'll do for a vote and flowers isn't one of them.'

With that my mobile phone rang, 'twas the Mother. She wasn't able to come and collect me, could I get a lift home. I was explainin' my predicament to Liz when who came along but that wretch of a Pipplemoth.

'Ah, my dear Councillor Maurice,' he exclaimed, full of his usual plawmaus, 'how wonderful to see you.'

'Excuse me Councillor Davis,' interjected Liz, 'Are you going home to Honetyne?'

'Indeed I am, Elizabeth. Why do you ask?'

'Councillor Hickey needs a lift to Killdicken, can you oblige?'

'Why, of course,' he replied. 'Maurice, you can join me in my 'advertisemobile'. What an excellent use of resources. My transport and advertising are all part of the one package. Let's do a round of Clonmel and give the people an opportunity to see the new face of Dáil representation.'

I turned to Liz. 'Ms Cahill,' I hissed, 'I owe you for this. You wouldn't happen to have a balaclava handy?'

Pipplemoth did about four rounds of Clonmel, beepin' the horn and wavin' out the window of wanderly wagon. And there was I, propped up in the front seat like a big feckin' turnip.

I think I have no choice but run, if only to put a stop to this lunatic.

'TIS ALL IN THE PARISH NOTES

I occasionally get the job of writin' the Killdicken parish notes for the local paper, *The Weekly Eyeopener*. Mary Moloney normally does it, but she gets me to fill in when she's not around. Mary reports things as she finds them, but the divil gets into me when I get the pen in my hand and I like to spice things up a bit. Anyway, below is a sample of my attempts at local journalism.

Any Cause a Good Cause

Timmy Kelly is off on another holiday compliments of the Home for Lost Dogs in Ringthomas. He's collecting money for the home while taking a walking holiday in the Pyrenees. Those of you concerned for his welfare needn't worry too much: he's going in May so he'll be neither roasted alive or frozen solid. If you have loose change from which you are easily parted and want to see Tim's tan topped up then you can contribute to his heroic trek at collection points in the Post Office, Gleeson's Shop and Walshe's Select Lounge.

GAA Tracksuits

The Killdicken GAA tracksuit is now available. While people are happy with the design, unfortunately the garments are only available in extra, extra large (XXL). At a stormy meeting to unveil the tracksuits, some members protested loudly at the unavailability of smaller sizes. One woman left empty-handed after telling officials she came to collect a tracksuit and was presented with a two-man tent.

Parade Meeting

A meeting to explore the possibility of reviving the St Patrick's Day Parade in Killdicken will be held at the Community Centre on Monday night. In an ominous development Councillor Percy Pipplemoth Davis is to bring along an expert in 'Street Performance and Creative Community Expression'. Anyone wanting to make a spectacle of themselves should attend.

Christmas Dues

Canon McGrath was delighted with the Christmas dues. In a letter to parishioners he thanked them for their generosity, which surpassed anything he had witnessed in his thirty-five years as a priest. He is expected back from Barbados in February.

Weight Watchers

Weight Watchers is returning after the Christmas break. For those who put on the few pounds, the weigh-in begins at the Community Centre at 6.30pm on Wednesday. For those who went mad entirely and put on a few stone, there will be a weigh-in at 8.30pm at the weigh station in Horgan's Haulage yard on the Honetyne road.

Gun Club

A meeting of Killdicken Gun Club will be held at the Library in Killdicken on Friday night. Gearoid Mac an tSudaire, late of Long Kesh, will give a demonstration on gun maintenance and long-term storage of live ammunition.

Mick Magner will give a workshop on stalking and the art of remaining perfectly still for prolonged periods. After thirty years in the council his experience in the latter is unmatched.

Walking

A meeting to explore the development of walks on Crookdeedy will be held in the Community Centre on Saturday afternoon. The organiser, Pa Cantillon, is hoping another attempt can be made to develop the walks after a similar effort two years ago failed when the walking route was deemed too short. Those wishing to walk the proposed long route before the meeting are asked to gather at the Community Centre at 3.15pm. 'We should be back at the centre in time to start the meeting at 3.30,' promises Pa.

Active Retired

The Killdicken Active Retired Group calendar for 2007 is sold out. The calendar is a novel fundraising idea featuring photographs of the naked backsides of twelve members of the group. The project is entitled 'Known by your Bum'. Along with the calendar the group is running a unique competition: for an entry fee of €20, anyone who identifies the owners of all twelve backsides gets a prize of €100. Public Health Nurse Mag Lynch is prohibited from entry as it is reckoned inside knowledge gives her unfair advantage.

Planning Snags

The redevelopment of the Killdicken GAA grounds has been hit by planning problems. Detailed objections by former Chairman, Micksie Dunne, are holding up the process. It now appears that Killdicken could be without a home venue for up to two years. It has been suggested they negotiate with Glengooley GAA club for use of their facilities. However, there is widespread unhappiness at this prospect. According to some locals, asking Killdicken players to call Glengooley their home ground would be akin to asking Gerry Adams to sing *God Save the Queen*.

STUMPED ON THE STUMP

I was sittin' at home the other night and what came through the letter-box but election literature.

It brought the art of canvassin' to mind. The most important weapons to take on a canvass are the electoral register and a side-kick with local knowledge. That way you'll know the names of the people you're likely to meet and in many cases you'll know their political colour. If the register or the local sidekick is dodgy, the canvass can be a total feckin' disaster. Another big danger, especially for a new candidate, is advice and recommendations from 'well meanin' people'.

On my first election campaign after the father passed away, I was afflicted by all the things that make for disastrous canvassin'.

I had no problems when it came to the canvass in Killdicken. I knew everyone and they knew me. When I went out to places like Shronefodda, Glengooley, Teerawadra, Borrisnangoul and the outer reaches of Honetyne, I definitely needed a local guide and the electoral register. In those days the register was as reliable as the weather and some of my local guides were even worse.

I was particularly stuck as to how I'd get Shronefodda canvassed. An auld friend of the Mother's from Clonmel happened to visit and said she knew the man to help me, Timmy Hinchy. She organised for me to meet him at the Drippin' Tap public house in Shronefodda. He would do the drivin' and the introducin'.

I got to the pub at the agreed time but there was no car around. I went in and the only human bein' in the place was a skinny cratureen of a man leanin' up against the counter smokin' a Woodbine and finishin' a pint.

'I'm Maurice Hickey,' says I, 'and I'm lookin' for Timmy Hinchy.'

'Your search is over,' answered the man at the counter, 'I'm Timmy Hinchy.'

I felt like the Fugitive meetin' face to face with the one-armed man.

'Maurice,' he asked, 'Will you have a pint?'

'No,' says I.

'Fine so,' says he, 'We'll get to work. We'll drink enough when we get you elected.'

Out we went. I hadn't noticed the Honda 50 parked outside the pub and Timmy didn't see me go a whiter shade of pale as he kick-started it and shouted, 'Get up and hould on!'

I realised fairly lively that my guide had a dodgy style of motorbike ridin' and an even dodgier knowledge of the area. Accordin' to him every house we stopped at was Ryan's.

'This is Tom and Mary Ryan's, great supporters of your father,' he'd shout as he brought the Honda to a halt at each gate. But at the first three houses, not only was there no Tom or Mary; there were no Ryans. There were Hogans, Regans and Barlows.

I knew I was in deep trouble when Timmy sent me into one particular Ryan establishment to greet more 'great supporters of my father.' It was a Ryan house alright; the home of Mick Ryan, a sittin' FF councillor who offered me fourteen kinds of tay, drink and grub.

'Twas time to look at the register, but tryin' to do that on the back of the bike was like tryin' to read a map in an Atlantic gale.

After three hours of uselessness we arrived back at the Drippin' Tap havin' littered the countryside with pages of the register and done woeful damage to my electoral chances. To add insult to injury we had dishonoured the memory of my father. I was told in one house that I wasn't half the man he was: 'at least he knew his neighbours.'

We were sittin' havin' a very silent pint when in walked a commercial traveller. He looked at Timmy in surprise and said:

'Begod Hinchy, you're a long way from Clonmel.'

'Erra,' says Timmy, 'The Aunt gave me a few pound to drive this fella around to do a bit of canvassin'. I hardly know anyone around here but he's a total feckin disaster, he knows no one.'

God between me and well-meanin' people. Isn't it a wonder I ever got elected?

MORe PARiSH NOTeS

Goin' through my files I found another sample of my contributions to the parish notes for the *Weekly Eyeopener*.

ICA Amalgamation Talks Stalled

Amalgamation talks between the ICA (Irish Countrywomen's Association) guilds in Honetyne, Killdicken and Glengooley stalled during the week. Maude Reidy led the Honetyne contingent out of the negotiations accusing Moll Gleeson, President of the Killdicken Guild of engineering a coup. 'That lady has been in secret discussions with Glengooley to divide up the big jobs and leave Honetyne out in the cold,' she claimed. 'They have a hatched a plot to set up a rotating presidency between the two of them. Well they can rotate, rotavate or vegetate all they like but Honetyne will stand alone.'

Organic Course

A ten-week course on 'earth friendly planting' hosted by Percy Pipplemoth Davis will begin in the Community Centre, Killdicken on Monday night. The first session entitled, 'Being Gentle with the Soil' will be given by the host himself. Homework will probably consist of stripping off and rolling naked around the garden. Thank God the nettles aren't due back for a few months.

Booze Bus

The outcome of a day-long meeting to establish a pilot rural pub transport scheme for Honetyne, Killdicken, Glengooley and Shronefodda continues to be shrouded in secrecy. The gathering held in 'The Dripping Tap', Shronefodda on Friday last was attended by all local publicans. However, the conclusions are a mystery to everyone including those in attendance. The gathering lasted late into the night and taxis had to be brought from Clonmel to ferry the publicans back to their respective establishments. When asked to comment, Tom Walshe of Killdicken declared, 'Nothing is agreed till everything is agreed and as we have difficulty remembering anything that was said you can take it nothing is agreed.' It's great to get a bit of clarity.

Pot Holes

At a meeting to draw attention to the potholes on the Borrisnangoul Road, farmer Pa Cantillon described the road in terms of a World War I battlefield, 'Tis like a place that got on the wrong side of an artillery sergeant,' he exclaimed. 'The road is so uneven when I go to feed the cattle I have to take seasickness tablets to cope with the swaying of the tractor as it negotiates the craters.'

Sympathy

Sympathy is extended to the Roche family whose aunt, Anna Betty died in Lancaster last week. Her life's achievements were celebrated at a Mass of remembrance held at Killdicken Church on Thursday last. Afterwards at a reception in Walshe's Lounge Bar, Anna Betty's exploits as a champion hurdler and all-round athlete were recalled. In an eloquent address, popular local councillor Maurice Hickey described her as 'the Carroll's Boomerang of the women of the parish.'

Race Night

A race night will be held on 10 February in aid of the Killdicken Graveyard Committee. Sponsorship for races and horses is being sought at the moment. Chairperson Monica Reilly say the committee has big plans. 'The current growth in the local population means things are getting tight in the graveyard. People will have to start doubling up if we don't move into Hayes's field sooner than planned,' she declared. 'With the help of a good race night we'll be able to move it on fairly lively. It's not fair that people who are dying have the prospect of being buried with strangers added to their worries.'

Marriage Support

'Don't be scared, be prepared.' This is the message from Agnes Delahunty of the Regional Marriage Support Group. A series of marriage support weekends are being organised by the group at the Sunset Retreat and Holistic Centre, Kilnaroe beginning on Friday 9 February. Agnes

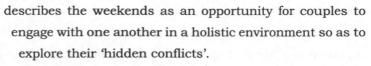

describes the weekends as an opportunity for couples to engage with one another in a holistic environment so as to explore their 'hidden conflicts'.

Poor auld Agnes means well, but if I was in a stormy marriage I'd be inclined to leave well enough alone. Most married couples have enough to do to handle open conflict not to mind digging up hidden ones.

SLEEP TALKIN'

Thinkin' out loud is very common. However, when it's combined with day dreamin' you have a dangerous mixture.

Tom Cantwell is a hoor for it. He ends up in awful trouble for tellin' the truth in the wrong places. For instance, one day he was in the Post Office enquirin' about a parcel of computer bits he was expectin' from Dublin. It had gone astray. He was leanin' on the counter waitin' while Lily Mac made a phone call tryin' to trace the missin' item. Now, Lily is not what you call a small woman, she carries a bit of condition. Not to put a tooth in it, she's feckin' huge. Anyway while she was on the phone she turned around to have a look for the parcel in the boxes on the ground behind her. As she bent over Cantwell found himself starin' at the enormity of her west end and went off into a daydream. Unknown to himself he began to think out loud and talk out loud. He failed to notice that Lily had finished the phone call.

'By God' says he, 'that's one big arse. I think it's the biggest I've ever seen in my life.'

'How dare you, Thomas Cantwell,' barked Lily, 'Who gave you the right to make comments about my person?'

Cantwell was stuck. His big gommy mouth had landed him in trouble again. In fairness he only said what everyone thinks around here. The size of Lilly's hind-quarters never ceases to amaze the natives.

'I'm sorry, Lily,' says he, 'I was only day-dreaming.'

'Well you can daydream about somethin' else besides my backside, you dirty article,' snapped a fierce cross Lily. 'Get out of my Post Office. If your auld computer yoke turns up I'll make sure it doesn't go astray again. In fact I'll put it under my fine big arse, the biggest one in the world accordin' to you: that should keep it safe and sound till you decide to come lookin' for it. Now, feck off!'

Cantwell didn't have to go back to Lily for his parcel. When Pa Quirke delivered it the followin' week it had all the appearance of somethin' that spent a few hours under the weight of a backside of substance.

Another day Cantwell was in the local enjoyin' a quiet pint in the middle of the afternoon. Tom Walshe, the publican was at the other side of the counter readin' the paper. Now, at that time Walshe had a set of false teeth that he liked to keep exercised. Every now and again he'd send them on a lap of his gums before slottin' them back into place. He fairly put them through their paces when readin' the newspaper: the teeth would be flyin' around the mouth as if they were bein' chased by Ger Loughnane with a cattle-prod. Any stranger lookin' at him would think there was somethin' live tryin' to break out through his face.

Cantwell was nursin' his pint and starin' over at Tom. The only sound to be heard was the rattle of Tom's gallopin' dentures. Not realisin' he was broadcastin' Cantwell started thinkin' aloud with near disastrous consequences.

'You're too feckin' mean to buy a set that'll fit you. That's the holy all of it. If you're not careful you'll swally them and they'll eat you alive.'

'Are you talkin' to me?' asked Walshe.

'Who's talkin?' asked a puzzled Cantwell

'You were talkin' to me in a manner that was far from complimentary,' declared Walshe.

'You're goin' off the head, Tom Walshe. You're hearin' voices,' replied Cantwell, 'I said nothin' to no-one.'

He finished his pint and departed, convinced that Tom Walshe was losin' his marbles. Walshe was left scratchin' his head, convinced that the drink was havin' a serious effect on Cantwell's brain.

Anyway, since then the publican has a new set of false teeth that appear to be nailed in place. Cantwell has taken up yoga to cure his day-dreamin', but Lily Mac is still a slave to the cream buns.

COMETH THE TIME

I'm takin' soundin's among my people to see if I'll run in the general election. You're probably sick to the back teeth listenin' to me ditherin' about this, but I've never had to take a decision like it before. You see, I walked into the council seat when my father passed away.

Takin' on the general election is a different kettle of fish. I'd have to go outside my comfort zone and canvass in places I wouldn't be known. I had a long chat with my kitchen cabinet, Messrs. Cantwell, Cantillon, Walshe and Quirke over a few pints the other night. There was general agreement that if I didn't go this time I'd be too old when the flag went up next time.

It's a good job my skin is fairly thick as my cabinet members were not what you'd call complimentary.

'Maurice,' says Pa Cantillon, 'You're a bit like a turkey a fella wins in a card game in October. If the bird isn't killed for Christmas, by the time February comes decisions have to be taken as to whether he's destined for the oven or for life as an ornament in the farmyard. It's the same with you now, Maurice. Either you take a run for the cauldron of Leinster House now or you prepare yourself for to be a big auld turkey cock struttin' around the confines of Killdicken, Honetyne and Glengooley.'

'Begod,' says Tom Walshe, 'if those were the choices facin' me I think I'd prefer to be on one leg in a hen run than facin' the heat of an oven.'

'Indeed,' says Cantwell, 'It's the choice at the heart of the human condition: do you let life slip away in a quiet backyard or do you go out in a blaze of glory?'

Everybody called a pint for him: Cantwell makes no sense when he's sober.

'What does your Mother think?' asked Quirke.

Now, that's the most fundamental question to ask an Irishman when it come to him makin' decisions.

'Well,' says I, "tis hard to know. Sometimes I think she'd love to see me in the Dáil but things are grand for us at the moment. She drives me around to every auld function I have to go to and I'm home for the dinner every day. She has me for company and I have all the comforts of home. Except when I make a public eejit of myself: then it's like havin' Vincent Browne with a sore head parked beside the fire every time you come in the door.'

'But what does she think?' insisted Quirke, 'Have you asked her?'

'On a good day she says it wouldn't do any harm to run. On a bad day she says 'tis bad enough havin' a local gobshite in the house without havin' to live with a national gobshite. On balance, I'd say she'll go along with whatever I decide.'

Cantwell had downed his pint and was beginnin' to settle.

'Listen,' says he, 'Why would you want to run? Is there an agenda or a manifesto you have? Are there things you want to achieve? If you're only runnin' because you have nothin' better to do with your time then how do you expect people like me to wear out shoe leather for you, climb poles with posters and collect a few pounds for the funds?'

There was silence for ages. Eventually Quirke spoke up. 'I hate basic questions, they take the fun out of everything.'

Just then the door flew open and two carloads of men and women from the other side of Clonmel invaded the pub. They were at a weddin' in the village. As they ordered a drink they recognised me.

'Aren't you Maurice Hickey,' asked one of the women, 'the man who wants to bring back the plastic bag?'

'That's me,' says I.

'Well if you can bring back the plastic bag and get rid of the smokin' ban then you're our man,' she declared.

As they all lifted their glasses Quirke looked at me.

'Game on,' says he.

OH NO YOU WON'T!

Killdicken hasn't had a local pantomime in years, due in large part to an outbreak of that common Irish condition known as the split. About a decade ago a row on stage spilled over into the crowd, out on to the street and only came to a halt when the Parish Priest and the Sergeant baton charged the crowd.

The panto that year was based on the story of Goldilocks and the Three Bears. As usual there was fierce competition for the leadin' part, Goldilocks. Now, the producer wasn't lookin' for a blonde little girl in pigtails: he wanted a big bulky hoor who was willin' to wear a dress. Believe me, you'd be amazed how many big bulky hoors of fellas want to wear pretty dresses.

Anyway, Mick Regan and Tony Nolan were in the runnin' for the part. Both were built like Russian tanks and driven by two very ambitious mothers. The producer was local impresario, Aloysius Segan Doyle who worked for years as a stagehand in the West End. He settled back home and brought with him an accent, a double barrel name and a cravat.

Unfortunately, Aloysius, who produced all the pantos in the area, had one major weakness; he took an obvious shine to people he thought had star quality. Durin' the auditions for Goldilocks he reckoned Mick Regan had a future under the bright lights. The only future under bright lights we could see for Mick involved him beatin' bullocks around the ring at the night mart.

Anyway, Tony Nolan's mother was like a divil when her boy failed to be cast as Goldilocks. She nearly went mad altogether when he got Daddy Bear's part, a role that would hide him under a full costume for the duration of the show. Mammy Nolan didn't rear her Tony to be hidden under anythin'.

On the first night of rehearsals she slipped quietly into the hall. Aloysius Segan Doyle was on stage addressin' cast and crew in advance of rehearsals. He loved this bit; he always wanted to be in the limelight himself and gave a speech fit for an openin' night in the Abbey.

He was in full flight about 'ort and the stage' when Mammy Nolan burst out of the darkness at the back of the hall. 'What would you know about it?' she shouted.

'Who dares interrupt me? Desist at once,' he demanded.

'You're nothin' but a bag of double-barrelled wind,' she shouted. 'You know as much about talent as I do about deep-sea divin'.'

She eventually left when her son Tony begged her to go. However, after she had gone he overheard his rival sniggerin' at her. From that moment he planned to take revenge the man who would be Goldilocks.

On the second last night of the show he cut loose. He was playin' the part of Daddy Bear and had the famous lines, 'Who's been eatin' my porridge? ' Who's been sittin' on my chair?' and 'Who's been sleepin' in my bed?' When he got to askin' who'd been sleepin' in his bed, he went off-script.

'I've got it,' says he, 'sure there's only one family in this parish who could eat all that feckin' porridge, make shite of the youngfella's chair and leave a bed like mine saggin' in the middle. There must be one of them big fat feckin' Regans somewhere in the house.'

With that Goldilocks Regan jumped out of Baby Bear's bed and made a go for Daddy Bear. Mammy Regan beat her way up one side of the crowd and Mammy Nolan beat her way up the other. They met in the middle and all hell broke loose. First cousins, second cousins and neighbours got involved as they beat one another down to the square where peace was restored by the combined forces of the law and the church.

We were reminiscin' about it in the pub the other night when someone suggested we should revive the panto. The very mention of it was met by a chorus of: 'Oh, no we won't.'

THE POWER OF PRAYER

There was a time in this village when you could set your watch by the family rosary. At seven o'clock every evenin' the cowboys and Indians rode off into the sunset and we, the youngsters of the parish, pulled our backsides after us into kitchens to endure the eternity of the daily rosary. We'd throw ourselves across chairs while parents knelt upright like soldiers and prayed like monks. We'd be kneelin' there, bored out of our minds while the prayers rose and fell like the wind in a mild storm. Decade followed decade until we arrived at the trimmin's, totally exhausted and convinced that life was easier for pagans.

Of course if there was any kind of an audience there'd be devilment. Occasionally, bein' an only child, I'd be allowed stay at a neighbour's house for the rosary. I often found myself at Quirkes' or Cantillons' and became an expert in each family's particular way of prayin'.

The Cantillons had what you'd call a very natural method. Their lives and the farm found their way into the most sacred of the prayers. They'd remember things durin' the rosary and unless they mentioned them there and then they were afraid they'd forget them. Both the father and mother were distracted by the farm and were likely to say anythin'.

This is one of many versions of the rosary you could hear at Cantillons':

'The first sorrowful mystery; Our Lord goes into the garden. Oh Cripes, did anyone close that gate? If the pigs get in again we won't have a spud left.'

'Why didn't you close it yourself if you are so worried? – Hail Mary full of grace ....'

57

'The second glorious mystery; the ascension into heaven – I'll have to get that ladder back from Gleesons', they're surely finished white washin' by now? That crowd would borrow your eye and come back for the socket – Our Father who art ....'

'You're a bigger fool to be givin' them anything. They've plenty money to buy their own feckin' ladder – Hail Mary ...'

The Cantillons' dog often found his way into the prayers. He was useless on the farm but a divil for followin' birds, especially swallows. He'd spend the summer runnin' around the yard after them yelpin' and snarlin':

'Holy Mary Mother of God – lie down you useless mongrel or I'll get the gun – pray for us sinners ...'

'Glory be – that dog is one useless hoor – as it was ...'

The Quirkes were different, they were very strict when it came to prayin'. Everyone had to kneel straight up and anyone who happened to call in had to take part no matter what they believed. Auld Quirke loved religion and thought he had the makin's of a bishop. When it came to prayin' out loud he developed an accent befittin' a high-rankin' man of the cloth.

One evenin' Cantwell and myself were at Quirke's at rosary time when who dropped in but local character, Mick Ryan. Mick wouldn't be renowned for his religious beliefs and that evenin' he was well oiled after spendin' the day at a funeral in Bally. We were all ordered to our knees when the clock struck seven.

Auld Quirke, who was grander than usual now that he had an audience, opened proceedin's with great gusto: 'The Fawst Glawrius Mystereh our Loood rises triumphantleh.'

'Yehoo, ya boy, ya! Good man yarself!' shouted Mick Ryan.

Cantwell, Quirke junior and myself got such a fit of laughin' we had to hit for the door and hide in the bushes. By the time we found the courage to come back auld Quirke had other problems on his hands. Mick Ryan had fallen sound asleep durin' the remainder of the rosary and they couldn't wake him.

'I wonder,' says Cantwell, who was always a pup, 'If we had another go at The Fawst Glawrious Mystereh would he rise triumphantleh?' After that we were never invited back to pray with the Quirkes.

LOST IN TRANSLATION

St Patrick's Day falls at the worst time of the year. The rain, wind and cold is enough to kill a nation and yet we expect people to parade up and down windswept streets with little or nothin' on them. No wonder the common cold flattens half the country in March.

Everyone I meet has a bad cold. No matter who I talk to gives me a run-down on the state of their health, their coughs and sniffles. The Mother has been in the scratcher for the past two weeks with a hot water bottle and a bucket of Lemsips. I'm killed from cookin', cleanin' and bummin' lifts. I've no one to take me anywhere and have missed a heap of auld meetin's.

I did get to one council meetin' and you wouldn't hear yourself thinkin' in the chamber with the splutterin' and the coughin'. The state of the councillors' health didn't stop a row breakin' out between members from Glenhoran and Cappamoggle. When the Glenhoran boys found out Cappamoggle had jumped the queue for a new sewerage system there was open warfare.

The Cathaoirleach, who had a particularly bad cold, took a fit of sneezin' as the row started and was helpless when rival Councillors started climbin' over seats to get a dig at one another. Luckily the Director of Services, a referee in his spare time, had a whistle in his pocket. One blast and they all came to their senses.

We should never underestimate the power of the common cold. The Cathaoirleach's dose nearly led to chaos at the heart of local government in our particular corner of the democratic world.

Of course, there's a whole language used to describe the symptoms of colds and flus and everyone seems to know what you mean when you describe yours. However, as they might say on RTE, the language of the common cold is not universal.

A few years ago this English lady doctor came to the village to do locum for Doc Doherty who was away on holidays. She arrived durin' an outbreak of the common cold in all its forms. The waitin' room was full and Monica Whelan, the secretary/receptionist got fierce concerned when she noticed that people who went in to the doctor were bein' sent back out to the waitin' room. After a while the queue of splutterin' adults and whinin' children was out the door as the whole system clogged and there was no movement in or out.

Monica, who's as good as any doctor, took matters in hand and went in to the surgery and found the poor visitin' doctor in floods of tears.

'Why didn't somebody tell me that Gaelic is the first language around here?' the distressed doctor cried, 'What's more, if you don't mind me saying so, Monica, I think there's a danger of an outbreak of sexually transmitted diseases. A lot of these men seem to be dabbling in the sex industry.'

Poor Monica nearly fell into a heap but held herself together. She phoned her daughter to come and take over at the reception desk while she sat in with the doctor to do the bit of translatin'. She was sure the patients wouldn't mind as they always give her a full account of their ailments on their way in and out from the Doc Doherty.

Herself and the doctor started again from the top of the queue and recalled Mickey Mullins. He told them he had a 'rasper of a rattle' that was 'tearin' the gizzard' out of him and he didn't know where he got the 'hoorin' thing'.

The doctor looked fairly relieved when Monica explained that Mickey didn't have any unusual disease in his undercarriage and wasn't 'playin' away from home'; he simply had a bad cough.

She guided the doctor through the multitude of patients who had a 'smotherin' hoor of a dose', 'a fecker of a nose', 'a bastard of a throat', 'a gravel pit in me chest', and 'a melted hoor of an earache'.

'Tis no wonder there's still no cure for the common cold.

WHAT A WEEKEND

Paddy's Weekend was a weekend of three halves. We had a parade, a plague and sobbin' session.

The big day itself was great. This year the local parade went off with little or no fuss. 'Twas organised by the teachers in the national school with none of the usual politics, shenanigans and tomfoolery. They invited all the other clubs and organisations to participate and everyone had great fun. We adjourned to Tom Walshe's for a few very pleasant pints.

On Sunday there was a challenge match between the junior hurlers of Glengooley and Killdicken. That too was a fairly quiet affair. Well, sort of, if you take into account the long tradition of hatred between the two clubs. These matches rarely get to half-time. On Sunday the game lasted up to ten minutes into the second half before it was abandoned. In case you jump to conclusions, it wasn't a row on the field of play that led to the abandonment: no, 'twas a dose of the scutters did the harm.

Stickie Stakelum's chip wagon was parked in Killdicken the night before and whatever was in the curry sauce it ran through the two parishes. 'Twas like a cross between a volcano and a flood. Ten minutes into the second half Stickie's scutters struck all members of the two teams that had dined on his dodgy delights. Fellas took off runnin' for the jacks and the bushes clutchin' their rear ends in desperation. As the players dropped like flies, the ref blew the whistle and collapsed into a heap on the pitch. There was no ambulance available so the civil defence sprang into action and held the fort till the Doc Doherty arrived with his bag of tricks.

On Monday the place was very quiet. The ones that were home for the weekend were gone back while me and the few auld faithfuls were left

holdin' up the counter.

'I'm glad this weekend is over,' says Quirke, 'I hate the Paddy whackery of it all. What gets me is the auld come-all-ya songs. They'd put years on you.'

'Begob,' says Cantillon, 'I think they're great. I love nothin' better than a good cry when I have a few pints in me. You can't bate "The Old Bog Road" to turn on the waterworks.'

'Ah no,' says Cantwell, 'My favourite is "A Mother's Love is a Blessin'", that's a dead cert for the blubber lips.'

He started singin' in a lonesome voice that would put a banshee to shame:

A mother's love is a blessin'
No matter where you roam,
Keep her while she's livin'
You'll miss her when she's gone.
Love her as in childhood
Though feeble old and grey
'Cause you'll never miss a mother's love
'Till she's buried beneath the clay.

As he finished he put his head down on the counter and did a fine imitation of a distraught son mournin' in death the mother he neglected in life. He got a standin' ovation from the rest of us, but when the applause died down all we could hear was the sound of snifflin' comin' from behind the counter. I leant over and there was Tom Walshe sittin' on the floor and he cryin' like a baby. We all looked at one another and didn't know what to do.

There was dead silence until Tom stood up and straightened himself. No one said a word as he busied himself behind the bar washin' glasses. After about ten minutes Cantwell broke the silence:

'Give us four pints, a bag of peanuts and what were you cryin' about?'

'Tis that song,' replied Tom, 'I had an auld pet ewe one time and I loved her. She had twin lambs and not long after they were born she died. That

song was a hit at the time and whenever it came on the radio I melted. What's worse, the lambs never took to me after the mother died. Jaysus, I'm still heartbroken.'

Everyone has their own troubles.

WHAT HAVE I DONE NOW?

Did you ever walk into somethin' you know you will regret? To make a long story short, I decided I not to run in the general election, but threw my lot in with another candidate; none other than the bould Breda Quinn, Superquinn. 'Twould've been an easier job to run myself.

I'd better fill you in on the background. Last week I ran into Breda in Clonmel and she spittin' fire about the health service. Her mother had to go to hospital recently and after four days on a trolley she was sent home and told she'd be called for an ultrasound when they'd get the machine workin'. Eventually Superquinn threatened the hospital authorities that herself and her mother would picket the place until she was seen. They got sorted out, but she's still as cross as a bag of cats.

'Only that you might be runnin' in the general election yourself, Maurice,' says concluded, 'I'd be tempted to put my hat in the ring.'

I spent the rest of the day thinkin' about her closin' remark. The more I thought about it the more I liked the idea of Superquinn the candidate. To be honest, I'm in no humour for an election; the prospect of gettin' literature together, printin' posters and tryin' to gather money puts years on me. On the other hand 'twould be great to be part of the action and if Superquinn ran, I could have the best of both worlds.

When I ran the idea past the Mother she seemed relieved.

'I'm glad,' she said. ''Tis bad enough bein' a councillor, but if you went to the Dáil, we'd be pestered entirely.'

Even though she has no great love for Superquinn, she thinks she'd be a good candidate.

'There's no law that says you have to like the people you vote for; as long as they're good at their job, that's all that matters. For instance, I think Mick Healy the butcher is the most ignorant hoor this side of the Cliffs of Moher but I won't buy my meat anywhere else. It's the same with Breda Quinn, I mightn't like her but if she was a TD I'd go to no one else to do a job for me.'

The followin' evenin' I made it my business to call to Superquinn. She poured me a drink and we settled down to chat.

'I came to tell you,' says I, 'that I won't be runnin' in the general election. What's more, followin' our conversation in Clonmel I think 'twould be a great idea if you threw your hat in the ring. You'd be a mighty candidate.'

She stared into the fire and after about five minutes she spoke. 'Twas clear that she had already given this serious consideration.

'I have been thinkin' about it,' says she, 'and now that you're not runnin', I most certainly will. Since Dixie died I've been badly in need of somethin' to revive my interest in life. Maybe this is it!'

'That's the stuff,' says I, 'I'll be your campaign manager and we'll frighten the life out of the lot of them.'

'Hang on now, Maurice,' says she, 'I'd advise you to consider that offer carefully. This will be fierce hard work and your track record in that department isn't somethin' for the Guinness Book of Records. In fact if you were shot for bein' a hard worker, 'twould surely be a case of mistaken identity.'

I was gobsmacked, but before I could unsmack my gob she put the bottle of whiskey back in the press and handed me my coat.

'Go home and get a good night's sleep. Be back here tomorrow evenin' with a copy of the electoral register, a list of people that might help us, an estimate of how much this will cost and a list of fundraisin' ideas.'

I tried to explain that I was busy but she cut me off.

'I want results, not excuses. Good night, Maurice.'

I should've kept my mouth shut.

TRAPPED

Oh God I'm killed. Superquinn has taken to electioneerin' like a kangaroo takes to jumpin', except she's jumpin' all over me. I had an awful job to lay hands on the electoral register. Twice she sent me in to Clonmel for it and twice I came back without it: I was sent in a third time. The women at the reception desk in county hall were gettin' worried about me; I obviously looked to be under terrible stress.

Jack Neylon, the porter came to me durin' my third visit and whispered, 'Jaysus Maurice, did you get married on the quiet or somethin'?' You're like a man livin' in the shadow of a cross woman.'

'You don't know the half of it,' says I.

'There's only one thing for that,' says he, 'and that's an escape hatch.'

'What are you talkin' about?' I asked.

'Well,' Maurice, 'as you know, my woman is not known for her mild manners and her gentle ways so over the years I've had to invent an escape hatch. I work as a volunteer with the local senior citizens group. They meet once a week but as far as the wife is concerned there's three meetin's a week: one with the senior citizens and two meetin's of the committee. That gives me cover to get away and have a few quiet pints with the lads.'

'I might need a place like that,' says I, 'except I'll need it for six days a week.'

When I got home Superquinn wanted the names of every contact I had in the electoral area, all my family and friends, every dog and devil I knew. After an hour I had a pain in my hand from writin'.

I needed an escape hatch and I needed it now. 'Twas time to run. As luck would have it, Cantwell rang me on the mobile phone askin' if I was goin' to the match on Sunday. Poor Cantwell didn't know what was happenin' when I answered the phone. This is how the conversation went.

Cantwell: 'Maurice, are you comin to the match? I need to know.'

Maurice: 'Well, the poor woman; this looks serious. What did the doctors say?'

Cantwell: 'What doctors? You mad hoor. We're goin to a feckin' match, not a hospital.'

Maurice: 'Ah sure, twould be an ease to her. We'll be over as soon as we can. Good Lord, we can only hope and pray she'll hold out till we get there. Bye, bye now and God bless.'

I'm sure Cantwell was lookin' at his phone as if it had been taken over by aliens, but I had my escape hatch.

'Breda,' says I, 'my Aunt Madge in Kilkenny has taken bad, I'll have to go. I'll give you a ring when I find out how things are.'

I didn't wait for he response. I took off runnin'. My next problem was to find a place to hide. Passin' the post office I bumped into Pa Quirke, the postman. He was finished his rounds for the day and goin' to Limerick to buy a greyhound.

'I'll go with you,' says I, 'I need a few hours away from this place.'

We took off for Limerick but I forgot to tell the Mother anything. When I got home that night she was sittin' by the fire with a face like a fiddle on her.

'What kind of lies are you hidin' behind?' she barked. 'I met Breda Quinn today and she was surprised I wasn't gone with you to Kilkenny to be at the bedside of your 'sick and dying' Aunt Madge. Like a fool I tried to ring Madge and could get no answer. I thought the worst, so I drove to Kilkenny only to find she was gone to the races. When I came home I rang Breda to tell her your 'sick and dyin' Aunt Madge is in the full of her health. When she lays hands on you, she'll tear that lyin' tongue out of your head. If she doesn't do it, I will.'

I'm afraid my escape hatch has landed me in solitary confinement.

BEWARE OF THE LIVE MIKE

Aside from the nuclear bomb, live radio is the most dangerous thing on the planet. This is especially true for the politician. It should be avoided completely but I still manage to walk myself into trouble at least once a year.

On Good Friday I was invited by Willy De Wig Ryan to do an extensive interview live on our local radio station, The Sticks FM. The programme entitled: 'The World According to Maurice Hickey' was advertised heavily for two weeks and was broadcast between 8.00pm and 9.00pm on Good Friday.

I arrived at the 'studio', a disused hairdressers in Honetyne, at quarter to eight on the evenin' in question. Willy De Wig rushed in with two minutes to go and put me sittin' at an old kitchen table facin' a microphone perched on top of a pile of auld telephone books.

The eight o'clock news finished and we were on.

'Good evenin' listeners and friends,' he began. 'Welcome to dis special Good Friday programme featurin' yours truly in conversation wit wan of de legends of dis area; none udder dan dat well know Councillor, de King of Killdicken, Maurice Hickey. Good evenin' to ya, Councillor Maurice.'

With an introduction like that I couldn't go wrong. I was just settlin' down when he hit me with a walloper.

'Maurice, as you know we've been advertisin' dis programme all week and we've had numerous messages for you includin' dis wan here from Mick Gilhooley of Shronefodda. 'Willy, when you get dat useless hoor Hickey on de programme ask him what he's doin about my son's plannin' application. He's been fartin' around wit dis for two year makin' all kinds of promises and deliverin' nothin'. Votin' for Hickey is as useful as votin' for my auld dog, Shep.'

'Now Maurice, what have you to say to Mick? He's not what you'd call a fan.'

I was stuck to the chair. I muttered somethin' about the complexity of plannin' and every case bein' different. I did remind Willy that I was involved in getting' Mick Gilhooley a new toilet.

'Dere ya go, Mick,' interrupted De Wig, 'you ask the good Councillor Maurice for a house and he gets you a jacks. You should've asked him for a hotel and you might've got the house.'

Things could only get worse, and they did. One dirty question followed another till the final scud caused me to explode.

'Maurice. Why aren't you married? Dey say you're too much of a Mammy's boy to ever get yourself hitched. Is it true dat de Mudder will have to be six foot under before you'll pop de question to anyone?'

That was enough for me. He went too far.

'Listen, Willy,' says I, 'I know that politicians are supposed to handle the media with kid gloves, but I left mine at home tonight. I just want to tell the listeners what I'm lookin' at. I'm lookin' across at a fella that's at least a decade aulder than myself. The wig plonked on his skull looks like somethin' dropped by a cow on fresh grass and he's wearin' a trousers that would have been too tight for him when he was a teenager nearly fifty year ago. 'Tis no wonder he has failed to father a child, despite all his efforts. You've only to look at the trousers and you'd know that it has squeezed the life out of whatever was inside in it.'

Willy De Wig was lost for words. I was on a roll.

'As for Mick Gilhooley and his son's plannin',' I continued, 'the son in question has three houses in Clonmel, one in Bulgaria and one in Tanyourbottie on the Canaries. Givin' him plannin' permission would be like rubbin' lard into a fat pig's arse. Now Willy, you can take your radio programme and your microphone and—' someone pulled the plug before I lost the rag entirely.

I left the studio havin' broken all the rules about dealin' with the media, but I felt feckin fantastic.

AND THEY'RE OFF

The election trail started in earnest this week when Superquinn decided 'twas time to kick-start her campaign. She chose to launch herself on the electorate outside the Post Office on Friday mornin' while the senior citizens were collectin' the pension. We sent a press invitation to the papers and the radio station.

I've discovered that bein' director of elections is goin' to be easier than I thought. Superquinn likes to control everythin' so all I have to do is nod in agreement. For the launch she had everythin' organised while I'd be thinkin' about it. She got posters made, she put an ad on The Sticks FM and borrowed a public address system from Pee Hogan and the Blueboys.

In an attempt to make a pitch for the green vote she enlisted the services of an ass and cart to act as a platform. The animal and transport came compliments of Reggie Ingham, a retired Englishman who runs a home for animals in Cossatrasna.

Everythin' was in place at 9 o'clock Friday mornin'. Formalities were to begin at ten. At quarter past the place was like a ghost town, and by half ten the press were gettin' edgy so we decided to get the ball rollin'. I kicked matters off with a fine speech delivered to an empty street. Mag Richardson and Bridie Sheehan came along, one of them is as deaf as the other. They stopped to look at me as I addressed the absent multitudes from behind Pee Hogan's microphone. After a minute or two Mag shouted at Bridie, 'I never knew the Hickeys could sing.'

'And they can't,' answered Bridie, 'I pity the poor ass havin' to listen to him.'

They disappeared into the Post Office and I was left talkin' to the wall

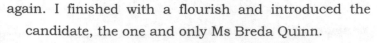

again. I finished with a flourish and introduced the candidate, the one and only Ms Breda Quinn.

Superquinn launched into her speech and no sooner had she started than Tim Delaney pulled up in his ancient Zetor tractor. He seemed confused by all the fuss and quickly retreated into Post Office to collect his few pounds. However his battery must be dodgy because he left the tractor runnin'. No one could hear or see Superquinn with the splutterin', coughin' and belchin' of Tim's auld machine. After a minute or two she called a halt to her speech, jumped off the ass and cart and pulled the plug on the tractor.

She was back in full flight when Tim came out to find his Zetor stopped. As he stared in amazement at the silent antique one of the photographers approached him, whispered into his ear and pointed at Superquinn. Tim began to shout and wave his fists at her. The cameras snapped and the journalists scribbled furiously as he called her every name under the sun includin' an interferin' auld biddy. When she accused him of single-handedly causin' global warmin' with his splutterin' tractor a full-scale row broke out.

I got down from the cart to make the peace but there was no talkin' to Tim. He pushed me aside and gave the poor ass a wallop on the arse. The frightened animal took off with Superquinn on board, but she held on and continued her speech. In fairness to her not only did she bring the ass under control, she managed to turn him around and came back up the town with her theme tune, Abba's 'Super Trouper', blarin' out of the sound system.

Meanwhile Tim enlisted the support of myself and the assembled members of the media to give his tractor a push. When it finally rattled into life it did so with a massive bang that frightened the life out of the returnin' ass and the beast took off again without givin' Superquinn a chance to dismount. This time he meant business and there was no controllin' him as he galloped out of sight.

However, 'tis an ill wind that doesn't blow some good. By the time the gallopin' ass arrived back with Superquinn he had certainly raised her profile in at least four parishes.

AN HONEST POLITICIAN

Campaignin' with Superquinn will be the death of me. The amount of jobs I get to do is astronomical. Every complaint or query she gets on the doorsteps is handed over with the instruction, 'Make a note of that Maurice and follow it up.'

The list of jobs is so long I'll have to hire a secretary to get through it all; otherwise I'll burst. Although 'twill do me no harm for the local elections I hadn't intended fightin' that campaign for another two years.

The worst thing about canvassin' with Breda is that she's too honest. She breaks the first rule of politics by sayin' what she thinks. Every politician gets fed up of the whingin' you get on the doorsteps and there comes a point when you want to tell the complainers to cop on and get a life. However, accordin' to the golden rule you must hold your tongue and keep your advice to yourself. There's no such rule for our Breda.

Callin' to a house in Borrisnangoul the other day we had to beat our way through an overgrown hedge to get beyond the gate. We were met at the door by a yelpin' Jack Russell and a woman who was eatin' her way through a lump of sponge cake that would feed a house full of children. She started complainin' about the potholes on the road, the state of the hedges and the fact that the council wouldn't come to clean the chutes on the house. Behind her, lost in a cloud of smoke in the sittin' room sat her husband in his vest watchin' telly.

When she finished with the council she tore in to the health services.

'My poor Fred there,' she said, pointin' to her husband, 'He needs a chest x-ray and they won't send a taxi for him, how are we supposed to get him to the hospital? I'm waitin' for an appointment with a chiropodist for me poor feet and I don't know when I'm goin' to get it.'

Superquinn listened for about ten minutes and then cut loose. She pushed the woman aside and walked straight into the sittin' room, threw back the curtains, opened the windows, took the fag out of Fred's mouth and flung it into the fireplace.

'What your Fred needs is some fresh air and a bit of exercise,' she declared, "tis no wonder he has chest problems if he spends his days in this gas chamber.'

Fred looked at her as if she was about to send him to Siberia. She made him put on his shoes and dragged him out to a shed where she found a slash hook and a hedge clippers. 'Now cut back that hedge and when you're finished, pull the weeds, clean the chutes and work up a sweat. You don't need a chest x-ray; you need to get off your arse.'

She then turned on the woman with the sponge cake, told her if she lost a heap of flab her feet wouldn't be killed from carryin' her around.

'Now,' says Superquinn, 'Councillor Hickey will call back here in two weeks' time and if that hedge is cut, the chutes are clean and the air in this house is fit for human habitation then I might do somethin' for ye. But if ye're intent on killin' yerselves by sittin' on yere backsides while eatin' and smokin' yerselves into an early grave then all the county councils and health boards in the world wont be able to do anythin' for ye.'

She left the two in a state of total shock. The woman of the house was standin' with the lump of sponge cake hidden behind her back. Himself stood in the yard in his vest starin' at the hedge clippers and slash hook as if they had fallen from outer space. Even the Jack Russell was frightened, he cowered behind an overflowin' bucket of ashes.

I'm lookin' forward to goin' back in two weeks time to see how they got on with the hedge. I'd say 'twill remain untouched by human hand and there'll be no answer at the door.

BIG BALL BLUES

The sportin' season is in full flight. Last weekend it began with a disaster when Killdicken junior footballers lost badly to the Bally boys.

Now, football wouldn't be the natural game around these parts, fella's prefer to have a stick in their hands when they put on a pair of togs. Anyway, there's always a handy auld cup to be won and a few medals to be collected for the game with the big ball.

A huge crowd turned up on Saturday evenin' to see the teams take to the field on neutral ground in Honetyne. We got off to a flyin' start with two quick points but the Bally boys cut loose and let us have it. First came a catastrophic goal. The ball was droppin' into the square and our full back was in reverse as our goalie, Tom Shine, caught it. The full back couldn't stop himself and reversed into Tom whereupon the two of them, ball and all, tumbled into the back of the net.

Worse was to come. After the Bally full forward got his third point in a row Marty Quinn, our corner back flattened him. Marty got his marchin' orders but the hoor of a Bally boy made a miraculous recovery and went on to play a blinder.

Our goalman, Tom Shine, featured prominently again. His wife arrived on a bike and as he tried to keep his eye on play she began shoutin' at him:

'Where did you put the keys of the car? I've to take me mother to Mass.'

'What?'

'Where are the keys of the car?'

'How should I know, I'm drivin' the van?'

'You had them last when you went to get your feckin' smelly gear out of the boot?

'They must be in my pocket ... oh jaysus ...'

With that a ball broke at the edge of the square and before

Tom could disentangle himself from the conversation with the wife the ball was in the back of the net. Killdicken were in deep trouble, by half time we were down two ten to three points; 'twas fairly dismal.

The second half was even worse. A man down and thirteen points in arrears our lads had to face Everest, and face it they didn't. By the time the last fist flew the Bally boys had banged in three more goals and fired over twelve points. We had added only a point. It ended five nineteen to four points. We were feckin' mortified.

Two nights afterwards, trainer manager and coach, Billy Hinchy, called a meetin' of the team. He brought them together in the hall, lined them up in their playin' positions and walked in and out between them as he carried out a post-mortem.

Everyone was asked for his opinion about what went wrong in his particular position. When Marty Quinn, the corner back was asked to assess his contribution he reminded Billy that he had been sent off twenty minutes into the match. In his opinion this had a serious impact on his performance for the remainder of the game.

We had a new knacky little corner forward, Deane Murray, who had just moved down from Dublin. When he was asked what he thought went wrong he remarked that he'd have seen more ball if he'd stayed on the subs bench.

When Billy got to Tom Shine he stood in front of him and boomed, 'Besides your wife on a bike what else caused you to let in five goals?'

Tom declared that as far as he was concerned his own back line were a bigger danger to him than the Bally forwards. At that point Marty Quinn made a go for Tom, callin' him a hen-pecked nancy-boy. Billy tried to intervene, but came in the way of a haymaker intended for Marty. He keeled over, the team scattered and when he recovered he was in the arms of his dodgy goalie. He decided that neither he nor Killdicken football was in safe hands and the game with the big ball has been put to bed for a long sleep.

STRAY VOTES AND WANDERIN' BULLOCKS

It has been an eventful week on the national hustin's. While the media have been followin' Bertie like a pack of hounds, Superquinn and myself have been followin' bullocks around Teerawadra.

No matter what people ask her to do she tries to follow it up. The most ludicrous of requests are chased: fellas convinced they've been done out of a will in America, people wantin' to get on *Winnin' Streak*, even people lookin' for a letter from the Bishop sayin' they were never properly married in the first place.

Saturday evenin' was the last straw. My legs were worn up to my arse from canvassin' and I was ready for a pint and a sleep. We were finishin' a canvass around the back end of Teerawadra when we met this fella who was far more concerned about five bullocks that went missin' than he was about the state of the nation. Superquinn quizzed him about when and where he last saw them.

After five minutes talkin' to your man she thought she was in for a barrel full of votes and decided we'd give him a hand to look for the bullocks. I couldn't believe my ears. Here I was, at the height of an election campaign, wanderin' around the most isolated, godforsaken, back end of the constituency. There was about six potential voters in a ten mile radius, the rest was furze bushes, goats and possibly five wanderin' bullocks.

The farmer, delighted with this unexpected help, decided to split us up and send us off in different directions. Superquinn refused and told him she wouldn't be parted from her director of elections at such a crucial time. She didn't seem to mind bein' parted from the electorate.

We took off together in the direction of nowhere with me cursin' and Superquinn salivatin' at the prospect of a vote. 'All you'll get from him,'

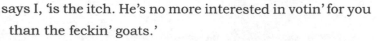

says I, 'is the itch. He's no more interested in votin' for you than the feckin' goats.'

'Every vote counts,' she answered, 'and the vote won hardest is the sweetest of all.'

'What a load of shite,' I thought. 'The sweetest vote is the one that falls into your lap when you least expect it.'

We spent two hours wanderin' around the wilderness till we spotted the bullocks in a field across a stream.

'Come on,' says she, 'Take off those shoes and socks and follow me.' She was about to remove her footwear when I spotted a few stones we could step across. We were halfway to the other side when I took a tumble and brought Superquinn with me. The two of us ended up in our backsides in the stream. As we straightened ourselves I looked up to see the five bullocks headin' straight for us at full speed.

'Come on,' says I, 'let's get out of here, this is a stampede.'

We took off runnin' in the direction we came with the bullocks in hot pursuit. Occasionally they'd pass us out and other times they'd dance a round us. We kept goin, wet, sore and half frightened of these mad cattle.

We arrived back to a hero's welcome from the farmer. After he got his wanderin' stock safely into the haggard he invited us in for tay and we gladly accepted.

'Watch this,' says Superquinn, 'We'll get the tay and I'll squeeze his vote out of him and the vote of everyone who belongs to him.'

The minute we got inside I knew 'twas goin' to be hard to squeeze the number one out of this character. The place was like a shrine to Garret Fitzgerald, there was even a picture of Garret over the Sacred Heart lamp.

Superquinn was like a lunatic when all she could get from him in the shape of a vote was a vague promise that he'd 'look after her'.

As we left the house I remarked that despite all our efforts she didn't squeeze much out of him.

'If I could lay hands on a suitable implement I'd squeeze him where he squeezed the feckin' bullocks,' she barked.

LOUD & CLEAR

This election campaign is goin' from bad to worse. Durin' the week Superquinn decided we weren't makin' enough of an impact so she tried a variety of stunts. The Moloneys down the road had twin boys a week ago and Breda borrowed the whole family for a half an hour. She had a picture taken outside the maternity with a child in each arm. An advertisement appeared on this week's *Eyeopener* showin' Superquinn with the babies under the caption: 'You Push and I'll Deliver.'

I got an awful slaggin' in the pub. 'Should we expect news from yourself and Superquinn?' I was asked.

'I hope you aren't getting' too close to the candidate?' remarked Cantillon, 'we don't need any more scandal to distract us from the key issues in this election.'

That was bad enough. Superquinn managed to get a loan of a Transit van from an auld friend of hers and she stuck posters to the side of it. She got a loan of a PA system from Pee Hogan and the Blueboys and on Sunday went around the place blastin' out her message:

If you vote for me be sure you will see
Prosperity flow like a river,
With jobs by the score and houses galore
Vote Breda, the one who delivers!

Everythin' was goin' grand, but unfortunately, Breda hadn't time to record her message and so was broadcastin' live from the back of the transit. She couldn't see where she was goin' or who was listenin'. They were goin' past the church in Honetyne after Mass on Sunday when the van, driven by Tom Cantwell, swerved to avoid a dog. Breda, with microphone in hand let out a string of curses that nearly sent the parishioners dashin' back into the church to save themselves from burnin' alive.

'Jesus, Mary and Joseph,' she screamed at Cantwell, 'What kind of a stupid hoor are ya?' She forgot the mike was open and her tirade of the abuse was broadcast to the whole country.

'Don't blame me,' shouted Cantwell, 'that was Moll Gleeson's mongrel.'

'That one and her mongrels,' responded Superquinn (still live on air), 'She'll get some fright when I'm elected and take my seat in all my finery in Dáil Éireann. She'll be green with envy – that stuck up auld bag of wind. That mongrel of hers would have more of a chance of gettin' elected than she has.'

She continued broadcastin' her rhyme in the sweetest little voice you ever heard. You'd think butter wouldn't melt in her mouth: that same mouth that had just sizzled Moll Gleeson.

She ordered Cantwell to pull over to the shop so she could buy the papers. She got some frosty reception in the shop. Honetyne is home to a lot of Gleesons and they were far from happy with the public attack on one of their own.

Superquinn then went on a bit of a house-to-house canvass but she might as well have been tryin' to sell ski holidays in the North Pole. One fella told her his greyhound had more of a track record than she had even though the hound in question had never run a race.

A woman met her at the door with a bottle of holy water and told her she should rinse her mouth out before she handled the microphone again.

'My poor mother was just out of bed after a dose of the nerves,' she barked at Superquinn, ''Twas her first day at Mass in months and your language from that loudspeaker has put her back to square one. You should take yourself off to Lough Derg and not be pesterin' the people.'

Breda couldn't wait to get back to the van. She found Cantwell had gone for a pint so she went in to the pub and pulled him out by the ears. They took off in such a hurry they didn't notice the van had been spray painted with the slogan: 'Stay Clear: Mad Cow in Transit.'

'TIS OVER

Well, thanks be to all that's good and holy this cursed election is over. I'll give ye a full account of the result next week. All I know as I put pen to paper is that my legs are worn up to my tail-end and my heart is broken tryin' to cover up for Superquinn as she put her foot in it mornin' noon and night.

You wouldn't know what she's goin' to do next. Durin' the week she took part in a debate in Walshe's pub with Percy Pipplemoth Davis where she inflicted some serious damage – on herself. She stole all my political clothes and proposed the reintroduction of the plastic bag and the reversal of the smokin' ban.

Her promotion of these policies came from what you might call the 'Cranks' angle. Percy Pipplemoth Davis attacked her over the policies sayin' they were the most irresponsible and dangerous he had ever heard. She replied 'tis people themselves are irresponsible and dangerous.

'The problem with politicians like the Pip here,' says she, 'is that they think we, the people can't think for ourselves. They think 'tis their job to babysit us as if we hadn't a brain in our head. I don't fancy bein' babysat by the Pip and his likes, you'd be a long time waitin' for a good feed of meat and spuds. They'd be pourin' leeks and carrot juice down your gullet pretendin' this kind of scutter is good for you.'

The man from the *Weekly Eyeopener* was writin' furiously and I saw disaster loomin'.

'Listen,' says she, 'let me tell you what I think of the smokin' ban. If some gobshites want to poison their lungs and wheeze their way into eternity; then off with them. What we should have is a combination of smokers' pubs and smoke free pubs. If you are a non-smoker and want to enjoy a drink without the prospect of contractin' a terminal illness then you can go to a smoke free pub. If you want to join the gobshites on a fast track to see St Peter, then off with you to a smoky kip where you can get as sick as you want as quick as you want.'

She then advocated the return of the plastic bag. I was delighted with this, 'tis great to have your policies endorsed by another politician. 'As ye know, my friend and colleague, Maurice Hickey, has been advocatin' a return of this most useful shoppin' tool since the government chose to take it from us.'

I was feelin' very chuffed until she explained where she was comin' from. 'Every one with a brain in their head knows that plastic takes forever to decompose. So I suggest every plastic bag should have the slogan: *Let your children's children pay for it.* Then you can let people use the bag or not, leave it up to themselves if they want to poison the next generation.'

The last topic of the night was the Eurovision Song Contest and should Ireland ever bother enterin' again. Percy Pipplemoth thought this year's song was great and went on about the importance of participation. 'A load of bull,' retorted Superquinn, 'Winnin' is all that matters. If we have no hope of winnin' we shouldn't bother our backsides. It's the same with this election. I'm not in it just to participate; I'm in it to win. I haven't worn out five pairs of shoes and given Councillor Hickey fourteen kinds of windgall in his undercarriage simply for the joy of participatin'. I'm in to win.'

'As far as the Eurovision is concerned,' she continued, 'Ireland's problems with that started when the Iron Curtain was pulled back and the communist governments of Eastern Europe fell. I will campaign for the return of the Iron Curtain and the reinstatement of the Cold War. Otherwise we will be waitin' forever to win the Eurovision. Lettin' that crowd into the Eurovision was like lettin' Man United into the Eircom League. Till we keep them out we haven't a hope.'

With statements like that you could see why I couldn't wait to see the end of all this.

ELECTORAL FALL OUT

You probably have enough of elections to last you a lifetime. Well, I'm lucky to have escaped with my sanity. To get straight to the point Superquinn didn't win a seat. When the boxes opened she got a spatter of number ones everywhere, but when added together they weren't worth a curse.

The first count went on for seven hours due to a mistake when countin' the boxes. 'If they can't count the boxes properly,' says I to Superquinn, 'how do they hope to count the votes?' I was to regret those words.

The result of the first count came and Superquinn polled a total of 201 votes, the quota was 8,050. She was devastated. We were commiseratin' with her when all of a sudden she dried her tears and demanded a total recount. We nearly calved. She was in danger of bein' lynched by everyone.

When I asked her to reconsider she quoted my own words back at me in the presence of my friend, Patsy Geary, the returnin' officer, 'Sure wasn't it you who said if they can't count the boxes there's little hope of them bein' able to count the votes?' I wish the ground could have swallowed me as Patsy glared at me. 'Twill take a dose of pints to bring him back on side.

When the recount was finished Superquinn ended up with 195 votes, six less than she started out with. She was doubly disgusted and left in a huff. I went home and put my feet up, glad the whole feckin' thing was over. I went back in time for the final result only to witness Superquinn cut loose on everyone.

In her closin' address she described the electorate as a bunch of ninkumpoops who wouldn't know a decent politician if he or she sat up and bit them on the arse, 'Ye've got what ye deserve,' she shouted, 'I hope ye enjoy the misery ye've elected for yerselves.' The boos and hisses didn't knock a feather out of her. After a performance like that she hasn't a hope of a vote if she ever again runs for public office in this area.

I need a holiday after the campaign. I said my sanity is badly affected by it and I'm not jokin'. In fact for a few nights after the whole thing finished I couldn't sleep a wink but then, when I started to sleep I took to sleep walkin'.

In the early hours of last Wednesday mornin' it seems I left the bed at about one o'clock in the mornin' with an overcoat over the pyjamas. I walked down the village, sat into Tinky Ryan's taxi and demanded to be taken to the county hall in Clonmel. By the way, Tinky is the local undertaker and taxi driver: they say that alive or dead, he'll take you wherever you want to go.

Tinky was half asleep and didn't realise that I was completely out of it. As he drove he kept talkin' and never copped on to the fact that he was gettin' no answer from me.

He pulled up at county hall and let me out. I tried four doors to get in and couldn't. I eventually went out to the front and picked up a big stone to throw it through a glass door. Tinky saw what was happenin, ran over, caught me around the waist and pulled me to the ground. I woke up and whatever put it into my head I thought Tinky was tryin' to force me into a coffin. I hit him a few slaps but he had me held too tight for me to do damage. 'Twas then a squad car pulled up and arrested the two of us for disorderly behaviour. It took us three hours to explain everything. At one stage the guards were about to charge Tinky with kidnappin' me.

All's well that ends well, but there was a sting in the tail. We got home safe but Tinky, the hoor, left the feckin' meter runnin' for the duration of our ordeal and by the time we got back I owed him €150. That's the last time I'll sleep walk.

BEWARE THE FOOD POLICE

When I get a chance I like nothin' better than to read the odd magazine. Of late I've had time to flick through some of the latest glossies and I can't get over the amount of guff that's written about food.

As far as I'm concerned food writers and diet merchants have taken the good out of eatin'. Those of us who enjoy plain wholesome grub are made to feel guilty every time we even think of eatin' the kind of fodder we love. Admittin' that you like fare from the fryin' pan is like admittin' you have an embarrassin' itch. The cholesterol police are liable to be at your door within minutes.

This week I'm writin' my own food column. If you're a health freak, a heart surgeon or a vegetarian, I suggest you stop readin' now and go for your usual forty-five-mile jog. This column is for real grubbers.

My Day at the Table

A good breakfast is vital, 'tis like drinkin' brandy before you go on the batter. As they say, if you light the fire well you can burn anythin' in it.

A dacent breakfast should start as soon as you get up. The boiled egg smothered in butter is your only man. Follow this with a bowl of porridge buried in sugar and wash it down with a pot of strong tay. Then you're ready for the full Irish.

A real Irish breakfast should be fried in a pan, in lard or butter. Make sure 'tisn't grilled: the grill is a posh word for an incinerator: many a juicy sausage is turned into a dried stump by a red hot grill.

Any respectable fry will have the followin':

4 rashers (at least)

83

6 sausages

2 eggs

5 slices of black puddin'

5 slices of white puddin'

A fistful of mushrooms

2 potato cakes

Half a sliced pan, buttered and toasted

Optional extras include chips and tomatoes.

This of course would be described as kamikaze fare by your average food writer but to your average Irishman and woman, 'tis heaven on a plate.

Now for the dinner: the dinner is meant to be eaten in the middle of the day and should consist of as many courses as you can fit in.

Start with soup, anythin' out of a packet is fine as long as it is as thick as a bull's neck and accompanied by any amount of buttered rolls.

After this the spud is essential, preferably with bacon and cabbage. Now the spuds should be balls of flour the size of a sliothar and smothered in butter. There should be no limit to the amount of spuds eaten. I suppose when the pile of skins is high enough to defy the law of gravity it's a good indication that you might have enough.

The bacon should be cut in long thick slices with plenty of fat. There is nothin' in the world tastier than fatty bacon accompanied by cabbage cooked within an inch of its life and mashed with lashin's of butter.

Dessert has to be bread and butter puddin' with custard followed by a pot of tay and four or five slices of buttered spotted dick.

Now that's a dinner.

The supper is always a bit of conundrum. 'Tis fierce hard to put a good supper together. I find the best thing is a few rasher sandwiches with plenty of brown sauce washed down with a few mugs of tay and a feed of madeira cake. That should see you right till you go for the few pints and of course when you get home the hungry grass hits again. It's then the toasted cheese sandwich comes into its own along with a few bags of Taytos and a bar or two of chocolate.

Let me tell you, there are people up and down the country who will be delighted to read this. I have championed the plastic bag, I'm workin' on the smokin' ban and my new cause is the salvation of dacent Irish grub. It's time for the food police to get worried.

HOW MANY SHADES OF GREEN?

Superquinn called in durin' the week for a bit of a post-mortem on the election. I was mightily relieved when she declared she'd never to run for public office again: I had visions of havin' to compete with her on my patch in the next local elections.

'Do you know somethin',' says she, 'lookin' at the kind of people drafted in to support this pick'n'mix government, if I was goin' to run for election again I'd be sure to make a public disgrace of myself first. It's a ticket to a Dáil seat and might even get you a hotline to whoever holds the power.'

We were wonderin' how Councillor Percy Pipplemoth Davis, our local tree hugger might react to the Greens in government. We hadn't started givin' out about him when the man himself arrived at my door with a bag of smelly cheese, a box of rice cakes and a gallon of his home brew.

I thought he had arrived to celebrate the entry of the Greens into government. 'If you're comin' here to celebrate anything, Councillor Percy,' says I, 'you've come to the wrong house. Your crowd have feckin' well sold out.'

'Councillor Maurice,' replied a very drained and tired lookin' Pip, 'You don't understand, I've never been a member of any party, I have my own little alliance known as 'The Friends of the Sunflower'. People connect me with the Greens and to be honest, I haven't denied a sort of spiritual connection with them. However, their decision to take part in a threesome with Bertie and the Harney lady has scandalised me. That's one bed I'll not be found in. Can you imagine trying to get a corner of the duvet with Jackie Healy-Rae pulling at it from the other side? What Sargent and company have done reflects badly on me. I need some friends tonight, as I now know what it feels like to be independent, isolated and alone.'

I brought him inside for fear the stink of his cheese would cause the Mother's roses to wither. Superquinn tore into the cheese and the rice cakes while myself and the Pip tore into the wine.

Before the home brew took us off into the land of gobbledegook I had an interestin' conversation with the hoor of a Pip. He comes across as an innocent abroad, but he's as clever as a cut cat. He did much better than Superquinn in the election gettin' more than 1,000 votes after a campaign that had more in common with a circus than a serious attempt at takin' a seat.

While the rest of us struggled with canvass cards, posters and press releases, the Pip was distributin' lollipops, balloons and daisy chains. However, he had a strategy for every electoral area. 'I made it my business to know the chair and secretary of every community council, every residents' association and every pressure group from anti-dump to anti-mast groups,' says the Pip.

'Is that so?' says I.

'Indeed it is,' answered the Pip, 'But I think the lollipops, balloons and daisy chains did the damage. They got me the lefty trendy vote that would've come my way anyway. Every ounce of hard work I did with the associations and pressure groups went off into thin air with the blasted balloons. My next campaign will be a collar and tie job with the spectacles on top of my nose. Besides, since the Green crowd slipped in under the quilt with Bertie, if I try to push the green agenda the electorate will think I'm an FFer in a woolly jumper.'

I wasn't long soberin' up. I realised that if this fella moves too far into the middle ground he could sweep my little seat out from under me. After he left, Superquinn confirmed my fears: 'Maurice,' says she, 'you can't afford to take your eye off your political nest for a second. There are cuckoos everywhere waitin' to relieve you of your perch and the biggest cuckoo of them all has just walked out that door.'

AN ART ATTACK

There's a fierce flurry of activity in the council at the moment as we prepare for the summer holidays. We're tryin' to pack three months work into one and the meetin's are takin' place mornin' noon and night.

As a councillor I am a member of what is called a Strategic Policy Committee, or to give it its short handle, an SPC. There are four of these talk shops on the council made up of councillors, business people and community activists – you know the kind – stuck in everythin' in the parish and the county.

Anyway, I'm on the Social, Cultural and Housin' SPC chaired by our local FG councillor, Moll Gleeson. Moll has completely lost the run of herself since she took charge of this august body: she thinks she's runnin' the cultural affairs of feckin' Vienna. You always know when there's a meetin' of our SPC because Moll arrives dolled up like a film star and drippin' with enough jewellery to finance a small war.

She forgets that housin' is an essential part of our brief and for most of us 'tis the most important part. We couldn't give two shites if the RTE concert orchestra forgot this neck of the woods existed or if we never saw another play in our lives. We're concerned the people on our housin' lists get houses. Moll is only worried about what she refers to as: 'the cultural desert we live in.'

Things are so busy in county hall at the moment that our SPC had to meet at half eight in the morning. We had a heap of housin' issues to get through includin' a policy document providin' for a huge increase in affordable housin'.

Moll's arrival at County Hall was not just ministerial, 'twas feckin' regal. Perched like Lady Muck in the back seat of the Volvo, she was driven to the entrance by her husband. When the car came to a halt, the eejit of a husband came around and opened the door for her. She stepped out in all her finery carryin' a leather briefcase and lookin' like the mother of the bride.

We were fit to explode when Moll produced an agenda she must have borrowed from the Wexford Opera Festival The first item was a proposal from an artist friend of hers to open a series of art galleries in the area. 'The visual arts are the poor relation here as elsewhere,' she declared, 'a series of small art galleries in our towns and villages would form a necklace of priceless jewels around the county.'

'They'd be more like a millstone around our necks,' says I, 'Who'd pay for these things? Let me tell you, we have a whole heap of things to discuss about housin'. At the rate we're goin' half the county will be homeless and we'll be fartin' around talkin' about modern art. As far as I'm concerned modern art is a con job. Fellas in woolly jumpers and sandals gettin' thousands for firin' blobs of paint at blank canvasses. They must be laughin' all the way to the bank when they find clowns like county councils queuin' up to pay for the scutter they produce.'

'You're such a Philistine,' declared Moll as she called me to order.

'Philistine?' I gasped, 'I don't even know where Philistinia is, but I can assure you that angry constituents will turn this place into the Gaza strip if we don't stop gabbin' about art and do somethin' about the housin' list!'

The meetin' finished soon after with no discussion on the affordable housin' policy. Despite a blazin' row Moll saw no point in meetin' again until September.

I softened her cough. That evenin' myself and the other councillors on the SPC phoned the people on our housin' lists and gave them Moll's mobile number. We told them she was holdin' up the whole show and they should contact her.

I got a phone call at midnight from a very stressed Moll who said we needed an urgent meetin' of the 'Housin' SPC'. She obviously had her cultural wings clipped by people with more urgent problems.

HIS WORSHIP THE MAYOR

To everyone's surprise, includin' my own, I was elected Cathaoirleach of the council this week. I now proudly carry the title of Mayor. I never expected it, but Percy Pipplemoth Davis fell out with the FFers and refused to back their candidate. I had been lined up as a stalkin' horse, but when Percy cut the bellyband under the FF contender I won the race by a head.

As it dawned on me that I might be elected I phoned Superquinn to break the news to the Mother. I also asked her to go around and collect her, grab my good suit, polish my shoes and come straight in.

They arrived just in time. I changed clothes in the jacks and the outgoin' Cathaoirleach was callin' order as I hopped in to the council chamber on one leg tryin' to get my foot into the second shoe. In my rush I forgot to zip up my fly and passin' Moll Gleeson she advised me to shut the stable door, 'This is no day for that horse to bolt,' she whispered.

I was proposed by the same Moll who waxed lyrical about my father and his father before him and our proud family tradition of public service. I started cryin', the Mother started cryin' and before we knew it there wasn't a dry eye in the chamber. The FFers were cryin' so much I thought they were goin' to vote for me. I had just about composed myself when the numbers were counted and I won by a single vote. I was the proudest man on the planet when it came time to accept the chain of office.

Makin' speeches is no bother to me so when I stood up to give my *Cáirde Gaeil* I was in flyin' form. As I launched into my impromptu 'programme for government' there were smiles and nods all round the place. However, as the details came into my head and straight out my mouth I could see the County Manager goin' pale at the gills.

I promised to fill every pothole, tar every road, straighten every bend, do away with house waitin' lists and repair every window, door and drainpipe in the county. I promised to fight the good fight for the hard-pressed pub smokers and for the poor shoppers deprived of their plastic bags.

The Manager started to shake uncontrollably when I promised that every plannin' application would be fast-tracked under my mayorality. However, he wasn't the only one with the shakes when I announced my 'flagship project'. In a stroke of inspired genius, I promised that our county would lead the way in the fight against global warmin' by makin' a site available for the first nuclear-powered electricity generation station in the country.

I wasn't out of the chamber when my phone started ringin' and within two hours I was on every radio station and TV station in the country. Even the BBC interviewed me.

That night I came home to Killdicken to a hero's welcome. There were bonfires all along the road and a session in Tom Walshe's that went on till two in the morning. 'Twas half three when I got to the scratcher but I woke at half eight to the sound of drums in my head. 'Oh Jaysus,' says I 'the first mornin' of my mayorality and I have the double first cousin of a hangover.' I never had such a poundin' in my skull.

I threw back the curtains to find the poundin' was not in my head. Every eco warrior and every hairy drummer in the country had landed in my front garden to protest against my nuclear energy proposal. They carried all kinds of posters with slogans such as 'No to Nukey Hickey', 'Maurice's Furnace will Fry Your Future'.

The Mother was waitin' for me in the kitchen with a face that would split the atom. 'Look at what your big mouth has drawn down on us. If you don't back-pedal on this nuclear power plant fairly lively, the first bit of fallout will take the form of your eviction from this house.' 'Twill be an eventful six months.

WHISTLESTOP HICKEY

This Mayor's job will kill me. The diary is full from mornin' till night. Every minute is taken up with openin's, launches, photo opportunities and meetin's. As I write this it is noon on Wednesday and I'll give ye a rundown of my day so far.

7.00 am Breakfast meetin' with Tipp In Business.

These local business people think they're feckin' Tony O'Reilly with their dawn breakfast meetings. The last time I was up this early I hadn't been in bed at all. The Mother warned me to have a speech prepared, but I was in Shronefodda till two o'clock in the mornin' officiatin' at the openin' of the annual Wellie Racin' Festival. I was too knackered to be writin' any speech.

I got to the breakfast meetin', had the full Irish and felt all right. But once the speeches got goin' things went downhill. If I heard the phrase: 'sustainable goin' forward' once I heard it fourteen hundred times.

I nodded off and soon I was snorin'. I woke to the sound of my name boomin' out over the sound system, the MC had to call on me three times. He was too polite to give me a dig.

I got straight to my feet: 'A Cairde Gaeil,' I started, 'None of ye got up at sparrow-fart this mornin' to listen to me ramblin' on about high economics. If ye did, ye came to the wrong breakfast. However, let me say, from what I've heard at this function ye are a very excitin' and lively bunch of people. I'd just like to wish ye the best in your work and, as Mayor, it is great to know that the business life of the county is sustainable goin' forward. Now ye'll have to excuse me, I've to go to Teerawadra to officially open Tim Hayes's new milkin' parlour.'

9.00 am Teerawadra

When I arrived in Tim Hayes's yard he was finished the milkin'. A few of the neighbours were there along with their new curate, Fr Willy Naughton. The milkin' parlour was empty except for two cows waitin' for a visit from Willy De Wig Ryan, our local broadcaster who doubles as the Artificial Insemination man, or the bull man, as we call him.

Tim opened the formalities and I gave a short speech. After that Fr Naughton began the prayers. He has a voice like a foghorn and when he started callin' down the Lord's blessin' he literally frightened the shite out of the two cows. They drove spatters in every direction and we were all decorated. Tim, who's not known for his diplomacy, roared at the priest, 'In the name a' Jaysus, Father will you calm down. Since when did God go deaf?' As soon as the poor priest finished I headed off for the launch of Ladies Day at Beechmount Golf Club with a fine smell of cowshite off me.

10.30 am Beechmount Golf Club

At Beechmount I was greeted by the Lady Captain, Greta Nestor. I knew by the nose on her that she could smell the cowshite. The women golfers were in the clubhouse ready to tee off and I gave what I thought was a fine spake. I said how great it was for them to get away from the kitchen for a few hours. "Twas an ideal time of the day for a bit of badly needed exercise and they'd be home in grand time to get the dinner for himself and the children.

The reception I got was as frosty as a polar bear's paw. The Lady Captain responded by wishin' me a speedy journey into the twenty-first century and, as the women filed out towards the first tee I thought they were goin' to lay into me with their clubs. 'Tis hard to know when you're sayin' the right thing.

And there's more!

This afternoon, at two o'clock I have to open a summer camp in Borrisnangoul, at 4.00 I launch a local history book in Bally, at 7.00 I'm to open a hurlin' tournament in Honetyne and at half nine, if I'm still alive, I'll give out the prizes at a Feis in Cossatrasna.

This Mayorality will be the death of me.

HOME JAMES

I never realised there's so much happenin' all over the place. As Mayor, I'm invited to everythin' that moves includin' summer schools, festivals, vintage shows and donkey derbies.

However, I am a bit worried about the Mother; she's worn out from drivin' me everywhere. The cousin rang from Kilkenny wonderin' why they hadn't heard from us. The Mother explained that she's on the road mornin', noon and night since I became Mayor. The cousin suggested that her son Manus, who's home from college and at a loose end, would love to drive me and give the Mother a break.

The Mother left for Kilkenny on Sunday evenin' and young Manus landed at my door on Monday mornin' ready to be my chauffeur for the week. He's some sight with his blond hair, a pair of Bono sunglasses on his head and a black suit. He looks like one of them fellas that minds Bush. 'Good morning, Maurice,' he chirped, 'I have a timetable from your Ma so let's move. We have places to go and people to see.'

I grabbed my coat and my chain of office and followed my new driver to the gate. I nearly collapsed when I saw the car. 'Tis one of these boy racer yokes; all white with silver wheels, aerials at all angles, a big tail fin on the boot and a pair of silver exhausts comin' out the back. The thing looks like the car in that film *Back to the Future*.

The inside is a cross between a space ship and a house of ill repute with bright red upholstery and white fluffy trimmin'. As soon as the ignition is turned on the thing lights up like *Star Trek*. The body is so low to the ground you'd think you were sittin' on the feckin' road.

'Strap yourself in and hold on,' shouted Manus as he revved the engine makin' it roar like a lion. 'Twas then the stereo kicked in and blew every bit of wax out of my ears. The car vibrated from stem to stern to the beat of what Manus calls 'dance music'. All I could hear was 'bumpadda, bumpadda, bumpadda, bumpadda'. I'll tell you, if you had constipation twouldn't be long about shiftin' it.

We took off down the village and sped through the countryside. Manus thought he was feckin' Michael Schumacher revvin' and changin' gears and doin' handbrake turns at every sharp bend.

As we got near Gurtnamucca, our first port of call, Manus remarked, 'Hey, Maurice you're one important dude. Look behind, we have a police escort with flashin' lights and the whole bit. This is cool.'

'That isn't cool at all,' says I lookin' back, "tis feckin red hot. Them guards are tryin' to catch up with you. Turn off that feckin' music and slow down. I'll put on me chain of office, it might do somethin' for us.'

'Don't worry, Maurice,' Manus replied, 'this is what they call a police escort and we are the main vehicle. Man, how coooool.'

As we screeched to a halt outside the Gortnamucca community hall the squad car screeched in behind us. Two breathless guards ran up and opened the car doors at either side. 'Get out ye pups before ye kill yerselves and half the feckin' country! Get out!' There was a crowd outside the hall starin' at the drama unfoldin' before them. The guards nearly died when I extricated myself from the machine, decked out in my chain of office. I suggested they have a good long talk with the young cousin, 'If ye can give him half the fright he gave me,' says I, 'ye might get him to slow down.'

In all the confusion I had forgotten what I was supposed to be doin' in Gurtnamucca. As the guards were gettin' stuck in to Manus I went over and asked him to look at the timetable the Mother gave him. 'Oh,' says he, as he pulled the list from his pocket, 'You're openin' a Macra conference on road safety.'

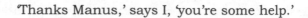

'Thanks Manus,' says I, 'you're some help.'

I'VE A MAN IN MY LIFE

I feel like Robinson Crusoe, not because I'm stranded on a desert island, but because I have my own Man Friday in Manus, the cousin's son who is drivin' me to my mayoral functions. He is some sight; his chariot is a jazzed up car with go-faster stripes, tail fins, chrome and white wheels.

Aside from last week's close encounter with the law we're doin' fairly well. We have become somethin' of an odd couple around the county. To be honest, we resemble the original Odd Couple more closely than I'd care to admit.

Manus is stayin' at home with me for the duration of the Mother's absence and, while he's only supposed to drive me around, he has taken complete charge of my political and domestic affairs and is drivin' me mad. The breakfast is on the table at cockcrow every morning, my clothes are ready and my diary for the day is read out while I'm tuckin' into the egg. He's a cross between a butler, a secretary and a reverend mother. I don't know where he was got.

As a teetotaller he doesn't understand my fondness for the few pints and insists on waitin' in the car outside the pub with a face like a fiddle on him. He's a tidiness freak, but he's also a great cook. As soon as we come in the door the apron goes on, he does a quick clean up and can produce a dish from any corner of the globe in a matter of minutes. I'm the opposite; there's bits of me thrown in every corner of the house and as for cookin' I never go beyond the two pans: the fryin' pan and the sliced pan.

While he has his advantages he's worse than the Mother for fightin' with me. In an argument he's like a dog with a bone.

Last Thursday evenin' I was openin' the annual Pig's Crubeen Festival in Lisbanniv and lookin' forward to a great night. He dropped me off and told me he'd pick me up at eleven o'clock. I told him this was goin' to be a late one and I'd find my own way home. He insisted he'd be back for me at eleven and reminded me I was due to chair a meetin' of the Glengooley Sewerage committee at half nine the followin' mornin'. 'You've done so much shoutin' about sewerage problems you'll have to be there or the media will make mince meat of you,' he warned. We tore into one another for about ten minutes until I eventually pointed out he was my driver, not my wet nurse.

'Wet nurse! Is that what I am.' He left in a huff and I began to enjoy my minder-free night out.

I don't know what time Tinky Ryan dropped me home, but the birds were singin'. I knew 'twouldn't be long till Man Friday would be callin' me.

I heard nothin' till I woke suddenly at quarter past nine. I jumped out of the bed shoutin' for Manus, but there was no reply. Oh Jaysus, had he gone back to Kilkenny in a sulk? How was I goin' to get to Glengooley for half nine? Why didn't I listen to the little hoor and come home at a respectable hour? I dressed myself as quick as I could and ran out the door only to find Mr Manus waitin' in the car with 'I told you so' written all over his smug face.

We drove to Glengooley in total silence. The sewerage meetin' had no sooner started than I began to have even bigger regrets that I didn't listen to Man Friday the night before. The discussion of raw sewerage, solids, liquids and run-off sent my stomach into somersaults as the Lisbanniv porter, poteen and crubeens went in search of my own personal sewerage system.

I must have passed out because I woke to see Manus leanin' over me like Jackie Kennedy in Dallas. Someone asked him if he was my doctor. 'No,' he replied, 'I'm just his wet nurse.'

A CLOSE SHAVE WITH DE WIG

I knew 'twas comin. Monday mornin' I got the call from Willy De Wig Ryan of The Sticks FM. 'How is de Cathaoirleach?' said the voice at the other end of the phone. I recognised De Wig's rasp and wanted to hang up but I'd only be puttin' off the evil day.

'Who's this?' I asked, pretendin' I didn't know. 'Mayor Maurice, dis is your auld friend, Willy De Wig Ryan of The Sticks FM. Let me say how delighted I am wit your recent bit of ladder climbin'. It couldn't happen to a nicer fella.'

I wanted to tell him to take his sweetness and stick it up his hairy nose. He's a treacherous hoor and liable to say anythin' on the air. I held my fire: you have to keep on the right side of the media. 'Oh thank you for your kind words, Willy. Now, what can I do for you?'

'You've probably guessed what I want,' he replied. 'I was hopin' you might come in and talk to me on de radio. I'd come down and do de interview in your own house but I was kicked by a cow in Borrisnangoul last week and I'm not very mobile.'

'A sore place to get a kick,' says I. De Wig is a part time AI man. Around here an AI calf is called 'a Willy job'.

'I don't know if I can fit you in,' I continued, 'I'm up to me tonsils at the moment, the diary is full.'

'Ah now, Mayor Maurice,' pleaded De Wig, 'As de Mayor I tink 'twould be vital to appear on my flagship breakfast programme, *De Top of De Egg*. De people will expect it.'

'Well,' says I, 'I'll see what I can do. I'll talk to my private secretary.'

I spoke to my right-hand man, Manus and he suggested I do the interview and get it over with. By the way, he is spendin' an extra week with me.

The interview was arranged for Wednesday mornin' and Manus drove me to the abandoned hairdresser's in Honetyne where The Sticks studio is located.

As I arrived De Wig was on air concludin' a telephone conversation with Bridie from Glennabuddybugga who's havin' difficulty gettin' Polly, her she-goat in kid. He had obviously asked listeners to ring in with their suggestions. One caller suggested Bridie should get De Wig to take the she-goat in hand since he has a proven track record with cows. 'Well ladies and gentlemen,' says he, 'I'd be delighted to give Bridie a dig out as long as I have a place to hang me trousers.' The man should be arrested.

He then turned his attentions to me like a fox stalkin' a lame chicken, 'Ladies and gentlemen, I have here in studio wit me, none udder dan our new mayor, Councillor Maurice Hickey. You're welcome Mayor Maurice.'

'Thank you, Willy, I'm delighted to be here,' says I, lyin' through my teeth.

'Let me begin by congratulatin' you on your excavation to de high office of Mayor,' began De Wig.

'You probably mean my elevation,' I interrupted.

'Dat's de word I was lookin' for. I gets confused in de presence of greatness. Anyway congratulations on gettin' de leg up, you must be delighted with it.'

'I'm sure you mean my election and yes I am delighted,' says I.

'Dat's what I meant. Sure you have no use for any udder kind of a leg up.'

The interview was in a speed wobble. How was I goin' to avoid bein' destroyed by this notorious hoor?

The cavalry arrived in the most unlikely shape of Bridie from Glennabuddybugga and Polly, her she-goat.

The door of the studio flew open and she stormed in with Polly on a rope. 'Good man, Willy,' says she, 'I decided I'd save you the trip to Glennabuddybugga and so I brought Polly to you. You surely have somethin' in the boot of the car to cure what ails her. Meself and the Mayor will say nothin' to no-one.'

You wouldn't see me leggin' it out of the place leavin' De Wig to deal live on air with a persistent Bridie and the emotional needs of Polly.

THEN THERE WAS THREE

The Mother came back on Sunday evenin'. As you know she has been away visitin' the cousin in Kilkenny and in her absence the cousin's son, Manus, took up her chauffeurin' duties.

On her return she was shocked to see how tidy the house was. She wanted to know if I had hired contract cleaners to do the job, 'It's a certainty you didn't do it yourself,' she snapped.

Anyway I explained that Manus, along with his chauffeurin' tasks had put himself in charge of the house, in charge of my diary, in fact he had taken charge of every feckin' thing. I was explainin' this to her when the lad himself appeared through the back door with an armful of washin' from the clothesline.

'Oh, Auntie Biddy,' says he to the Mother, 'it's great to see you. Give me a sec to put this washin' down and I'll greet you properly.'

He put the clothes into the ironin' basket and gave the Mother a peck on each cheek. I could see she was charmed, not just by the pecks on the cheeks, but at the sight of a clean house and an empty washin' line. 'Twas like a glimpse of heaven.

'Sit down, and rest yourself, Auntie Bid,' he continued, 'I'll put on the kettle and you can give us all the news from the Marble City.'

'Begod,' I thought to myself, 'if that fella stays around any longer he'll seriously raise the standard for the male occupant of this house. I'll be under fierce pressure to lift my game.'

After sittin' through a half an hour of family gossip I announced I was goin' for a pint. Manus reminded me that I was to be in Rathgubbin at noon the followin' day for the openin' of their *Golden Years* art exhibition.

'Of course,' says he, 'that's not my job anymore, I'll be handin' over to you in the morning, Auntie Bid.'

'We'll talk about that tomorrow,' says she.

I thought no more of it and went for my pint. When I got back, the Mother was still up and readin' the paper.

'I thought you'd be in dreamland by now,' says I.

'No. I had plenty of sleep while I was away. Do you want tay?' she asked.

An offer to make tay at that hour of the night is a sure sign the Mother has business to discuss.

'I'm not gettin' any younger,' she began as she put on the kettle, 'and while I don't mind drivin' you on your normal council business, this Mayor job is a big undertakin'. You could say that bein' the mayor is a horse of a different colour. The prospect of drivin' you to every cock fight in the county from now until Christmas makes me weak at the knees. However, I've spoken to Manus and he's takin' a break from college and is hopin' to go abroad in the New Year. He'd be delighted to drive you for the few months. He could live with us and the travel expenses would provide plenty money for him.'

I was thinkin' fast. 'Twas one of those moments when you're not sure if the light at the end of the tunnel is daylight or the headlamp of an oncomin' train. Havin' Manus around was fine for two weeks, but the prospect of bein' wet-nursed till Christmas wasn't too attractive. On the other hand, I had to consider the Mother, there's no point in pushin' her too hard when she's beginnin' to burn a sup of oil.

'Well,' says I, 'if you feel under pressure, then Manus is the only solution. But I wonder how you'll cope with havin' a lodger in the house?'

'Haven't I had you lodgin' here for decades and I'm still fairly sane after it?'

'This is a lodger with a difference,' I cautioned, 'you could come home some day and find him organisin' your wardrobe and ironin' your smalls!'

'Well,' says she, 'if Manus is that kind of man I've only one question for him.'

'What's that?'

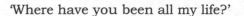
'Where have you been all my life?'

HOT GOSSIP

Manus, my driver and right-hand man, is typical of young people today: as soon as I gave him a job he took holidays. He had booked a week in Ibiza before he realised he'd be workin' with me. Anyway I hadn't much on the agenda for the period in question and the Mother could drive me to the few functions listed in the diary.

I was about to make arrangements with her when who appeared on the scene but Superquinn. We hadn't seen her for weeks and she arrived with a head for news on her.

'Who's this fella drivin' you around, carryin' your school books and wipin' your nose for you?' she asked in what appeared to be a fit of high dudgeon.

'Oh that's Manus,' I answered, 'he'd be somethin' of a cousin of mine.'

'Hmm,' says she, 'that's what they all say.'

'What do you mean?' I asked.

'Now Maurice, if you have somethin' to tell me I'll understand perfectly. I'm just disappointed you didn't feel comfortable enough to share this with me before now. I thought we were friends.'

'There's nothin' to tell you, Breda,' says I, fairly lively, 'Manus is the son of my Mother's first cousin in Kilkenny. I don't know what kind of a relation of mine that makes him, but he's probably some breed of cousin once, twice or three times removed.'

'Oh, I don't mind at all, 'tis none of my business,' says Superquinn. 'People are just wonderin'.'

'Tisn't often I get into a rage, but I felt this one startin' under my toenails and eruptin' through my throat like a volcano.

'So people are wonderin', are they?' I shouted, 'Well, they can wonder all they like, but this is the story. Listen carefully so that when you're natterin' with the nosey parkers of this village you can put them straight.'

I was in my stride and for a change I had Superquinn under pressure.

'As it happens, the drivin' associated with my Mayoral functions was too much for the Mother so she decided to take a holiday in Kilkenny. Manus came here to drive me in her absence. She then took an extra week and when she came back and heard how well Manus did we agreed I'd keep him on until Christmas.'

'Oh, I'm sure everythin' is above board,' said a slightly embarrassed Superquinn.

'It most certainly is,' I continued, 'but just in case you're still not sure let me tell you another thing or two. Manus is a great lad, a good driver and a topper at lookin' after me, my paperwork, my diary and my wardrobe. He's also very neat, very tidy and very fussy, I knew this would get people talkin', I partly guessed they'd be wonderin' if he had 'a girlfriend or what'. As far as I'm concerned whether he's fond of women or men or both doesn't matter a damn to me, all I know is that when it comes to doin' a job he does the work of five people. Am I makin' myself clear?'

'I suppose I was out of order,' admitted Superquinn.

'You most certainly were,' says I, 'and if you hear anyone makin' snide remarks about that young man you should put them in their place as only you can.'

With that the Mother came in from the backyard enquirin' as to what all the shoutin' was about.

'Ah,' says I, 'Breda has agreed to drive me around for the week while Manus is away. I want to pay her, but she won't take a bob. She's fierce nervous in case people will start talkin', claimin' we're havin' an affair. Before you know it her car will be seen parked in every lane with steamy windows and bockedy suspensions. I've been tellin' her not to worry about that kind of auld thing, people will talk anyway.

'You're right too,' says the Mother. 'They will talk, but at least if they're talkin' about the two of ye they might stop talkin' about yourself and Manus.'

Good lord, I give up!

TEARS IN TEERAWADRA

We have our very own local version of the Shannon-Heathrow crisis. I'm referring to our local rural transport scheme that serves Glengooley, Killdicken and Honetyne, the 'Pothole Express. A few times a week it carries people to Clonmel to do the shoppin', get the hair done and have the dinner.

You might also remember that Superquinn is drivin' me around while Manus is away sunnin'· himself in Ibiza. I nearly died last Monday mornin' when she arrived to take me on my official duties in her VW campervan. What were the locals goin' to say when they see me in this hippie-wagon?

'You don't expect me to go and perform my official duties in that thing?' I asked when Superquinn pulled up in her jalopy.

She wasn't impressed: 'Take a look at your feet,' says she, 'and now take a look at the van: which of them will get you to Clonmel faster?'

There was no competition and so, with a bould face on me, I got in to the campervan and we took off. About two miles out the road my mobile phone started hoppin' mad with calls from people in Teerawadra. It emerged that the 'Pothole Express' is about to abandon its weekly service to their village and switch to a new stop in Glenbreen where a whole estate of sheltered houses for older people has been built. There are far richer pickin's to be had there.

Because of holidays and all sorts of things it appears no one turned up for the bus in Teerawadra over the last four weeks and the management committee decided to pull the plug. The new crowd in Glenbreen have been negotiatin' for their own stop for a long time and now they have it, at Teerawadra's expense.

There is uproar in Teerawadra. I was told in no

uncertain terms that if I don't do somethin' about it I needn't appear in that parish again. They must think I've a second magic wand.

After openin' a children's art exhibition in Clonmel, we went straight to Teerawadra to meet the abandoned passengers and the irate community. As we got near the village the roadside posters left us in no doubt but that local feelin's were runnin' high; you'd imagine the populace was about to be starved into extinction. *'Teerawadra: abandoned by the world'; 'Will the last person to leave Teerawadra please turn off the lights!' 'The Pothole Express takes up where Cromwell left off.'*

'Cripes,' says I to Superquinn, 'They're takin' this fairly seriously.'

'The crowd in Teerawadra are not to be messed with,' says she, 'Even the Tans were afraid to go in there. Two truckloads of them who went in on a raid one night ended up walkin' back to Clonmel in their underwear. Their trucks, guns, uniforms – everythin' disappeared. The followin' day they had to be shipped straight to England and not one of them ever fired another shot. Most of them finished their days in a home for the bewildered.'

'In the name of God what am I goin' to tell them?' I asked Superquinn.

'What you need to do is buy a bit of time,' says Superquinn. 'Tell them you're doin' all in your power to help.'

I arrived to a great welcome and assured the community council I was doin' my level best to solve their problems. However, they wanted to know what immediate help I could give. It was Friday and there were four people who needed a lift to Clonmel.

Superquinn, who sat in on the meetin' suggested we bring them in the campervan. 'Twas a stroke of genius. By the time we arrived in town there was a posse of reporters and photographers waitin' for us and the local headlines this week were worth 500 votes:

'Hickey Saves Teerawadra Stop-over: Next Stop Shannon-Heathrow.'

Look out, Bertie.

A CHAIN OF EVENTS

I took a bit of a holiday this week. I wasn't up to goin' anywhere and decided to stay near home. The only mayoral event in my diary was the 'Times Past Festival' in Honetyne on Sunday evenin'. The festival marked the beginnin' of Heritage Week and I used it to mark the beginnin' of my week off. The event included displays and demonstrations of rural traditions such as churnin' milk, bakin' soda cakes, pulpin' turnips, tossin' sheaves and all kinds of pursuits that are now the stuff of history.

I was in holiday humour when I got to Honetyne and enjoyed a fair few pints and small ones as I toured the village. The atmosphere was great and the craic was mighty.

One of the highlights of the festival was the revival of a horse race known as the Honetyne Harness Gallop. This used to be an annual event held at the end of August after the hay was brought home. Local people raced their horses around the village and the winner received a bit of new horse harness, hence the name. A parish priest banned the event in the late sixties after it became notorious for bettin', nobblin' and skulduggery. It caused fierce rows and to this day certain families are not talkin' to one another.

Stories about drugs in the horsey world are big news at the moment, but they are no surprise to anyone in this neck of the woods. Horses and riders were at it here in Honetyne forty years ago in the heyday of the Harness Gallop. Poteen was the drug of choice. If you wanted to cause a horse to slow down you put it in the feed and if you wanted to speed it up you rubbed it in to the tailend. Pa Quirke told me his father was nearly killed by a badly drugged horse durin' the 1965 race. It appears his nag was a hot tip to win the harness but half way round the circuit the animal pulled up mysteriously and trotted into Sam Wilson's yard where he fell sound asleep against a reek of hay. Auld Quirke was nearly smothered.

Whatever about times past it was my job on Sunday night to present prizes for the 2007 sheaf tossin' and the horse race. By the time it came to the awards ceremony I was in great form, the pints and the small ones ensured I was feelin' no pain.

Three men from Shronefodda won the sheaf tossin' but my prize givin' speech got the organisers into big trouble. In the course of my few words, I remarked that it was no surprise the Shronefodda men won the event in question since their parish had produced its fair share of tossers over the years. The crowd from Shronefodda took exception to my few words and only agreed to accept their prizes after bein' promised a feed of porter.

When it came time to the prize for the horse race the organisers suddenly realised they had no bit of horse harness for the winner, 'Erra, Maurice,' says Pa Cantillon, whose son Vinnie had won the event, 'Put your auld chain of office around the nag's neck, isn't that the finest bit of harness in the county.' Everyone shouted encouragement and of course I played to the gallery. When young Cantillon led the horse to the stand I put my mayoral chain around the animal's neck. As soon as I did, a big cheer went up and one of the offended tossers from Shronefodda gave the horse a hefty slap on the hindquarters. The frightened animal whinnied into the air, took off down the street and disappeared into the wilderness that once was Tim Hanley's farm.

I've spent my week's holidays lookin' for the horse and my chain of office. I'll have to go on the radio with Willy De Wig and make an appeal if I don't find them soon. Should anyone see a horse wearin' a fancy necklace give me a shout, in the meantime say a prayer to St Anthony and make it a big one, it's a horse I'm lookin' for.

ANGEL DUST

Pa Cantillon's mad nag turned up two days ago, but there was no sign of the blasted chain of office. I'm in deep trouble; what will I tell the powers that be in County Hall? If it gets out I'll be the laughin' stock of the country.

I had no choice but to tell Sergeant Miller. He suggested we conduct what he called a discreet search and after three days if it didn't turn up we'd have to go public. I enlisted the help of my friend, Pa Quirke the postman. He travels every boreen and lane in the parish.

For three days we searched high up and low down and were just about to give up when Quirke came back with a bit of news. As Eamon Dunphy might say, 'twas good news but 'twasn't great news. He found the chain alright, but it was in the possession of Wild Willy Roche who lives at the backend of Glennabuddybugga. Wild Willy is a recluse, a bit of a religious freak, and a major consumer of magic mushrooms.

Quirke was on his rounds in the locality when he spotted Wild Willy walkin' backwards around a fairy fort with my mayoral chain hangin' round his neck. When he asked him where he got his necklace Willy explained 'twas given him by an angel who appeared in his haggard in the shape of a horse and ordered him to wear it until the people turned their backs on drink and sex.

Quirke knew this was a tall order and suggested a more reasonable ransom such as a hundred euros, a council house or shares in a good greyhound. Wild Willy was havin' none of it. He wanted sackcloth, ashes and abstinence.

When Quirke came back and told us his story I knew I was in real trouble. This fella could demand the conversion of China before he hands over the chain.

Sergeant Miller decided we should take a softly-softly approach so the two of us went to visit Willy in the Sergeant's family car. He reckoned the squad car could 'inflame the situation'.

When we arrived we found Wild Willy with the chain around his neck and he diggin' spuds. After some small talk about the weather and the blight Sergeant Miller asked him where he got the chain. He told us the same story he had told Quirke and added that the arrival of community leaders like the Sergeant and myself was a further sign that the angel was genuine. He instructed us to go back and tell the people to sleep in their own beds and stay out of the pubs.

Sergeant Miller informed him we were there to retrieve the chain, which he described as the property of the County Council. 'As I told you,' declared Wild Willy, 'this chain was given me by an angel of God who appeared in this very haggard and told me to wear it until the people renounce drink and sins of the flesh.'

'Well,' says the Sergeant, 'I have information that the horse in question got that chain from Councillor Hickey. Now be a good man and hand it over.'

'Handin' it over to you won't make me good,' replied Willy, 'holdin' on to it will make everyone good. So there.'

After two hours negotiatin' we left without the chain. The Sergeant gave Willy twenty-four hours to hand it back, otherwise he'd get a search warrant and retrieve it by force of the law. Willy told him he only obeyed the law of God. We'll need a theologian and an exorcist to get it off him.

As we left Sergeant Miller declared, 'We'll have to get Canon McGrath involved and maybe the Vatican will send the Swiss Guards to get your chain back. You're some eejit, Maurice. If the papers get hold of this you're fecked.'

Isn't it well I know it, my political career is hangin' around the neck of the most unpredictable man in the constituency.

MOTHER ON A MISSION

In the end it was the Mother who retrieved my chain of office from the clutches of Wild Willy. After the attempt by myself and Sergeant Miller to get it failed I knew I was in deep bother.

I had hidden the crisis from the Mother for a few days until Pa Quirke called with the post and asked her if there was any sign of the chain. She knew nothin' about it, Pa told her everythin', she was furious and I was devoured for actin' the fool with council property. When it dawned on her that I might have to face the monthly meetin' of the council without the chain she went into orbit entirely. I was afraid she'd crash into the international space station.

'Gettin' that chain back from Wild Willy will be no easy task but it will have to be done,' she warned. 'There's no point in sendin' yourself or that useless Sergeant Miller, 'tis like usin' cotton wool in place of sandpaper. I'll have to do it myself.'

She was up at cockcrow the followin' mornin'. I heard her stirrin' and thought she was goin' to Clonmel for first Friday mass. As she left the house I took a peek through the curtains and saw her gettin' into the car with an ash plant in one hand and a bottle of holy water in the other. 'Twas clear she was a woman on a mission.

I became concerned and asked myself whether I should have let her off on her own. I needn't have worried, she returned before the breakfast with the chain in her fist. I was afraid to ask how she managed to get her hands on it but after she calmed down she filled me in on the details.

First, she did her research about Wild Willy and found out that he goes for a skinny dip in the Dribble every First Friday morning. Winter or summer, frost or shine, he does his monthly penance in the nip. The Mother got her information from the women in the Post Office, who claimed to have witnessed Wild Willy in full monty – they'd all been down for a peep. So on the first Friday of September she hit for the spot beside the river where he is reputed to perform his ablutions.

'Well,' she explained, 'I waited in the rushes and sure enough along he came. After bowin' three times to the north, south, east and west the hoor took off everything, includin' the chain and waded into the water in all his nakedness. As soon as his leathery arse went under water I made my move. I grabbed the chain, flung his clothes into the river and took off.'

'However, he spotted me and scrambled out of the water to follow me,' continued the Mother 'but the briars and the nettles were too much for his tender parts and he gave up.'

When I asked her why she carried holy water and ash plant with her she replied, 'I took the holy water in case I needed divine intervention and the ash plant in case God was slow about intervenin'.'

'Fair dues to you,' says I 'you're a mighty woman.'

'And you're a mighty eejit,' she responded, 'I've done many a thing for you in my time, but havin' to hide behind a bush and watch that hairy hoor strip to his pelt beats all. I'm warnin' you, if you lose that chain again you'll find yourself in the river splashin' around beside Wild Willy and I'll be splashin' your name all over the papers.'

The chain will be minded with my life.

HuNGry FOR HEADLINES

I was mightily relieved the local papers and radio didn't get a whiff of the chain's disappearance or they'd have made a show of me. And this brings me to what's botherin' me now: politicians and the media.

Us politicians have a love-hate relationship with the media: we can't live with them or without them. When I turn up at an event the first thing I look around for is a reporter or a photographer. A hack or a snapper at an event can multiply your audience by hundreds if not thousands.

However, since I became mayor this relationship between the media and politicians makes life very difficult, especially when it comes to chairin' council meetin's. Councillors intent on makin' the news can be impossible to control. The more the reporters scribble the more the chamber turns into a classroom of bould children and I end up like a stressed out headmaster.

Chairin' last Monday's meetin' was like herdin' cats. The first row started with the openin' prayer. Councillor Percy Pipplemoth Davis refused to stand or pray declarin' the practice to be 'sectarian and divisive in the new Ireland'. Councillor Moll Gleeson was havin' none of it and grabbed him by the ear shoutin', 'Stand up you pagan and pray like the rest of us.' I reminded Moll 'twas my job to call order. 'Well do your job,' she snapped, 'and get this pagan to his feet.'

After numerous demands Pipplemoth stood up only to declare, 'While I respect the wishes of the Chair I object in the strongest possible terms to the imposition of a specific form of religious practice on this council—.' 'Councillor,' I interrupted, 'Just stand up, shut up and leave the prayin' to the rest of us. At least the good Lord will be spared havin' to listen to you, the rest of us aren't as lucky.'

Durin' the prayer I noticed there was no one from the press in the chamber to witness Percy's carry-on. I couldn't wait to break the news to him. As proceedin's begun I innocently enquired if there was a reason there was no media in attendance. When Pipplemoth turned and saw the empty press chairs he went pale; the crafty hoor thought he had next week's headlines in the bag but his pagan tantrum was lost to posterity.

Ten minutes after the meetin' kicked off the press trooped in; they had been at a press lunch given by a new PR agency in town. As soon as they took their places all hell broke loose and every item on the agenda caused trouble. Even good news like the new playground in Honetyne raised a row. Moll Gleeson wanted to know if the paint on the equipment was lead free so as not to poison the children, 'Listen Moll,' says Councillor Peter Cleary, 'The children won't be eatin' the shwings and shlides!'

When Moll accused him of bein' careless about children's health Cleary remarked that the crowd in Honetyne 'are probably hungry enough to eat the shwings and shlides.'

Moll attempted to climb over her bench to get at him and only for the efforts of colleagues and the restriction of a very tight skirt she'd have been dug out of him.

Even when it was announced that the council would be takin' over a number of water schemes early there was major trouble. This should've been great news: the council gettin' around to anythin' ahead of schedule is as rare as a total eclipse.

All of a sudden the rows died down and we were gettin' through the agenda in jig time. I couldn't figure out the cause of this sudden change in atmosphere until I looked at the press chairs and saw the assembled ranks of the local media in slumber deep. The councillors were savin' themselves until the hacks woke up.

The PR lunch had obviously taken its toll and the councillors' efforts at makin' the headlines had gone completely unrecorded. The Manager is seriously thinkin' of organisin' a press lunch before every council meetin'.

A CROWDED HOUSE

Manus, my trusty driver, is home from his trip to Ibiza and back at work. Things were quiet up to recently and I hadn't much need of him but I'm flat out again.

When he returned from the holidays the question arose as to where the young man would live. At first we agreed that he would move in with us and we'd all be one big happy family. In fact the Mother was delighted at the prospect of havin' a man like Manus around the place, as she said about him: 'he's better than any woman in the house.'

Manus thought he might move into a flat in the village but that was easier said than done. We looked at a few places and most of them were fine if you were a lump of mould with no place to stick yourself. I've seen better cow-houses. When we failed to find suitable accommodation Manus moved in with us.

There's a lot of truth in the old sayin' that tells us: 'If you want to know me come and live with me.' For the first few weeks after Manus moved in the Mother and himself and myself were like Jesus, Mary and Joseph; we got on grand. The Mother was charmed with Manus: she no sooner had a wash on the line than he took it in and ironed it; whatever she polished he shined, whatever I dropped he picked up. 'Twas goin' great, but was it too good to last?

It seemed the Mother and Manus were made for each other, in fact at times I felt left out, I was a bit like Princess Diana, 'There were three of us in the relationship, it was a bit crowded.' However, as time went by I began to notice risin' tension between the pair of them. Durin' the dinner Manus might say, 'That was lovely, Auntie Bid, a bit salty for me, but tasty all the same.' You'd hear the Mother's false teeth grindin' like the tracks of a bulldozer.

When he'd cook the dinner the Mother would be sure to get her own back. One particular exchange was fairly lively. 'That was grand, Manus,' says she, as she poked her dinner around the plate, 'The carrots could have done with another few minutes, but sure you can't keep an eye on everythin' and aren't I lucky my false teeth are up to the job of crunchin' them.' Manus put his head down and swallowed hard.

Over the weeks the tension grew until the house began to feel like a gas cooker with a leak: all it needed was a spark and the place would explode.

I got up one mornin' at about half five to water the pony and found the Mother ironin' a heap of clothes. 'What are you doin'?' I asked, 'Do you realise what time of the mornin' it is?'

'Oh,' she said, 'Manus is tryin' to do too much, he'll be worn out. I decided I'd get the ironin' done before he gets up.'

The next mornin' at half four I heard a clatter in the back-kitchen and came down to find Manus peelin' vegetables for a stew. When I asked him what he was at he explained he wanted to get a head start on the dinner. I suddenly realised I was caught between two people competin' for the Killdicken Housekeeper of the Century award.

A few nights ago the Mother sat me down and told me I'd have to find other lodgin's for Manus. 'Now Maurice, don't get me wrong,' she explained, 'Manus is a lovely boy but he's drivin' me mad. I know I've spent years givin' out about you and men like you but God preserve me from the modern man: give me a useless hoor like you any day.'

You'd need a pint of caustic soda to wash down a compliment like that.

FROM THE FRYIN' PAN TO THE FIRE

I've been fierce bothered about the tension in the house between the Mother and Manus. In the pub the other night Superquinn noticed I was out of sorts and asked, 'Who ate your bun?'

'No one,' I answered, 'but I'm caught in the middle of a bun-fight between the Mother and Manus. They are getting' on one another's nerves and I need to find a place for him to live before I have a crime scene on my hands.'

'Well,' says she, 'Isn't that a coincidence. I'm fed up of the quietness in my own house and only last night I was thinkin' 'tis time I took in a lodger. Wouldn't my place be ideal for your Manus?'

'Begod,' says I, 'that would be great. Sure he'd be just down the road from me and he wouldn't have to live with his work.'

'Indeed,' says Superquinn, 'and if I need a partner for a night out won't he take the bare look off me?'

'Whatever you're havin' yourself,' says I, 'But how will I explain this to him without him feelin' he's bein' thrown out!'

'That's your problem,' says she, 'I'll get a room ready and you can send him over when you've talked to him.'

I wasn't lookin' forward to that particular chat until an ideal opportunity presented itself when we got a puncture on the way home from a meetin' in Rathgubbin. In the course of the wheel changin' I broached the subject: 'Manus,' I began, as I leaned against the car, 'do you find it hard livin' with myself and the Mother?'

'What do you mean?' he asked.

'Well, you're a young man,' I explained, 'meself and the Mother are kinda set in our ways and I'm sure we might be gettin' on your nerves.'

'What are you talkin' about?' he asked, 'I'm perfectly happy with the two of you?'

'Well,' says I, 'I was just thinkin' that a young fella like you might like to be doin' things that are – I suppose – not the sort of things meself and the Mother might do, like.'

Manus stopped for a moment, looked at the ground, turned and pointed the wheel brace at my nose, 'Are you askin' me to leave or are you throwin' me out?' he asked. I suppose tellin' someone you're evictin' him when he has a wheel-brace in his hand isn't what you'd call great timin'

'Now, now Manus,' I replied, 'I'm not throwin' you out on your ear, I'm doin' it in a way that ensures you will land on your feet.' I told him about my chat with Superquinn and suggested he might move in with her. He said nothin' only sat into the car and zoomed off leavin' me stranded on the side of the road. It took me an hour and a half to walk home and by the time I got there he had taken all his stuff and left.

I was in an awful state and thought he was gone altogether, but later on the Mother told me she saw his car outside Superquinn's place. He came back that night and apologised for abandonin' me in the middle of nowhere. He also agreed it was a good idea to move out and said he should get along grand with Superquinn. Above all he was wonderin' if he still had a job. I assured him he had and we shook hands.

It doesn't end there. Superquinn has taken quite a shine to Manus, so much so that she's dressin' like a teenager: the hair has been

straightened, the jeans have got tighter and the belly is exposed for all the world to see.

Manus must think he's gone from the fryin' pan to the fire. When you see a fella hidin' behind a wheelie bin while there's a woman goin' up and down the street callin' his name you know the hide and seek is fairly serious.

Sergeant Miller took his life into his hands on Saturday night when he met the all-new teenage Superquinn outside Walshe's, 'Begod, Breda,' he commented, 'I hope you never get a puncture: that spare tyre of yours is fairly bald.'

WHAT A PICTURE

Durin' the week, Manus and myself found ourselves at the launch of a campaign called 'The Apple-a-Day' campaign. Run by local apple growers and the regional health promotion unit it is meant to encourage people to eat apples and keep the doctor away.

Anyway, the launch consisted of a photo-call at a local orchard last Monday week and I showed up as requested. Myself and Manus were greeted by the sight of a number of gorgeous models swannin' around with little or nothin' on them bar a bikini. 'Jaysus, Manus,' says I, 'some days 'tis great to come to work.'

'Mornin' girls,' I chirped, as I got out of the car, 'Ye're not afraid of the goose-bumps I see.' Tim Tomlinson, head of the growers group and Miriam Hinchy from the health promotion unit came to greet me as I filled me eyes with the gorgeous view.

'Now, Councillor Maurice,' says Miriam as she hauled me away from where the lovely models were preenin' themselves, 'We'll get this started, I know you're a busy man. Let me introduce Rob, he's in charge of the photo-call and will call the shots from now on.'

'Lovely to meet you, Your Worship,' said Rob. 'Now I hope you don't mind, but we have some very physical stuff lined up for you.'

I didn't like the sound of it so I called on Manus for a bit of support. Himself and Rob got into a huddle and sorted everythin' out – they seemed to talk the same language.

The first photo involved myself and one of the bikini-clad models, Nikki, standin' beside these mediaeval stocks – you know what I'm talkin' about – the contraption they used for publicly punishin' petty criminals durin' the middle-ages. I remember them from Robin Hood films; fellas' heads and hands would be locked into a block of wood and people would throw rotten vegetables at them. The way things are goin' we could do with a set of them things in every village. Anyway meself and the gorgeous Nikki were photographed standin' at either side of the stocks eatin' apples while a fella dressed in a doctor's white coat was locked in the stocks.

'Begod,' says I, when the photo was taken, 'I've always wanted to know what 'twould be like to be stuck in those things.'

'Go ahead and try it,' suggested Rob. They locked me in and took a heap of pictures with Nikki on one side and Lexi, her model partner, on the other.

The next photo was bound to cause bother. Meself and the bikini models had to get into this big barrel of apples. We were up to our waists in the things. They gave me a pair of football togs to wear before I got in.

Anyway it all went fine till one of Lexi's earrings fell down into the apples. She asked meself and Nikki to stand still while she rummaged around lookin' for the missin' jewellery. However, she went slightly astray in her search and I let out a little 'Whoop' which drew everyone's attention to what had happened.

Lexi eventually found her earring and we all got out of the barrel. Fair dues to Manus, he had my trousers waitin' for me and we made a quick escape, but 'twas too late!

The followin' Wednesday and Thursday I made the

front pages and the two centre pages of every local paper in the region followed by appearances in many of the Sunday tabloids. One of them referred to me as, 'Hickey: the Kinky Councillor'. There were shots of me with Nikki and Lexi in 'bondage' in the stocks, pictures of me in football shorts gettin' into and out of the barrel with the half naked Nikki and Lexi. And of course, on the front page of all of them was that moment in the barrel when Lexi grabbed the wrong piece of jewellery.

I'm the laughin' stock of the place; even the Mother can't look at me without a smirk on her face. I won't be seen in the pub till Christmas.

OPENIN' SHOTS

The local elections of 2009 are beginnin' to raise the temperature and certain people around here are gettin' several varieties of the electoral itch. Councillors that haven't been heard of in three years are rousin' themselves. One of them in particular, Mindy Morrissey, an independent from Glennabuddybugga is rattlin' her cage after a long silence. Aside from an occasional outburst about indecency and filth and odd accounts in the paper of her frequent pilgrimages, little or nothin' has been heard from her since she got elected. She has decided to revive her political fortunes and seems to believe that attackin' my performance as mayor will put her back in business.

I should expect nothin' else from her. In the election for Mayor followin' the 2004 council election she deserted me along with independent Terence Bullockfield and Percy Pipplemoth Davis. More recently these three turned on their FF allies and voted for me in the July mayoral election.

Before I get on to Mindy's antics I should fill you in on Terence Bullockfield. He is a sort of new age gentleman hippie who was elected as an independent and, while he turns up for council meetin's, he has been off the political radar since the count. People reckon he contested the council seat simply to get access to a steady stream of clients for his new age quackery and cures.

He spent the last two years promotin' a therapy he calls 're-birthing', claimin' it wipes out all your mistakes and lets you start life again with a clean sheet. I'd love to believe it. Anyway, he developed a contraption he called the 'new womb'. This thing was like a hollowed-out round bale and people crawled into it while he induced their 'new labour'. They were encouraged to squeal like a pig while Bullockfield was outside shoutin' 'push, push' and howlin' with pretend labour pains.

Anyway, he thought he'd get an endless supply of people with more money than sense to pay €150 for two hours of screamin'. When it dawned on the clients that all they got for their money was a hoarse throat and a light pocket the business dried up. Bullockfield took a leaf out of the HSE book and closed down his labour ward; he is now concentratin' on his political career and his face is plastered all over the papers for the past few weeks.

But let me go back to Mindy Morrissey. She has decided to revive her political fortunes by attackin' me. In an interview with this week's *Eyeopener* she accused me of bringin' the office of Mayor into disrepute. 'The track record of Mayor Maurice Hickey is one of shame and disgrace,' she told the paper. 'He recently lost the mayoral chain on a horse and was splashed all over the local and national media in the company of scantily clad hussies. It's no wonder the moral fabric of our society is falling apart when community leaders like Councillor Hickey actively promote low standards in high places.'

When I read that on Wednesday evenin' it took the wind out of my sails. I adjourned to the pub for consultations with my kitchen cabinet. Cantwell, the shrewdest of them all advised me the only way to defend myself from the religious right is to out-flank them. He suggested a photograph with Canon McGrath was in order and said that a unique opportunity would present itself in the church the followin' evenin'. A local priest home from the missions was celebratin' his golden jubilee and the place would be alive with photo opportunities. Manus, who is a dinger with the camera, accompanied me to the celebration and photographed me with everyone we could find in a collar. He took a great shot of myself and Canon McGrath in deep conversation in the pews.

That particular photo appeared on the front page of the *Eyeopener* this week. It would've been fine except for the caption *'Bless me Father for I have sinned: Hickey to mend his ways?'* I can feel Mindy Morrissey linin' up for another attack or claimin' credit for my conversion.

IN PRAISE OF THE MIDDLE GROUND

The Mindy Morrissey campaign against me continues with a vengeance. In the last election she campaigned and was elected on a 'public decency' platform. In particular she campaigned against the skimpy attire of the modern woman describin' it as an assault on public morality. I think 'twas her husband she was most concerned about, his wanderin' eye is legendary. Anyway, she's now concentratin' her fire on me claimin' that as Mayor of the county I spend half my time hangin' around in barrels of apples with half dressed 'young hussies'.

In my years in politics I have come to the conclusion that most of the trouble in the world is caused by people on the extremes. It's not a place you'll find me. I might have a pint or five too many and my love affair with the fryin' pan might play Russian roulette with my cholesterol but otherwise I hold the middle ground. My auld Latin teacher was a great supporter of this particular space in life, he used to say, *'Virtus in medio stat: too far east is west.'*

Most political commentators cast aspersions on the middle ground sayin' it's much too crowded. It's crowded because it's a feckin' great place. Every cute hoor in the country is to be found there. 'Tis a place where all disputes are solved in a cup of tay or drowned in a pint of stout; a place where hard principles and political correctness are used as cipíns to light the fire.

If I'm intolerant of anythin' it is extremism. I only get upset with people who upset people – if you get my drift. Mindy Morrissey is a case in point.

She's one of the crowd that goes around mindin' God. Now, if they believe God is all-powerful it puzzles me as to why they think he needs so much mindin'. They accuse anyone who doesn't march in step with them of 'flyin' in the face of God'. Well if a fella is flyin' in the face of God surely the Almighty is quite capable of swattin' him away without help from gobdaws with long faces and short tempers.

Then if you go to the other extreme, you have people who blame religion for everythin'. I read in the paper a few weeks ago where someone blamed the Catholic Church for the scourge of obesity. Now, I carry a fair bit of condition on my person, but the only one who puts food into my gob is myself, I can't blame anyone else for it. Come to think of it, I couldn't accuse Canon McGrath of feedin' me. I've done him a fair few favours in my time and except for an occasional cup of weak tay and one of Nell Regan's hard scones I haven't got a morsel from the man. I think a clerical lunch is in order.

Talkin' of clerical lunches and problems with extremists, I was havin' a cup of tay in Clonmel the other day when who walked in but our local Church of Ireland Rector, the Reverend Winifred Whistletweel.

'Maurice,' she sighed, 'may I join you?'

'Indeed you may, Winifred,' says I. 'Will you chance a cup of tay and a sticky bun.'

'I most certainly will,' she replied.

After I ordered the refreshments I mentioned she looked kinda flustered.

'Oh, don't talk to me,' she groaned, 'at this moment in time I could do with something stronger than tea.'

'What's botherin' a decent woman of the cloth like you?' I asked.

'Well,' she explained, 'some time ago two friends of mine, both men, asked me to perform a blessing of their civil marriage. I agreed, but certain members of the Church are none too impressed. This morning I had a delegation warning me if I go ahead with the ceremony I'll be flying in the face of God.'

'Well,' says I, 'that makes two of us. I too have been told that I'm flyin' in the face of God. Seein' we're goin' in the same direction can't we travel together?'

At that, we ordered Irish coffees and drank a toast to the middle ground.

THE MAKIN' OF A GHOST

At Halloween, conversation in the pub inevitably turns to ghosts, ghouls, and the boodie-man. We were in Tom Walshe's establishment on Friday afternoon gettin' a good run at the bank holiday weekend when the very topic came up for discussion.

'Isn't a ghost supposed to be someone who was unhappy at this side, or is it someone who's unhappy at the other side?' asked Tom Walshe.

'Well,' says Cantillon, "tis like a pub. There's no one happy at this side of the counter; but the fella at the other side is ecstatic as he takes money from gobdaws like us.'

Ignorin' Cantillon's dig the publican returned to his subject, 'I've heard it said that the Hammer Corcoran's auld forge at Borris Cross is haunted.'

'Well now,' declared Tom Cantwell, 'that forge is home to of a quare story full of happiness and unhappiness in this life and the next.' I could feel a local history lecture comin' on.

'Where do I begin?' he began. 'In the 1930s Tadgh 'The Hammer' Corcoran the local blacksmith lived and plied his trade at Borris Cross. He was a long-time bachelor and everyone thought he was married to his craft. At that time a girl called Bridgie Moloney from Cossatrasna, was doin' a strong line with a young Kennedy fella from Lisnagower. He was heir apparent to a huge farm. Anyway, his mother thought Bridgie wasn't good enough for Lisnagower House and the romance was forced on to the rocks of grandeur and notions. Poor young Kennedy never married and died alone in the big house. The most excitin' thing to happen him after he finished with Bridgie was his funeral.'

'Meanwhile,' continued Cantwell, 'poor Bridgie had given up on life and for years wandered around like a lost soul until she met The Hammer Corcoran at a threshin'. Within weeks she did somethin' that was unheard of at that time; she moved in with The Hammer, lock, stock and nightdress and they set up house at Borris Cross. This caused uproar among the clergy and disturbed the sleep of many so-called God fearin' lay people in the locality and beyond.'

'Well now,' interrupted Cantillon, 'there's a lot to be said for keepin' things proper. Sure nowadays when people talk about their 'portner' you don't know if they're referrin' to man, woman or poodle.'

'Be that as it may,' continued Cantwell, 'the parish priest at that time, along with the local curate and missioners from the town all visited the cohabitin' pair to get them to do the 'decent thing'. In one of his last altercations with the PP, The Hammer told him that himself and Bridgie were doin' the 'decent thing' a few times a week and 'twas marvellous for body and soul. He suggested the priest should try it himself, 'twould do him a power of good.

The enraged clergyman took drastic action and the followin' Sunday read The Hammer and Bridgie from the altar. He declared that with every pull of the bellows in his forge, 'Mr Corcoran is fanning the fires of hell that are waitin' to consume him and his 'cohabitant'.

The Hammer wasn't too put out. In fact he was more afraid of losin' custom than facin' the fires of hell. I suppose after a lifetime in the forge he was no stranger to heat. Anyway, the people kept comin' and he was never as busy; shoein' horses, makin' gates, mendin', bendin' and straightenin'. People came from miles around to get their ironwork done and to get a look at the man and the woman who were defyin' the laws of church and society and survivin' without as much as a singe mark on either of them. They had no children but lived happily into their nineties and died within weeks of one another.'

'Now, let me tell you,' concluded Cantwell, 'that place at Borris Cross is definitely not haunted. But there's a big auld house over at Lisnagower and they say that on certain nights a pale, sad faced young man can be seen goin' from window to window lookin' out for someone with whom he might do the decent thing.'

PEOPLE IN GLASSHOUSES

Pub talk, like many other pursuits, is always topical and seasonal. As my old English teacher used to say about poetry, 'it reflects the concerns of the day in tone, content and intensity.' Anyone who frequents licensed premises as regularly as I do will know that the best pub conversations happen between five o'clock and half nine in the evenin'. Before five there's no-one in the pub to talk to and after half nine the quality of discussion is diluted by drink and the arrival of the great unwashed.

Every possible subject from the copulation habits of water hens to the geo-political ambitions of China are parsed and analysed at the counter. Cast iron conclusions are never arrived at, which means every topic can be re-visited, re-used and recycled at any time in the future. Pub talk is very enjoyable as a spectator sport but when it forces one to tog out and play it can be lethal.

Last week I allowed myself the luxury of a few early evenin's in the pub as it was a light week in terms of council work. 'Twas great to sit at the counter and spend hours talkin' about matters of great indifference and while many local, national and international affairs got an airing, the major talkin' point of the week was the huge salary increases that Bertie and the boys gave themselves. Fellas got fierce excited about it.

To be honest I kept my head down. Well, you see, I'm gettin' a fine wedge of money for bein' mayor and instead of sittin' in the pub maybe I should've been out among my people. As all around me marvelled at how a fella as busy as Bertie would get around to spendin' €300,000 a year, I lost myself in a detailed examination of the bubbles on the top of my pint. At one stage I went to the jacks in the hope they'd have moved on to global warmin' by the time I came back.

On my return I found things were even worse, they had got into performance monitoring. The transport minister who wants to put 'L' drivers off the road was up for particular mention. 'Some transport minister he is. This know-all has frightened the life out of half the young drivers in the country,' thundered Cantillon, 'and yet he didn't know Aer Lingus was pullin' its Heathrow flights out of Shannon. To crown it all, in recognition of his brilliance he gets a feckin' massive pay rise.'

'I know,' says postman Pa Quirke, 'That would be like me arrivin' back at the sortin' office with half the post still in the van and tellin' my boss I didn't deliver it because I don't know where the people live. Wouldn't I be the happy camper when, after half-doin' my job I got a big raise. If I followed the government's line of reasonin' I wouldn't bother deliverin' any post at all; the less I delivered the more I'd get paid.'

'Councillor Hickey is fierce quiet over there,' says Cantwell, 'has the cat got your tongue, Maurice?'

'Why wouldn't he be quiet,' said Cantillon. 'Isn't he on a fine salary as mayor of the county and here he is sittin' at the counter drinkin' porter. Wouldn't you stay away from any conversation about soft money if you were him?'

'Well now,' says I, 'as I look around at all of you I suppose 'tis hard to believe I'm surrounded by such hard workers. There's you, Mr Publican who passes his time with his backside in the air leanin' over the counter talkin' through both ends. Opposite you is Postman Quirke who slaves away day after day shuttlin' around the country in a van sayin' "Howya Missus" and negotiatin' the occasional cross dog. Then we have Farmer Cantillon who never did much, but hasn't done a stroke at all since the single farm payment came along. Bringin' up the rear of this hard-workin' bunch is the one and only Mr Cantwell, a complete atheist when it comes to risin' a sweat. Lads, I think the lot of us should keep our heads down before we're all found out.'

NECK, JOCKEYS & PEN PuSHERS

The contents of my postbag would amaze you.

As an ordinary councillor I get a flood of letters but since I became Mayor it has turned into a deluge. You wouldn't believe the things people write to me about and the things they ask me to do. This week I got a particularly rare gem that has to be seen to be believed.

Rossflook
Shronefodda,

31/10/2007

Your Most Worshipful Worship, Mayor Hickey,

I follow your wonderful career with great interest. You are indeed a man of the people and spend your time tirelessly among them. Not a week goes by but you are to be found on every second page of the Weekly Eyeopener with your chest full of medals and you opening something, launching something, giving out degrees or handing over fat cheques to people worse off than yourself. You are involved in everything, God bless you. Nothing is a bother from old folks parties to the ICA, the GAA and the arts. Your dear mother's heart must burst with pride when she opens the paper and sees picture after picture of her fine son in his chain of medals. Wouldn't any mother be proud?

Recently I saw you pictured with a group of women who had just finished a mini-marathon in Clonmel. I showed it to my brother and said, 'Our Mayor Hickey is a wonderful man. Look, here he is in the paper having run the women's mini marathon and he didn't even have to tog out. Even though he carries a bit of condition it didn't rise a sweat on him.' The brother is not a very perceptive kind of man and muttered something about your neck and a jockey's undercarriage but I chose to ignore it. There are begrudgers everywhere, even under my own roof.

Now, Mayor Maurice, I won't waste any more of your precious time, I'm writing simply to let you to know that you have many an admirer throughout the length and breadth of the county. But, seeing as I have the pen in my hand, there is a little matter I would like to bring to your attention. It is a delicate financial matter, which could be resolved by a temporary injection of cash.

Let me put my case: I have a keen eye for the horses, people who know me will tell you I know my horseflesh and my horseflesh knows me. I follow the careers of successful horses as closely as I follow the successes of people like your good self.

To get to the point, I put a substantial flutter on a very promising mare, Lippy Lass, running in Newmarket last week. She was flying like a gazelle until the crooked snipe in the saddle pulled her back. I lost a tidy sum on her. However, there's an imminent opportunity to redeem my investment and indeed make a bit of profit for your good self.

Lippy Lass is running in the Curragh this coming Saturday and will be ridden by the Sangwich Grennan from Bally. He's one of the Batch Loaf Grennans and, like our Lord, he was born in the stable. With Sangwich in the saddle Lippy Lass is sure to do the business. She's at 33/1 as we speak.

I was wondering if by any chance I could have a short-term loan of one of those fine cheques you frequently give away. Perhaps you have one lying unused in a drawer, it could be most useful to me. The venture won't cost you a penny and if Lippy Lass does the business then we'll both be in business.

If you can find it in your heart to help me I guarantee you my No.1 vote and the first preference of my entire extended family for a lifetime of elections. (I'm afraid I can only guarantee a number 2 from my mother's people who invariably give the No. 1 to whatever kind of a yoke the

Blueshirts stick on the ticket.)

I look forward to your reply and to celebrating with you in the winner's enclosure.

Yours sincerely

Jeremiah Smith Kennedy

SILENT, O MOYLE, BE THE ROAR OF THY WATERS

I'm withered from people talkin' about men's health. You can't turn on the radio or the telly but there's someone orderin' us to go for a full service. Manus, my driver, has taken up the cause sayin' he's concerned at the way I'm waterin' the horse very often. 'Maurice, ' says he, 'I wont have a brake left in the car from stoppin' at every gap to let you out to do your jiminy riddle. You need to have yourself checked out.'

'Listen,' says I to him, 'all this talk about men gettin' check ups has nothin' to do with health and has everythin' to do with linin' the pockets of the doctors and chemists. You know well that between tay, porter and the occasional cappuccino I take on a fair volume of liquid and what goes in has to come out, that's all there is to it. It's not rocket science and I don't need to pay fifty yo-yos to the Doc Doherty to tell me that.'

A few days later the Mother entered the fray, 'How many times did you go to the toilet last night? How is it you can't get from the bedroom to the pot without knockin' half the house? Are you in such a rush? You should go and have yourself seen to.'

I said nothin' but the pressure was gettin' to me. I adjourned to the local hostelry where I bared my soul and my waterin' habits to Tom Walshe, the publican. 'Well,' he said, 'a fella should take no chances. Maurice, you can afford to pay the few pound for a visit to the Doc Doherty but I'm warnin you, he'll probably send you further and you'll end up on the ramp. This job will mean a bit of pokin' at the undercarriage.'

To cut a long story short Tom convinced me and I went straight to the Doc Doherty. The waitin' room was full and it looked like 'twould be hours before I'd be seen. Eventually my turn came but as I went in I knew everyone around me was mad anxious to know why I was there.

'What's the problem, Councillor?' the Doc boomed. As I sat down I had visions of the crowd in the waitin' room puttin' their ears to the door to find out what was wrong. 'Well, Doctor,' I started, 'I'm told I'm piddlin' too much,' I declared.

'And what experts are telling you this?' he asked, 'Has there been a sudden influx of urologists into Killdicken?'

'To be honest, Doctor,' I replied, 'I've noticed it myself. I'm piddlin' like a leakin' bucket for the past few months.'

'Well, I suppose at your age it could be the auld prostate.' he remarked. 'If it's a bit swollen it will put pressure on the bladder. Anyway, I'll have a look. I'll need samples. Have you something in your bladder?' he asked.

'Jaysus, I have,' I replied.

'Hold on for a few minutes,' he ordered, 'roll up your sleeve and I'll take bloods first.' By the time he finished bleedin' me my bladder was in danger of explodin'.

'Here,' he said, handin' me a bottle, 'go in behind that curtain and fire away.'

I could hardly wait. When I started 'twas as if the Niagara falls had broken their banks, the bottle was totally incapable of containin' the volume of what I had to offer. As the trickle turned to a flood the Doc panicked.

'In the name a' Jaysus, Hickey,' he shouted, 'put a cork on it till I get a bucket.' He opened the door and shouted at his receptionist through the crowded waitin' room. 'Maggie bring a mop, a bucket and the jeyes fluid before this hoor of a councillor floods the place.'

When we finished cleanin' up he told me he'd send off the bloods and make an appointment with a specialist.

News of my deluge spread like wildfire. I walked in to Tom Walshe's a few days later to be greeted by a chorus of the Rose of Mooncoin, 'Flow on lovely river flow gently along.' There's nothin' secret or sacred in this place.

FECK THE FACTS

Christmas is comin' and I haven't time to think with all the functions, parties and do's I have to attend. Myself and Manus are flat out goin' from one thing to another and what's more I'm near poisoned from ham sangwiches, deep-fried chicken pieces and cocktail sausages.

Among the functions I had to perform last week was the launch of a local history book entitled, *The Black and Tans in Glengooley* by local historian, Bill Regan. The whole parish was gathered in the library to celebrate the event and hear more about the happenin's recounted in the book.

I'm afraid however, there isn't too much to be learned from the bould Mr Regan. To call him a historian is very loose use of that particular title because when he is short a few historical facts Bill has no problem makin' them up. He'd build an epic around a half-baked rumour and can stand on his hind legs and give a two-hour lecture on people, places and events, ninety percent of which is composed on the hoof. You'll never hear him admit to not knowin' something.

His history of the Tans in Glengooley is a case in point. For years he has made a fortune from the eventful day when the brave men of Glengooley routed the entire force of Black and Tans in this part of the county. He has written numerous songs, essays and poems about the event and these are sold in all parts of the world where a wanderin' Glengoolian has chanced to settle. One of his more rousin' ditties boasts the followin' openin' verse:

Come all ye loyal Irishmen a tale I'll tell to you
About the day the Saxon sons were baten black and blue

When the brave boys of Glengooley set hearts and souls alight
And showed the hordes of Black and Tans how Irishmen can fight

Whenever this is sung locally the last line has a number of different versions, the most common of which transforms 'the hordes of Black and Tans' into 'them hoors of Black and Tans'.

Anyway, the only thing to recommend Bill's latest heap of scutter is its brevity.

In fact I don't know how even he managed to squeeze the makin's of a book out of the bare historical facts as we have them. These facts are well known locally, but either people prefer to ignore them, forget them or have decided that the place of Glengooley in the fight for Irish freedom is better served by the embellishments peddled by Regan and his likes.

The only the Black and Tans to come to Glengooley throughout the entire duration of the War of Independence was a truckload of the scoundrels who had gone astray on their way to Clonmel. They stayed all of ten minutes, but I suppose in fairness 'twas an excitin' ten minutes.

Auld Mick Gleeson was comin' up the village drawin' hay with his horse and haycar when the Tans arrived and the commandin' officer stopped him to ask directions. As Mick brought his mare to a halt the wary animal suddenly and violently broke wind. The Tans immediately hit the deck and opened fire breakin' every window on the street and sendin' people, pigs, dogs, and chickens divin' for cover. As fast as they could they mounted the truck and left at speed. From that day to this if you're ever in Glengooley when the locals have a few gallons on board you'll be deafened with auld 'come-all-yes' about how the boys from Glengooley sent the Black and Tans packin'.

The fact remains that the one who should get the credit for liberatin' Glengooley from the brief grip of the Tans is Mick Gleeson's windy mare. There isn't one mention of a horse in Bill Regan's book, that says enough about it.

A CHAIRDE GAEIL

When is a friend, a friend? Do you have to go to two matches and drink four pints with a fella before you call him a friend or would one match and two pints do? Bertie Ahern's contributions at the Mahon Tribunal has us all tryin' to figure that one out. I'll tell you one thing, anyone who'd give me €5,000 smackeroonies for nothin' is a friend of mine. I think the poor auld Bert is gettin' a raw deal. What was the man to believe when these people queued up to give him money, except that they were his best pals?

A single man like me depends a lot on his friends. I depend on them for company, advice, and the occasional kick in the tail-end when I'm a total gobshite. I suppose I'm lucky in that my stable companions at Walshe's bar perform all these functions and more for me. Cantwell, Cantillon, Quirke and Tom Walshe don't let me away with much. If I'm ever in danger of losin' the run of myself, one of them will stick out a leg and trip me up before I get too big for my boots. Whenever I'm headin' for trouble they try and steer me clear of it, but that's easier said than done. Sometimes they stand back and let me plunge into a mess of my own makin' and get a great kick out of tellin' me, 'I told you so.'

The Mother has never been too impressed with my friends. She refers to them as 'the usual dose' and blames them for leadin' me astray. You see, like all mothers she believes that her boy was the best boy in the world till his friends made a fool of him.

There's a certain amount of truth in what she says. Whenever me and the lads were mischief makin' as young-fellas I was detailed to act as look-out and so I was always the first to be caught and often the only one to be caught. You see I wasn't the athletic type, I carried a bit of condition and so if the lads were robbin' orchards or stealin' conkers I was sure to get stuck halfway up a tree or on top of a gate.

I remember one time we were robbin' Rev. Parker's orchard. His was the Rolls Royce of orchards and robbin' it was sweet. Not only had Rev. Parker the best apples in the parish, he also had pears, plums and gooseberries. Gettin' into his Garden of Eden was a major operation as it was surrounded by a high wall but if you got in and got out safely you'd have the finest of eatin' for weeks.

We were about to raid it one time when the lads decided that I should go first. 'We'll help you up this side and down the other,' said Cantillon as he gave me a leg up. Everythin' was goin' grand till I got on to the top of the wall where I froze and couldn't move backwards or forward. Who appeared around the corner at that very moment but the Rev. Parker himself. My loyal friends scarpered and I was left there lookin' down at the Reverend from atop his own wall. 'What are you doing up there, young man?' he asked. 'Oh,' says I, 'I was chased by a pack of wild dogs and I climbed up here to get away from them.'

'And what about your friends?' he asked, 'Did they not stay around to protect you.' 'On no sir,' I replied, 'Them hoors can't be trusted.'

'Indeed,' remarked the Reverend. 'Well, it's nice to meet you. Do be careful up there. Good day.'

To my horror the Reverend made no move to help me down and I was stranded on top of the wall until the Mother came lookin' for me after it got dark. When my three so-called friends appeared the followin' day to ask if I could come out to play they got a real 'whip around' from herself. By the time she was finished with them they most certainly needed a 'dig-out'.

HAVE YOURSELF A MERRY LITTLE MELTDOWN

Cantwell is not impressed with the array of Christmas lights adornin' every second house in the country. In the pub the other night he ranted on about our carbon footprint and the waste of scarce resources.

'This madness beats Banagher,' he fumed, 'our Environment Minister is in Bali tryin' to solve global warmin' while the Bally crowd here beside us are meltin' an ice cap all on their own. Every house in that village is lit up like a feckin' carnival.'

Manus suggested I should get a bit of publicity for myself and make a few remarks about this rash of Christmas lights. I was invited to launch the annual Christmas Sale of Work in Shronefodda and we agreed it was an ideal opportunity for a major speech. Manus wrote a few words for me.

The Shronefodda crowd are great organisers and had photographers and reporters of all kinds lined up so there'd be plenty of media coverage. I arrived in the village with a few pints in me and had a few small ones after I landed so the tongue was loose.

I wasn't there long when Mick Heenan, the chairman of everythin' in Shronefodda called on me do the openin'. Ready for my big moment I pulled the speech out of my pocket but unfortunately the combination of poor light and too much drink meant I couldn't see a thing. I had to switch to automatic pilot.

After complimentin' everyone on the Sale of Work I launched my attack on the Christmas lights and their impact on the environment. A few eyebrows were raised when I told the assembled Shronefoddites that puttin' a bulb under a plastic snowman's arse in the middle of a damp lawn for half the night wasn't the most sensible way to conserve energy. I went on to declare that flashin' neon ladders on the roofs of houses were not only wasteful but could cause a fire on a wet night. 'Some of these yokes are bright enough to attract aliens,' I warned, 'before we know it there'll be flyin' saucers hoverin' over our houses and little green men comin' down our chimneys in place of Santy.'

My next target was the neon Santys that wave at you on your way in and out of every village in the county. 'There's a ferocious lookin' fella outside Teerawadra,' I declared, 'he's like a mad guard tryin' to get everyone to slow down. The hand goes up and down at the rate of a mile a minute all day, every day. In fairness to him, I believe no one has broken the speed limit since he was erected in case they're scratched off his hit list as they fly past. He's not the kind of Santy you'd mess around with.'

'Then,' I continued, 'there was "Adolf Santy" outside my own village of Killdicken. Every few seconds this fella's hand would shoot up in salute like a stormtrooper at a Nuremberg rally. He had the scutter frightened out of half the feckin' country, but thankfully a direct hit put him out of action last week. Lil Moran took the law into her own hands and at dusk one evenin' when Adolf was in full flight she blitzed him with a bucket of water. He fizzled and sizzled till he went black and blue.'

I commended Lil's action and finished with a call on the Minister to come back from Bali and put a stop to this waste and lunacy. I felt like Al Gore – but not for long.

Chairperson Mick Heenan, who obviously hadn't been listenin' to a word I was sayin' came up to the microphone, thanked me for my few words and then handed me a remote control with an invitation to switch on the Shronefodda Christmas lights. My face turned as red as Rudolf's nose when I pressed the green button and the whole village lit up like feckin' Las Vegas. There was wavin' Santys, dancin' reindeers, wrigglin' snowmen and enough neon ladders to take a fella to the moon.

I asked Manus to put me into the boot and take me home.

Happy Christmas. Ho, ho, ho, feckin' ho.

QUESTIONS & ANSWERS

Because I'm Mayor, every newspaper and magazine in the county has been sendin' me questionnaires to fill in for their Christmas editions. I've been asked to reveal all about my favourite toy, my favourite pair of socks, my worst nightmares, my secret daydreams and my favourite TV programme. I was asked by a few publications to name my most embarrassin' moment, but there were so many events in the runnin' for that particular prize 'twould take a tribunal in Dublin Castle to pick a winner.

I thought my local rag, *The Weekly Eyeopener* knew everything there was to know about me but the editor sent me a questionnaire of her own and being the good boy I am, I filled it in.

What is your biggest fear?

My biggest fear is havin' to rely on Cantwell, Cantillon, Quirke and Tom Walshe for a dig out. Unlike Bertie's friends, these fellas have difficulty buyin' a round of drink not to mention partin' with cash for nothin'. On the other hand they'd be great fellas for a whip around; they'd be the first in the queue to handle the whip and take a few wallops at you. For all we know Bertie's friends might be the same – except for one, or maybe two?

Who is the biggest influence in your life?

If I didn't credit the Mother with bein' the biggest influence in my life she'd go mad. She feeds me, houses me and is leavin' me everythin' in her will, why wouldn't she have a big influence.

What is your biggest regret?

I was asked this question by another paper and without doubt my biggest regret is not bein' able to sit up straight on a horse. I would've been a champion jockey if I was able to do that but anytime I mounted a pony, an ass or a horse I had to put me arms around its neck and hold on for dear life. I could never manage to sit up straight. Cantillon and the boys tell me that no matter what way I sat on a saddle I wouldn't have been a champion jockey because my arse is too big.

What is your all time favourite song?

It has to be 'Lay the Blanket on the Ground' by Philomena Begley. When the boys and me were doin' the dance halls and marquees, that was our song. Whenever Philomena belted out the chorus promisin' to take the blanket from the bedroom she drove us mad with notions. She had us believin' that every woman on the planet was only dyin' to lay a blanket on the ground and have her wicked way with whatever man she could find to lie down beside her. How wrong could you be? Even though it only served to add to our frustrations and inflate our bullocks' notions, whenever I hear that song I still have visions of bein' led into the long grass by a leggy blonde carryin' a Foxford rug.

If you won the Lotto what's the first thing you'd buy?

I'd buy a plastic bag factory and distribute the bags free of charge. The disappearance of the plastic bag can only be compared to the disappearance of the wheel. It was the handiest yoke ever invented and you were never short when you had a plastic bag. You could walk into a shop with your two hands in your pockets and buy all round you with no worry about how to carry the messages home. The plastic bag could slide over the handlebars of the bike, fit on the carrier and if there had been a shower while you were in the shop you could put one over the saddle to keep your arse dry while you cycled home. Nowadays if you forget your shoppin' bags the messages are put into cardboard boxes and you end like a circus juggler tryin' to keep them straight while you attempt to ride your bicycle. If the saddle gets wet, by the time you've cycled home on a damp tailend 'twill take a pound of Sudocreme to cure the ring of fire created by the friction.

Any more questions?

NEW YEAR'S DISILLUSION

Durin' the Christmas while readin' one of the Mother's magazines I came on this article about 'transformin' your life.' It finished with a suggestion that you should write down your life achievements, write down a few ways you might build on them and finally make a list of the things you need to do to achieve even more. I didn't get beyond the first two steps.

Name Three Achievements in Your Life.

My first major achievement came in 1965 when I won the

under-eight egg and spoon race at the Killdicken festival. I was delighted, luckily my egg was cracked so it leaked a bit and stuck to the spoon.

The second thing that comes to mind is not so much an achievement as an endurance. In spite of all attempts to lose it, I'm still a virgin. When you come to my age virginity is like a stray dog that attaches itself to you: you can't shake it off no matter what names you call it or how many stones you throw at it. I suppose 'tis a rarity now for a fella of my vintage to be in this condition and sure, maybe I'm better off the way I am.

I was moanin' to Quirke about this the other night and he tried to put a positive spin on it. 'Now Maurice,' says he, 'If you had a 1958 Morris Minor in mint condition would you put a tow-bar on it and use it for runs to town or to the mart? No you wouldn't. You'd polish it and shine it and only take it out on special occasions. So, I suggest you treat your virgin status like you would a classic car.'

I reminded him that I can't drive and even if I owned a 1958 Cadillac 'twould be like my virginity; all dressed up and nowhere to go. Anyway, havin' trawled the fleshpots of South Tipp, Waterford and Lisdoonvarna for the best part of twenty-five years I think its some achievement to say my reproduction department remains in showroom condition.

To get on to my other crownin' glories: my career on the council and my election as Mayor is some achievement for a fella who never did a day's work in his life.

Build on your achievements.

Well, I suppose it's a bit late now to be buildin' on my 1965 egg and spoon success. It has always been a matter of some regret to me that I failed to repeat my under eight form when it came to the under-ten and under-twelve egg and spoon events. Whether it was the spoons or the eggs or the conditions under foot I'll never know.

If I had money I'd commission a Genesis report on it, just like the IRFU when they wanted to figure out what went wrong for the Irish team in the 2007 Rugby World Cup. But in fairness, I don't need any Genesis consultancy when I have the Mother, she's better than any expert for gettin' to the root of a problem, and she costs nothin'. When

I asked her why I didn't win an egg and spoon race since 1965 she told me my arse was too big. If anyone in the IRFU wants to know the truth about what went wrong in France I'll give them her number.

How do I build on the achievement of holdin' on to my virginity? How can you be a better virgin today than you were yesterday? I don't know the answer to either question. But I do know that the nearest thing I'll ever have to a full blown sexual experience is the pleasure I get from eatin' a juicy rasher sangwich drippin' with tomato sauce. In all fairness it's hard to beat that for satisfaction and you don't have to waste time on foreplay or after-sales-service.

As for buildin' on my political success, I'm now Mayor of the council and can't go any higher unless I want to become a TD. That won't happen because it's too much like hard work.

Happy New Year from your beloved Mayor, Councillor Maurice Hickey, public representative, virgin and martyr.

IT TAKES ALL KINDS

People nowadays are always moanin' about the disappearance of local characters but in this neck of the woods that's far from the truth. The place is full of them.

The first character that comes to mind is Mick Heenan, a fella we met recently at the launch of the Shronefodda sale of work. Mick is what you'd call a 'foosterer' who is secretary or chairman of every organisation in Shronefodda.

When he's not at a meetin', puttin' up posters or sellin' tickets he runs his own business; a mixum-gatherum of a shop that sells everythin' from bacon to barbed wire. 'Tis the most chaotic emporium this side of the Khyber Pass with hardware, food, medicines, lingerie and cleanin' agents sharin' the same shelves, the same counter space and the same floor space. People have been known to do serious damage to their teeth after buyin' a quarter pound of bulls-eyes from Mick only to find themselves bitin' into a stray gutter bolt.

He foosters around the place with bits of paper and a pencil mutterin' constantly and twistin' his false teeth around in his head. He talks to everyone with his eyes closed and when he's bein' spoken to he keeps repeatin' 'Ya, ya, ya, ya, ya, ya, ya,' in case he has to listen to what's bein' said. He's a man always on a mission and nothin' comes between him and it.

Mick does all kinds of things in Shronefodda, locals would tell you 'tis almost like havin a second parish priest in the place. In fact some regard him as a kind of a half-priest. For instance he's a great man to visit the sick. If you go to the hospital on any Sunday afternoon you'll see Mick scurryin' from ward to ward with a list of the Shronefodda patients in his hand and he tickin' them off as he finishes with them. He goes to every bed containin' a Shronefoddite and with his eyes closed he rocks back and forth on his feet as he spews out the news of the parish, which he has rehearsed and learned off in the car on his way in. He regurgitates it like a school poem leavin' no room for his listeners to get a word in edgeways. His recitation tells of who's sick, what ails them, who died, who sold land and what they got for it, what big events are comin' up in the parish, the size of the local lotto jackpot, how the PP's latest cold is and what the mart is givin' for cattle.

One day Mick was at the bedside of poor Lar Sheehan, rockin' back and forth recitin' the news with his eyes closed when the ward sister came over to him,

'Excuse me sir,' says she, 'you mightn't have noticed but poor Mr Sheehan passed away an hour ago.' Mick scratched Lar off his list and moved on. Another day he was visitin' poor auld Maisie Donoghue who had been in hospital for two months and was totally fed up. When Mick arrived to give his Sunday speech she closed her eyes and pulled out her rosary beads in the hope that he'd feck off. Not a chance, Mick had the news learned and rehearsed so Maisie was goin' to get the full treatment whether she wanted it or not. As he rattled off his recitation, whenever he stopped to take a breath Maisie would say, 'pray for us'. 'Twas the strangest litany you ever heard.

'The lotto jackpot this week is €2,500.'

'Pray for us.'

'Moll Doolan has pleurisy and Mag Ronan has to get the second hip done.'

'Pray for us.'

'Fr Ryan's head cold has turned to sinus and he's on his tenth antibiotic.'

'Pray for us.'

'Cattle were well back at the mart on Wednesday.'

'Pray for us.'

'They were up on Thursday.'

'Pray for us.'

'Sergeant Maher is retiring and they're holding a collection for him.'

'Feck him and the horse he rode in on.'

'Tis a great country.

LOW TACKLES IN HIGH PLACES

I thought my spell as Mayor was comin' to an end. If you'll remember, I was elected for six months and was due to hand over the mayoral chain by the end of December. However, we have a new county manager who plays everythin' by the book and informed me that there is no precedent for a six month rotation of the mayorality unless the incumbent resigns or dies. Whatever about resignin' I have no intention of takin' my last breath.

The Manager invited me into his office last week to talk about it. When he asked if any other councillor had designs on the mayorality I looked at him as if he had two heads.

'Has anyone else got designs on it? I gasped, 'With all due respect to you, Manager, that's like askin' whether a hungry fox would be interested in a lame hen.'

'I see,' he said, scratchin' his head, 'Which of them expects to be mayor if you resign.'

'Well,' says I, 'the death of former councillor Tom Heenan before Christmas delayed everything. Moll Gleeson believes she should be in the chair by now with the chain of office draped round her neck. What's more,' I continued, 'I have an unspoken understandin' with her and I'm not goin' to break it.'

'Fine,' said the Manager, 'your resignation will be top of the agenda at the next council meeting.'

The night before the council meetin' I went to the pub to toast the end of my mayorality. I was no sooner settled on my perch when Superquinn arrived with a ferocious face on her. She sidled up to me and whispered, 'We need to talk.'

'About what?' I asked.

'About Moll Gleeson and the chain of office,' she hissed. 'I've just come from an ICA meetin' in Honetyne where Moll Gleeson spent the evenin' boastin' about how she's goin' to be elected Mayor tomorrow. She told everyone that she intends to bring class and style to the office, unlike you who she described as an embarrassment.'

I was gutted. I always regarded Moll as a straight talker. I said nothin' for a minute but then I explained to Superquinn how the County Manager told me an election couldn't happen unless I resigned, 'After this story,' says I, 'I'm havin' second thoughts.'

'Hold tough,' she advised, 'at the meetin tomorrow ask the Manager to explain the protocol to the councillors. Leave the rest to me.'

The followin' day as the council gathered a very sorrowful lookin' Moll made her way to her seat. I called the meetin' to order and asked the Manager to give us a lead on procedural issues. He told the councillors they couldn't proceed with the election of a new Mayor unless the current incumbent resigned. What happened next astounded me; Moll Gleeson got to her feet and proposed that I should remain in the office. She was closely followed by Percy Pipplemoth Davis who seconded her proposal wholeheartedly. Moll's jaw dropped to her knees at Percy's intervention and was gaspin' for air when a majority of the councillors supported the motion.

After the meetin' Moll turned on me callin' me a dirty double crossin' hoor. I hadn't a clue what she was ravin' about till I met Superquinn who explained that she had planted a story with a crony of Moll's to the effect that Percy Pipplemoth had done a secret deal with the FFers and would be elected Mayor. Now, Moll hates the skin Pipplemoth stands in and would vote for a dog before she'd let him become Mayor. In the mistaken belief that the Pip was goin' to be elected she decided to snuff out his mayoral chances by proposin' that I stay on. When Pip supported me she realised she'd been stitched up.

As I left the chamber FF Councillor, Peter Treacy, came up to me and grinned, 'I see the most cunning and the most ruthless of them all has moved from Drumcondra to Killdicken. All you need is an anorak.'

'Or a dig-out,' says I.

HELP: I'M IN CYBERSPACE

The world is a different place since I was a youngfella. What changed things more than anythin' else is the computer and its off-spring, the internet.

I'm a recent arrival to the computer age even though, as a councillor, I was issued with a laptop two years ago. Until Manus came along the contraption was buried at the bottom of my wardrobe. He dug it out before Christmas and since then he has made me spend twenty minutes a day on email and the internet. The internet (or the web) is an amazin' yoke; it literally puts the world at your fingertips; as a councillor in the back arse of Killdicken I have as much information available to me as George W. Bush. Manus tells me that my little laptop is hundreds of times more powerful than the one that sent Apollo to the moon. Isn't that feckin' amazin'?

But it's not all positive, anythin' that's as powerful as the computer can be used for good and bad. For instance, fellas with a weakness for a flutter are in big trouble if they start at it on the computer. There's always a horse runnin' somewhere in the world and at four o'clock in the mornin' a fella in Honetyne could be losin' his shirt on a nag with a bad cough pullin' its arse around a race course in Sri Lanka.

Mick Gaffney, a retired council official in Shronefodda, got hooked on the internet and was glued to it mornin' noon and night. The wife thought he was lookin' at dirt and filth and took no notice until she saw the bank account gettin' tight. She sneaked down the stairs one night expectin' to find him starin' at half-dressed hussies gyratin' like pole dancers and drivin' him quare. Her worst fears were about to be realised as she rounded the landin' and heard him shoutin', 'Come on, come on you lovely thing, give it wellie.' When she burst into the room she found him cryin' over €150 he had just lost on a camel race in Bahrain. The credit card was given the scissors treatment and the computer was moved to the bedroom where she could keep a sharp eye on him and it.

Mick made the fatal mistake of tellin' his cronies about the camel escapade and earned himself the nickname 'Gaddafi'. He was in the council canteen for a cup of tay the other day and when he asked the woman at the counter for sugar she grinned and asked, 'One hump or two?'

The worst thing of all is the spam. When I was growin' up spam was ham in a tin, the kind of stuff the Brits fed their soldiers. In the world of email, spam is uninvited messages like the plague of catalogues and special offers the postman lands through the door with the post.

Every time I open my email there's sure to be three or four messages from fly-by-nights offerin' me all kinds of medicine for half nothin'. Every sort of tablet from Anadin to Viagra is available. But what really gets to me is the amount of emails I receive sellin' concoctions that I'm assured will enlarge a particular piece of my crown jewels. If I was given a euro for every time I got an offer to have a few extra storeys built on to my 'you-know-what' I'd be a rich man.

I was warned by Manus never to reply to these messages or I'd draw their senders down on me like a swarm of flies, but by last week I was fed up of them. I responded to all promises of enlargement with a request: I informed the senders that while I have no current need to expand my undercarriage I urgently need to do somethin' about the size of my head. I explained that I got a present of a very expensive hat for Christmas which is about two sizes too big for me. I wondered if they had anythin' that would enlarge my head to fit my new headgear. I haven't had an offer to have anythin' enlarged since.

AIRS & DISGRACES

Willy De Wig Ryan and The Sticks FM have hit the big time: they were recently awarded a community licence by the Broadcastin' Commission of Ireland (the BCI). However, the wild celebrations held at the station in Honetyne last week could prove premature.

I don't know whether the licence is good news or bad because as long as Willy De Wig was illegal there was always the possibility of closin' him down. Now that he has the blessin' of officialdom the hoor could do woeful damage to fellas like me; he's about as predictable as a heifer in heat when he gets behind a microphone. Anyway, there was a bit of a do last Friday to mark the entry of the station into the world of legal broadcastin'. Unfortunately, it turned into such a mad affair that De Wig is already in danger of losin' the new licence.

I was lined up to perform the openin' ceremony and arrived before one o'clock as instructed. The studios have been relocated to a house in Honetyne rented from Imelda Greene, a niece of the late Tim Greene. Imelda was born and reared in Queen's New York and moved to Honetyne about ten years ago. She's as daft as a brush but her Uncle Tim had a soft spot for her and left her everything. She works as a volunteer at the station and is rumoured to be Willy De Wig's occasional 'portner'.

Anyway, Imelda was in charge of proceedin's and just before one o'clock she gave me the signal to start talkin', 'Keep it short and sweet, Mr Mayor,' she ordered, 'or I'll cut you off.' I knew this was no idle threat. To be honest I couldn't give a damn if The Sticks FM is dumped in the dustbin of broadcastin' history but last Friday I wasn't goin' to say anythin' that would ruin their big moment. I shouldn't have worried; they're quite capable of doin' that themselves. I was in full flight praisin' the achievements of 'our little station' when Imelda shouted, 'Enough garbage from you, Mr Mayor, let's have the Shronefodda Ceili Band.' My closin' remarks were drowned by the strains of a Kerry slide.

As the afternoon wore on and the drink flowed the live broadcast began to wobble off the rails. Willy De Wig was on the hard stuff and gettin' more dangerous by the hour. Durin' an interview with Canon McGrath, De Wig asked him what was the worst sin he had heard in the confession box since he arrived in Killdicken. The poor Canon went pale and when no answer was forthcomin' Willy looked around at the gathered guests and began to suggest what the various members of the great and the good might have to confess. 'Look at Percy Pipplemoth Davis,' he mused, 'I wonder what dark secrets he might have, Canon? I can imagine his confession: "Bless me Father for I have sinned: I drove my car to Clonmel twice last week when I could have taken the bike. I ate a rasher sangwich and a small sausage roll and haven't been able to look a pig straight in the face since".'

'Begod, Canon,' continued De Wig, 'I'd say you've heard quare ones since you arrived here. For instance, there's Tom Walshe, the publican. The Good Lord might have made a name for himself turnin' water into wine but our Tom has made a career out of turnin' whiskey into water. That man could do with a strong dose of absolution.' Luckily 'twas time for an ad break and the Canon made his escape.

Next up was Sergeant Miller. De Wig opened the interview by suggestin' that as a young guard the Sergeant was 'a divil for shiftin' women in the back of the squad car.' Within seconds there was a mysterious power cut and the station went off the air for the rest of the day. By all accounts so many complaints went to the Broadcastin' Commission that De Wig might be off the air for the rest of his life.

THE BUILDER WHO KEPT ON DIGGIN'

I have been known to shoot myself in the foot on a regular basis. I've also been known to provide a handy target for disgruntled constituents and trigger-happy journalists. It was a relief recently to witness someone else doin' the same job.

To make a long story short, the Draft Village Plan for Killdicken was on display in the local library last Thursday. On Thursday night there was a stormy public meetin' attended by council officials and councillors. Contrary to what one might expect, it wasn't the councillors or officials who found themselves in the firin' line even though the Killdicken plan had the potential to antagonise many of the locals.

The planners suggested that the 'distinctive rural character of the village must be preserved.' They proposed that housin' growth be 'tightly controlled and limited to smaller developments sympathetic to the population structure and the close knit tradition of the area.'

Mick Twomey the builder was in the crowd with a face like a turkey on him. 'Do you mean to tell me,' he shouted at the top table, 'that ye intend to leave this isolated heap of stones the way it is? What in the name of Jaysus is the *distinctive rural character* of this village? Is it that ye want pigs roamin' the street, chickens perched on half doors and the smell of fresh cow-scutter perfumin' the place?'

'Every village in the county,' he continued, 'has new estates, new shops and trendy cafés, but what have we? Just look around the main street: we have a post office that belongs on the set of *The Quiet Man*; Gleeson's tuck shop, an emporium that might rise to a selection box or two at Christmas and finally we have Tom Walshe's hostelry; a dark dive that doesn't open till five in the evening. In fact that place isn't fit for human habitation till after seven o'clock when the fumes of Jeyes Fluid have evaporated. As for the rest of the village, if derelict buildings and chimneys with bushes growin' out of them are distinctly rural, then Killdicken must be the capital of them all.'

Those of us among the assembled councillors and officials were sure Mick Twomey's rant was the openin' salvo in a long line of assaults. However, when he sat down we couldn't believe our luck as the locals adjusted their aim and opened fire on him.

'How dare you talk about my post office in those terms, Mick Twomey,' thundered Lilly Mac, 'the buildin' might be quaint but we deliver an efficient service to all comers. We even serve builders who turn up with bundles of dirty envelopes ten minutes after we close. However, that service is suspended as and from now, you ungrateful slobber-awl. If it's *The Quiet Man* you want, you'll get the John Wayne treatment if you ever appear at my counter again.'

Lilly hadn't finished when Tom Walshe got to his feet. 'Through the chair,' he began, 'I know this meetin' is concerned with the contents of the Village Plan but I can't let the slur on my business and my premises pass. I don't open until five o'clock any evenin' because before that time the only people to darken my door are those who want to relieve themselves. As for the smell of Jeyes Fluid, when you have customers like Mr Twomey with huge capacity and a bad aim you need a powerful disinfectant to protect public health.' At this a big 'Yo-ho' rang out around the hall, but Twomey didn't give a damn.

Next up was Celia Gleeson of Gleeson's shop, a lovely lady. She complimented the councillors and council officials on the village plan and went on to make some suggestions of her own. As she finished she mentioned that she and the family were about to undertake a major extension to the shop. 'As local shopkeepers we like to keep business in the area,' she explained, 'and we had intended engaging our local builder. But following the remarks made by him at this meeting, people will understand if a contractor from further afield gets the work.'

That softened Mick Twomey's cough.

A RUMOUR OF ROMANCE

The Mother is a divil for readin' every word in the local paper. She reads all the ads, notices, obituaries and acknowledgements. Recently an advertisement put in by some hoor who's mad for a woman grabbed her attention. She is convinced it was me who put in the ad in a last desperate attempt to find a 'life partner', as Bertie might say.

Now, don't get me wrong, the Mother would love to see me hitched. Indeed there was a time she used to pay a nun in Limerick to do a novena to St Valentine that I might get someone to take the bare look off me. She believes deep down that I'm totally incapable of lookin' after myself and I need the firm grip of a woman to keep me in some sort of shape. Do you know somethin': the firm grip of a woman sounds like somethin' a fella could look forward to.

I'm wanderin' off the point. While the Mother might like me to find a woman she's desperately afraid I'll arrive home with someone she doesn't know from Adam (or Eve); someone who'll give her a run for her money. She's probably wound herself into a knot at the moment thinkin' the ad in last week's paper will attract a banshee from the other side of the mountain or a young featherhead from the town with a short skirt and a backside made for high stools.

Now, the Mother might have been anxious for me to get a woman, but she was always very choosy as to what kind of female would suit. Among the few girlfriends I had in my time there wasn't many she approved of. Whenever I was seein' someone we never really spoke about it until a certain point when she'd let me know she knew I was 'doin' a strong line'. What's more, as soon as she had some research under her belt I'd be treated to the seed, breed and generation of the woman in question.

She'd approach the subject of the current love of my life with all the subtlety of a Munster rugby tackle: 'The smell of Old Spice around this place is enough to give a woman a bad chest. I hope it won't do permanent damage to whatever poor girl has the misfortune to be keepin' company with you at the present time. I shouldn't complain, at least she's bein' spared the suffocatin' pong of your natural odours.'

That would be typical of the openin' shots in a campaign to flush out or dislodge any woman I had an interest in. In the course of the next few days she'd drip-feed what she knew about the pedigree of the most recent object of my affections. 'Her people came from Teerawadra, didn't they? They were sheep people.' That could mean that they were well known for dealin' in sheep or notorious for stealin' them. If she didn't approve of the stock or breedin' of the female in question she'd dig up some story about a relation that was jailed or sent to Van Diemen's land for highly suspect activities. If that failed she'd go searchin' for someone in the family tree that had been an agent for the local landlord or an informer.

Those days are over. Aside from a brief fling with Madge Quigley about two years ago my romantic life is all but history. I suspect the Mother had confined my marriage prospects to the back of the haggard until she spotted the advert in last week's paper. She's been on one leg since tryin' to find out if I got any replies. Poor Manus is interrogated by her every time he darkens the door and Pa Quirke has his hand taken from the elbow when he arrives with the post. It's such good crack I've decided to keep her guessin', I even bought a bottle of Old Spice just to keep the trail fresh.

BRIDESHEAD REVISITED

Every community has one or two characters who reek of auld money, but haven't a bob to their names. You know the kind: posh accents, worn tweeds and a weakness for sherry. Some of these are the last remnants of the landed or 'stranded' ascendancy while others are locals who have a university education and never did anythin' with it aside from learnin' how to read the *Irish Times*.

Around here, Percy Pipplemoth Davis fancies himself as the local bit of auld lace but he's only a bag of wind. As they'd say in Texas, 'he's all hat and no cattle.' However, the last of the genuine tweed brigade in these parts are the Buttonshots. The Mother spent years workin' for them as housekeeper, cook and secretary and while she has no time for grandeur she has great time for the Buttonshots, she visited auld Lady Marjorie once a week until she died in 1985.

There was one Buttonshot son, Cecil, who lived at home until he was twelve before he was sent off to boardin' school. Aside from a short visit back to bury his mother he wasn't seen here again until last August when he returned to claim what's left of his inheritance. There wasn't much to come back to except a big draughty heap of a house with a leakin' roof and about forty acres of wilderness on long-term lease to Tommy Nealon.

Since his return to Buttonshot Hall Cecil has become a familiar sight in the village. On good days he arrives on an antique bike he rescued from the basement of the house while on wet days a canary yellow Citroën announces his presence. When he got the land back from Tommy Nealon in November he took to drivin' around on a splutterin' 1950s David Brown tractor he found under a pile of auld tyres.

Everyone has taken to Cecil, especially the women. Lilly Mac in the Post Office goes weak at the knees when he comes in, 'I loves listenin' to him,' she sighs. 'When you ask him how he's gettin' on he'll reply, "How awfully kind of you to awsk." He sounds just like the BBC World Service. He sends letters to places like Pamplona, Verona and Buenos Aires, how romantic.'

Moll Gleeson, the FG councillor has developed a posh accent for her encounters with Cecil. When she greets him she shouts as if he's deaf, 'Oh Cecil dawling, how absolootely wonderful to see you. And how goes it at Buttonshot Hawl?' The poor man does his best to avoid her but it's difficult to escape Moll in full furs, jewellery and crimson lipstick.

Not everyone has taken to Cecil. For some strange

reason the Clonmel guards have a set on him and are givin' him hell. They've summonsed him for drivin' the Citroën without an NCT, for havin' no roll-over bar on the David Brown and finally the poor fella was pulled for havin no light on his bike and arrested on suspicion of bein' 'drunk while in charge of a pedal cycle.' The misfortune has taken to walkin' across the fields to get around; he'll turn into a recluse if this keeps goin'.

The locals are furious at this harassment so I decided to find out from Sergeant Miller why the man was bein' picked on. I called to the barracks and got a frosty reception from a young guard who informed me that while Cecil was not drunk on the bike, he was technically in breach of the law on all the other counts.

As I left, Sergeant Miller appeared and followed me out. In a whispered conversation outside the door he solved the mystery of Cecil's pestilence. He informed me that the bould Percy Pipplemoth Davis had made a call to the local Super advisin' him that Cecil should be watched. Obviously Pipplemoth, the hoor, is mad jealous that someone else has appeared in the locality with a woolly jumper and an accent.

Anyway, it's an ill wind that doesn't blow some good: when Percy crawls out on to a ledge, all I have to do is choose my moment and push. I can't wait.

KILLER CURES

I'm not at all well. I've a dose of the flu that just won't go away. I've tried Lemsips, Anadins, hot milk, brandy and port and half a gallon of hot whiskey but I'm still flattened. Poor Manus is worn out from nursin' me. His car is like a chemist shop with lozenges, rubs, and pills of all kinds.

Anyone that's been on the planet as long as me should know there's no cure for the common cold except bed and plenty of liquids. However, my current dose is so bad I'm willin' to try anythin' at all to get rid of it; and there's no shortage of remedies. Everywhere I went last week my drippin' nose and my red eyes seemed to attract people with cures.

I was openin' an art exhibition at the Honetyne day care centre on Wednesday and auld Lizzie Grehan gave me a remedy she swore was the greatest of all time. She told me to boil three peeled onions in milk, strain them, sprinkle the milk with pepper and drink every drop. I was so desperate when I got home that night I tried Lizzie's concoction. With tears streamin' down my face I peeled the onions and put them into a pot full of milk and laid it on the cooker.

After boilin' it for ten minutes I strained the milk into a jug and sprinkled it with pepper. It looked feckin' awful and smelled worse, in fact it smelled like boiled Wellingtons. It took me a few minutes of snortin' and gruntin' before I could summon up the courage to drink the stuff. 'Here,' says I, as I held my nose, 'kill or cure' and I swallowed the lot. 'Twas the hardest thing I ever did in my life; the concoction not only smelled like boiled Wellingtons, it tasted like a pair that had spent a month in a slurry pit. I felt as sick as a small hospital after the last drop went down my gullet.

I woke the followin' mornin' with a sore head, a cramped stomach and innards full of wind. I don't want to offend your sensibilities but Lizzie Grehan's cure started a series of nuclear explosions in my lower regions that went on for two days. Manus drove around with the windows of the car wide open otherwise the two of us would have suffocated. He suggested that I should forget about any more wild cures and just take to the bed like every other ordinary mortal afflicted by the common cold.

But there was too much to be done and I couldn't afford to take a day off. Besides, Moll Gleeson, my Deputy Mayor just loves gettin' her hands on the chain of office and paradin' herself all over the papers. I avoid lettin' her deputise as much as I can.

Anyway, the cold was only gettin' worse on Thursday night when who came to call but the bould Superquinn. She told me I needed to spend an hour in a sauna to sweat it out. Before I knew I was in the car beside her headin' for a new gym in Clonmel with a bag full of towels on my lap.

She marched me in and explained what I was to do. I nearly shivered to death in the dressin' room as I stripped to my skin. That was bad enough but when I walked into the sauna 'twas like walkin' into hell; I thought I'd fry. I couldn't see a thing with the steam and was sure some gobshite had turned up the temperature. I tried to find the door and couldn't so I began to roar like a bull. 'Turn it down or I'll suffocate.' Eventually I found the door and out I went. Well, the heat was bad but the cold was nearly worse. As I got dressed my teeth were chatterin' like a jackhammer.

I ordered Superquinn to take me straight home. I went to bed for two days, drank plenty of water, took a few hot whiskeys and I was right as rain in no time. There's no other cure for the common cold.

BURNIN' LOVE

Every day I live I'm becomin' more and more content with my bachelor status. In fact, the longer I spend on the planet the more I see that wedded bliss is a rare commodity. I know of many houses where the marriage is held together by friction.

One such place is the Kelly household located on the Honetyne road and inhabited by Maisie and Tom Kelly. Tom is a cantankerous hoor and why Maisie ever married him is an absolute mystery. He is a self trained mechanic who learned his trade in London fixin' dumpers and JCB buckets for McAlpine. In mechanical terms it's a long technical leap from a yellow dumper to the workings of a computer-controlled modern car and Tom never really made that leap. As cars became more complicated he became more and more cantankerous.

When people go to him with their sick machines he opens the bonnet, looks in and upon realisin' the problem is beyond him he tells the owner that only a pure eejit would buy a car like that. His next course of action is to reach for his miracle cure, a massive set of jump-leads attached to a battery that's big enough to kick-start a jumbo jet. Like one of them doctors you'd see on the telly administerin' resurrection shock treatment to a flattened patient Tom applies his wires to the unfortunate car. Within seconds the place is full of sparks and smoke and when the smell of burnin' gets to a certain level he pronounces the car clinically dead and tells the unfortunate owner he bought a dud.

The sparks in the garage are nothin' compared to the sparks in the house. The mechanical mayhem has turned Tom into a divil but Maisie is well able for him. She couldn't care less what he says. Luckily the children are grown up and gone so the pair can rise as big a row as they like and no one suffers but themselves.

Things have gotten so bad lately that Canon McGrath went to visit. His car needed a service and even though he always goes to the main dealer he decided to take his beloved Laguna to Tom as a sort of a Trojan horse to get inside the marriage. He reckoned a change of oil, plugs and points wouldn't be too much to ask Tom to do and the visit would give him an openin' to introduce Tom and Maisie to the idea of givin' their relationship a full service.

Last Monday mornin' the pair were at the breakfast when the Canon called with his Laguna. He joined them for tay and in the course of the small talk mentioned he was goin' to Cheltenham for a break and asked them if they ever take holidays. Well, if that didn't start a row. Maisie complained that the last holiday she had was her honeymoon in Blackpool in 1973, Tom told her she didn't need a holiday as her whole life was one and she wouldn't know what a day's work was.

When the Canon managed to get a word in he went the full hog and suggested they could badly do with some marriage counselling, 'It would be like a jump start for your relationship,' he explained. Maisie told the Canon she hadn't much faith in what he suggested as her husband regularly destroys perfectly good cars with jump-starts. Before another row erupted the Canon got them to agree to think about marriage counselling.

In case they might change their minds he decided to separate them sendin' Tom out to service his car while Maisie made more tay. The kettle wasn't boiled when they heard a huge bang from the garage. They went out to find Tom standin' there, jump-leads in hand and the bonnet blown off the Canon's Laguna. 'Canon,' says Maisie, 'If marriage counsellin' will do to him what he did to your car then it's my kind of a jump-start.'

MIXED MESSAGES

Parish halls and community centres are very busy places. There's so much goin' on it can be fierce hard to get a room for a meetin' and even when you succeed you can have fierce competition from activities in adjoinin' rooms. I had an example of it myself durin' the week. I was invited to a meetin' in Teerawadra community hall about a new scheme for older people in the area. Mary Treacy is puttin' an application together and asked me along to 'give the proceedings a bit of weight', as she said herself. To be honest, there was no shortage of weight at her meetin' before I arrived; no one in attendance would get a prize for slimmin'. However, next door in the main section of the hall another crowd was fightin' a fierce loud battle against the bulge.

The great and the good of Teerawadra had convened in the small meetin' room to discuss Mary Treacy's worthy project. When I arrived I was amazed at the number of cars around and puzzled as to where all the women in tracksuits were goin'. When I made my way through the side entrance to the meetin' room I found a small enough crowd there given the number of vehicles parked outside. The attendance included local PP, Fr Sheahan, the Reverend Whistletweel, Sr Jacintha from the convent, the Public Health Nurse, Dr Doherty and a fair sprinklin' of upstandin' community activists.

As soon as the meetin' began it was obvious that whoever booked the room didn't realise that Gladys Bardon was holdin' an aerobics class next door in the main hall. No sooner had Mary Treacy opened proceedin's at our little gatherin' than Gladys's music box started blarin' rock music that could be heard in Clonmel.

To make matters worse Gladys was shoutin' at the dancin' women like a drill sergeant; 'Come on ladies, if ye don't want ye're men to be lookin' at young wans ye better move them big tail-ends and shift them lumps of cellulite. By the time I'm finished with ye, ye'll look like pole dancers. Move it girls!'

I didn't know where to look. Why do these things always happen when you're surrounded by clergymen, nuns and the local clutch of holy water hens? Mary Treacy battled on bravely explainin' how this new fundin' would be of great assistance to the Meals-on-Wheels. Meanwhile, in the adjoinin' hall Gladys Bardon was roarin' at sweaty women who must have been regrettin' every meal they ever had whether on or off wheels.

Gladys's bellowin' and the sound of the music would've been bad enough, but what took the biscuit entirely was her choice of music. As Mary earnestly explained her project she pointed out that Teerawadra was home to a 'significant number of single elderly men living alone.' At that very moment Gladys's music box began to pump out the 1980's hit 'It's Rainin' Men, Hallelujah.' There was a big smirk on the Doc Doherty's face, but Mary kept goin'.

As soon as the song stopped, Gladys and her sweaty women took a break and takin' advantage of the lull, Mary ploughed ahead at breakneck speed givin' out as much information she could in as short a time as possible. When she finished her presentation she opened the meetin' to the floor.

Margot Delaney was first on her feet sayin' 'twas about time somethin' was done for the elderly.

'This godless Celtic Tiger has blinded us to our traditional values of modesty, moderation and carin' for our neighbours If people would only think of those less fortunate than themselves and not be spendin' their time watchin' filthy television programmes we'd be a far better country,' she said.

The words weren't out of Margot's mouth when Gladys was back on the air encouragin' her charges to 'get down and dirty' to the strains of Rod Stewart as he belted out 'If you want my body and you think I'm sexy.' Margot stopped suddenly and pointin' in the direction of the main hall remarked, 'Listen to that: need I say any more.'

There's a lot of life in one little community hall.

HOT MAIL

While letter-writin' is fast becomin' a relic of the past it's still a powerful way of communicatin'. I suppose people only take the trouble to write when they are passionate about somethin' and one thing most rural people are passionate about is plannin' permission. It is the hottest issue any rural councillor will have to deal with and it gets red hot entirely when the mother or mother-in-law of the plannin' applicant puts pen to paper: you'd need oven gloves to open the envelope. Here's a sample of what I got recently:

Talladuff
Honetyne

6 March 2008

Dear Councillor Hickey,

My son, Thomas, is getting married in October to Majella Clancy, one of the Clancys from Borrisnangoul. For the past two years he has been trying to get planning permission for a bungalow on one of the two acres I have with the house. He's a good lad and hopefully will be of help to me as I get more stiff and tired and sore. However, that blasted council of yours is doing everything in their power to stop the boy. At this stage he has dug so many soak holes the neighbours are convinced we're building a swimming pool.

Recently a young wan from county hall with a face like a fiddle on her came out on a site visit. Before she even got out of the car she told us that only people with 'an established housing need and a demonstrable connection to the area' would be allowed build. I brought her out into the yard and I put Thomas standing in the middle of the field.

'Now,' says I, 'there is my son Thomas, standing in that field. Can you see him?'

'Yes, I can,' she answered.

'And,' I continued, 'Does he have a house over his head?'

'No,' she answered looking at me as if I was gone off the deep end.

'That's right,' says I, 'That's my son who's getting married in a few months and is he going to bring his new wife into that field with no roof over their head?'

'I presume not,' answered Miss Know-all.

'That's right,' says I, 'so we have established his need and I have demonstrated it to you.'

'Well, Mrs Daly, that's not altogether sufficient,' she interjected.

'It's sufficient for me,' says I.

'Now that we have established his need,' I continued, 'we'll look at Thomas's connection to the area. He's my son, I'm his mother and here is his birth cert. I am the Margaret (Peg) Daly née Hartigan listed as the mother of one Thomas Mary Gerald Daly born on the 5th of June 1980. I live here in this house beside the field on which my son wants to build a house. Now if that connection isn't strong enough for you maybe I should go back to the hospital and get them to re-attach the umbilical cord or perhaps if the both of us went for a DNA test it might satisfy your requirements.'

I told her that as far as I was concerned I had clearly established my son's need for a house and his connection to the area. She replied that it wasn't as simple as that and, to add insult to injury she went on to suggest that Thomas and his new wife could move in with me.

Now, Maurice, you know them Clancy's as well as I do and while Majella might be a nice girl, her mother would go up your nose for news. As for the father, he has so many notions he'd need a trailer to carry them around. The thought of having to entertain that crowd under my *own roof is enough to drive me to drink.*

Maurice, if there's anything you can do I'd appreciate it. A lot of people around here say you're a useless hoor but I'm always willing to give a man one chance. Don't let me down.

Yours sincerely

Peg Daly

PS. I see a lot of you in the paper these days. That chain of office makes your belly look huge.

There's no doubt but Peg is an expert on makin' friends and influencin' people.

While much of my postbag concerns complaints or problems, I receive many a missive from people with suggestions as to how we might make the world a better place. It is hard to tell whether some of the authors are people of great imagination or have a slender hold on reality. This is one of the classics:

Sallymount

Honetyne

Dear Councillor Hickey,

In these days of global warming and declining fuel stocks may I be so bold as to suggest that the primary task of all political leaders from the King of Togo to Councillor Maurice Hickey is to encourage conservation. In the absence of any new sources of energy to replace coal and oil I believe the only way to save us all from freezing or frying is to conserve energy.

I intend to write to you frequently with short instalments outlining some of my proposals. Were I to put all my ideas in one document it would most likely end up as bedding for greyhounds before you would find time to read it.

My first set of ideas concern heating and cooling public buildings. Could I suggest that in winter we harness body heat to heat public buildings and in summer we use space to cool them. These buildings should be divided into summer quarters and winter quarters with summer activities held in big rooms with natural air conditioning, i.e. plenty of windows and doors. In countries such as Ireland it is surely the height of waste and foolishness to have buildings with air conditioning when all one has to do to get a blast of cool air is open a window. Air-conditioning should be banned.

In winter as many people as possible should be encouraged to squeeze tightly into small rooms so that the heat emanating from the human body would eliminate the need for fossil burning heating systems.

Now, to make optimum use of body heat, fatter people like your good self are particularly valuable as you are of a size and critical mass to generate copious amounts of heat. In fact, could I be so bold as to say that under full steam you are a veritable mobile incubator. Under my proposals people like your good self will be placed strategically at meetings and public gatherings in positions where you and your likes can provide all the heating requirements for those around you.

In this new dispensation our more rotund citizens will become highly valued members of society and should be spared the litany of dieting lectures they regularly have to endure from sour-faced, anorexic dieticians.

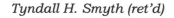

Placing people together at such close quarters may result in greater exposure to body odour and flatulence but, aside from a certain unpleasantness, these bodily activities do not inflict any lasting damage on man or beast and indeed are a sign of rude good health.

I shall be in touch soon again with further suggestions as to how we might save the planet using a modicum of common sense. In the meantime, if you would like me to address councillors or community groups on this topic I will be delighted to oblige.

Yours sincerely

Tyndall H. Smyth (ret'd)

Imagine bein' stuck in a lift with that fella.

INSIDER INFORMATION

Whatever about readin' your own post isn't it quare how we get a kick out of readin' other people's? I'm a hoor for it when I'm on my rounds. Very often when I call to a house there might be a letter from the Department of Agriculture lyin' on a table or a letter from the bank, or better still, a letter from the local TD. I'd be dyin' to have a look and the minute my host would go off to make tay or answer the phone I'd nearly twist my neck into a hoop to get a read. There's something in all of us that loves to poke around in the drawers of someone else's dresser.

As a politician a quick squint at someone else's post isn't necessarily a fruitless pursuit, it can deliver valuable information and priceless opportunities.

One such opportunity came my way recently and as a result I might pull off a great coup. I was doin' a clinic in Honetyne when I got a message from Toss Murphy askin' me to call to him; he wanted to talk about organisin' an official welcome for a crowd of high rankin' sheep farmers comin' to his place for a farm walk. When I called he was on the phone in the hall and pointed me in the direction of the kitchen. The missus, a secondary teacher, was at work and his children are grown up and gone.

As I sat down at the table I noticed a piece of Dáil Eireann headed paper stickin' out from under a pile of documents. Judgin' by the conversation on the phone I reckoned Toss wouldn't be finished for a while and I found myself starin' at the golden harp on the protrudin' Dáil letterhead. Eventually my curiosity and the devil got the better of me. I tugged at it and out it came; a letter from the desk of local TD, Ted Lynch:

Dáil Eireann
Dublin 2

9 March 2008

Dear Toss,

Further to your recent telephone call concerning your application for a small grant towards your forthcoming Sheep Festival, I have been in touch with my colleague in the Department of Arts & Culture (copy of letter attached.)

Unfortunately the closing date for these applications had come and gone a number of weeks before your application arrived and, much as he would like to oblige you and me, there is nothing the Minister can do.

I regret this is the case but if there is anything further I can do please don't hesitate to call me.

Mise le meas

Ted Lynch TD

Toss is a classic floatin' voter with family connections in all corners of the constituency. He is also stuck in every farmin' organisation in the country: he is the kind of voter a politician should mind. The letter I took a sneaked peek at wouldn't have done Ted Lynch any good in this house and beyond. I stuck it back where I got it and when Toss finished his phone call he came in and made tay.

I discussed the official openin' of his farm walk at some length in the hope that he might volunteer some information on his problems fundin' the Sheep Festival. As I stood up to leave I decided to take a more direct approach and asked him how preparations were goin' for the event. Well he flew into a rage, 'Maurice,' says he, 'that Ted Lynch is a useless hoor. He promised he'd have no bother gettin' me a grant for the festival and I heard nothin' for months 'till I got this,' says he pullin' out the letter I had just read. 'That's very disappointin',' says I as I read the missive with a big funeral face on me. 'I'll see what I can do, there might be a few pound in the council pot.'

'Well, Maurice,' says he, 'if you can put a few quid in my direction for that sheep festival I'll guarantee you every local sheep farmer's vote for the rest of your life. In fact I'll guarantee you the votes of their entire families, dead or alive, and if I can swing it I'll even get the feckin' sheep to vote for you.' My quick peep at that letter from the TD could see me elected from now to kingdom come.

I shook Toss's hand and left with the pure intention of findin' money in some pot for him. If he could only introduce an artistic angle of some kind to his sheep festival maybe the County Arts Officer might put her hand in her arts pocket for me?

HAVE ANOTHER WOMAN'S CAKE (BUT DON'T EAT IT)

The woman in her home is ferociously protective of her patch. This is particularly true in the home bakin' department: she mightn't care what comes into the house from supermarket or shop but she's fierce suspicious when anythin' made by another woman's hand finds its way onto her table.

My father, God be good to him, came afoul of this reality once too often. On his rounds as a councillor he'd be given the odd gift. Now before you jump to conclusions they weren't the kind of gifts that would land a fella in trouble with a tribunal or find him on the phone to Mary McAleese lookin' for his P45. No, often after a day on his rounds he'd arrive home with turnips, new spuds, the odd fletch of bacon, a few heads of cabbage, a bag of apples or even pears. The Mother never minded that kind of thing but when he'd bring an occasional pot of homemade jam or marmalade I'd know by the look on her face that it was a gift too far. From the way she'd react you'd imagine he was throwin' down a challenge to her, sayin': 'Bate that, if you can!'

I don't know if he was blind to her annoyance at havin' another woman's jam in her cupboards or whether he actually brought the stuff home to upset her, but he'd drive her mad altogether when he'd compliment it. As he'd smother his bread with this unwelcome condiment he'd be sure to say, 'I never tasted jam like this! 'Tis as good as you'd get anywhere in the world. The woman who made it should get a medal.' The Mother would be fit to boil over; she'd be bangin' pots and pans and slammin' cupboard doors as she fought the temptation to break the pot of jam over his head.

But by far the worst crime of all was to bring another woman's bakin' into the house. This had various levels of gravity: a tart or a sponge was bad enough, but puttin' another woman's brown bread on the table was worse than adultery; you might as well have brought the woman who baked it home and put her into the bed.

I remember well a series of incidents involvin' my father and the produce of Lil Keating's oven. Lil lived in Borrisnangoul and became a regular at my father's clinic after she ran into problems tryin' to buy her house from the council. About every six weeks she'd arrive at the clinic to see if there was any news and would load him down with plums, apples and pears.

The mother didn't take much notice of Lil's bounty till the first apple tart appeared. 'Faith and Lil Keating must have little to do to say she can bake for you,' she snapped, 'a man who has a woman at home already. Maybe she didn't notice!'

'She probably thinks I need a bit of feedin',' the father replied. 'If she thinks you need feedin',' the Mother shot back, 'then she needs new glasses, but I suppose her specs are constantly steamed up from all the cookin' she does for married men?'

The father wasn't listenin' at all; if he was he wouldn't have arrived home four weeks later with two cakes of Lil's brown bread. He might as well have come in with her lipstick all over his collar, the Mother went ballistic. She got the washin' basket, extracted all his dirty clothes and stuffed them into a pillow case which she flung at him with the words, 'If Lil Keating is so anxious to feed you maybe she'd like to clean up after you as well.'

He never brought another bite of food into the house. In fact he didn't even bring a thing from the shop in case he'd have to account for its origins. Funny enough, from that day on our dog started to suffer a dramatic fall into flesh and when his heart eventually burst he was as big as a bull calf.

BACK TO THE FUTURE

People are beginnin' to get excited about 2009 council elections. Political junkies are eagerly lookin' forward to the next crucifixion to be suffered by local politicians up and down the country in the comin' twelve months. I hate the long lead into these blasted elections, anythin' you say or do from now on will be seen as an attempt to hold on to your seat. Every conversation or phone call will begin with a menacin' probe; 'I suppose you'll be runnin' again next year,' and many will end with a veiled threat; 'If a fella like you is thinkin' of goin' before the people he'd want to be doin' somethin' about this.'

I feel sick at the prospect of the doorsteps, the demands, the pressure and the abuse. In fact I'm really tempted to declare I'm not runnin' and tell anyone with complaints about plannin', potholes or soak-holes to feck off and phone the council officials themselves. I'd love to be able to tell some of my regulars that I don't give two shakes of a scuttery cow's tail about their bellyachin'. Unfortunately, that's a luxury I can't afford; from now on I'll have to show interest in every cause that raises its head. I'll be expected to stand beside objectors to phone masts, to support campaigners for traffic lights in deserted villages and propose the construction of by-passes around settlements that have little or no traffic except for when the occasional funeral causes a blockage.

I was in the council the other day and had the misfortune to share a table in the canteen with Percy Pipplemoth Davis. The hoor must have taken the wrong tablets because he was like a greyhound with worms, he couldn't sit still for a minute. 'I'm getting desperately worried about the election, Maurice,' he muttered. 'What election?' I asked innocently, 'Has Cowen decided to make a go for the overall majority?' 'No,' replied Pipplemoth, 'I'm talking about the local elections. I'm so afraid the Green participation in government will alienate the local support I get from alternative types. I mean, they are horrified at our helplessness to stop that M3 motorway going through Tara.'

'Listen, Percy,' says I, 'the best thing you could do is go up to Tara and lie down in front of a bulldozer for a few days and that will surely harness the local alternative vote. You might as well be lyin' on the flat of your back up there as mopin' around down here with a face like a wet week on you.' Percy thought this was a great suggestion and took off for Tara with his woolly jumper, his sandals and his drum. He'll probably get the same four alternative-type votes he got last time.

Anyway, the nerves about the election must be contagious because no sooner had I dealt with Pipplemoth than I opened the local paper to see a cackle of the local FFers pictured at a local election plannin' meetin'. I began to get the shuckerin' duckers at the thought.

When I went home that night I couldn't sleep. I got up at about four in the mornin' and made tay. As I sat there I began to imagine what 'twould be like if I really decided not to run and, as I did, I began to relish the prospect of not givin' a damn. 'Twould be great fun meetin' people who constantly pester me.

For instance, there's Maggie Belford on the Bally road who has my ear twisted into a hoop about a pothole outside her gate. I'd get such satisfaction out of tellin' her to get a feckin' wheelbarrow and fill it in herself. And there's Marty Lenihan, who has more houses than I have teeth and wants the council to build two mile of a road up to his disadvantaged mountain farm. Everyone knows he has a queue of clients for sites the minute the road is finished. I'd love to tell him that the last thing the council should be doin' is rubbin' lard into his fat backside.

Maybe it's time I hung up the boots?

HAIR WARS

Nancy Spain is like a divil. Up to recently she was the only hairdresser in Killdicken, but Angela Purcell's new salon on the Bally road has shattered her monopoly. Angela has opened for business in the massive palazzo gombeeno herself and husband Tim built on a site given to him by his aunt. Like many another fella who got a site for nothin', he used the spare cash to build a monument to his notions of himself.

In fairness to Angela, she heard rumours that Nancy was on the point of retirin' but anyone who knows Nancy Spain knows she'll die with the scissors in her hand. In fact, if St Peter is in need of a trim when she arrives at the pearly gates he'll have a short back and sides before he has time to tell her whether 'tis up or down she's goin'.

I wouldn't have known anythin' about this loomin' hair war except for Manus who knows everythin' that happens in the three parishes. He is a hoor for news. He told me that Angela had decided to open up in the belief she was threatenin' no one, but that's not how Nancy sees it. As far as she's concerned, no jumped up snipper on the Bally road is goin' to steal her custom. She regards this as a direct attack and has responded fiercely.

She no longer waits for her customers to ring her for appointments, she rings them first tellin' them what time to come and warnin' them not to be late. Nancy is not the kind of woman you'd say 'no' to. In the last few weeks every female head in the parish has been blue rinsed, bobbed or permed, in fact there's often a queue outside her door like sheep waitin'

to be dipped. She has commandeered taxis, community cars and the rural transport bus to trawl far and wide and haul in her more isolated customers.

'Tis a military operation that even includes intelligence gatherin'; Nancy's nephew owns the land at either side of Tim and Angela's and has spent the last few weeks camped in the fields beside their house pickin' stones, pullin' weeds and repairin' fences while takin' note of every car that comes and goes through Angela's gates.

I was dragged into the affair when Angela decided to launch a fight-back by organisin' a fancy official openin' to which she invited the great and good of the whole region. She asked me to officiate at the event and, while I know for certain this could earn me the wrath of Nancy Spain and her long-tailed family, I couldn't refuse.

So last Friday afternoon the who's who of South Tipp gathered at Purcell's mansion for the big event. Nothin' was spared: there was a marquee, a caterin' company, a live band, champagne and all sorts of grub. While all in attendance were happily sippin' wine and nibblin' finger food I was engaged in a pursuit few politicians know anythin' about: I was desperately tryin' to avoid the photographer. Nancy Spain was well aware of the fact that I was doin' the honours at Purcell's official openin' but if I appeared on the paper beside a beamin' Angela she could do terrible damage to me in the ballot box: a sore place to interfere with any politician.

Anyway, just as the formalities were about to begin Nancy's nephew pulled into the field beside the house and proceeded to spread the foulest smellin' load of slurry that was ever spread anywhere on the planet. The marquee had to be abandoned and proceedin's were switched indoors but unfortunately, the pong followed. The photographer wasn't able for it and abandoned ship before the formalities began. The very minute the speeches finished everyone else followed suit. Tim and Angela's electronic gates were nearly torn from their hinges as the occupants of jeeps, mercs and beemers made a mad dash for fresh air.

I was feelin' sorry for poor Angela but she left me in no doubt that while Nancy might have won the first round, round two was only beginnin'. Stay tuned.

THE ENEMY WITHIN

They say a politician should be careful of those closest to him; he could be groomin' his successor without realisin' it. I'm beginnin' to think that Manus is learnin' too much too fast.

When he's not chaufferin' me around he does a bit of voluntary drivin' for Glenkilhone Rural Transport, the local rural transport association. He's one of a number of volunteer 'community drivers' who are paid a mileage allowance to take people who need transport to medical appointments and the like. The service is covered by the free travel and those not auld enough for the travel pass pay a small fare to the transport association.

Manus is forever ferryin' people to doctors, chiropodists, hospitals and chemists and consequently knows the pains, aches and treatments of everyone in the three parishes. In fact he is like one of them flyin' doctors they have in Australia, even when he's drivin me he gets calls from his community car clients who sound more like patients than passengers. They ring him up to ask his advice on all kinds of things includin' what tablets they should be takin' and in what order.

We were on our way to raise a Green flag at the national school in Teerawadra the other day when Tim Lenihan came on the car phone:

'Hello, hello, is that you Manus? Tim Lenihan here!'

'Hello Tim,' answered Manus, 'I hope you're not lookin' to book the community car. You'll have to ring the Glenkilhone office and they'll book one of the volunteers.'

'I don't need a lift anywhere,' replied Tim, 'I want to know about my tablets, the ones prescribed by Doc Doherty the other day; do I take three of the red tablets and one of the white ones or is it the other way round.'

'You take one red and three white,' answered Manus, 'a red one and a white one every mornin'' a white one with the dinner and another white one goin' to bed.'

'Oh, Jaysus,' says Tim, 'I've been takin' three reds and one white at one gulp in the mornin'.'

'For feck sake,' gasped Manus, 'ring the Doc Doherty this minute and make an appointment. I don't know what that concoction will do to you.'

The next thing we heard was the sound of the phone bein' taken from Tim by his strong-willed wife, Maura, 'Give me that phone you gobaloon,' shouted Maura, 'Hello Manus, 'tis Maura here. I'll tell ya what that new concoction of tablets is doin' to him; he hasn't slept a wink since he started takin' them and whatever has got into him he thinks he's a teenager in the undercarriage department. I have to take the cattle prod to bed to keep him away from me. Is there any chance you'd come over and take him to a doctor or the vet to quieten him?'

Manus patiently explained to her that he couldn't do anythin' but told her to ring the Doc Doherty and tell him what happened. 'Get back to me if you're stuck,' concluded Manus.

He had no sooner finished that call than the phone rang again, this time 'twas Bessie Johnson in Redbarn.

'Hello, Manus, Miss Johnson of Redbarn here.'

'Howaya Bessie,' replied Manus as cheeky as you like, 'and how're the bunions?'

'Well, Manus, the one on my left foot is beginnin' to pain me like you said it would, so I'm takin' your advice and have an appointment to see the chiropodist on Tuesday. Can you pick me up at 9.00?'

'Now, Bessie,' says Manus, 'you'll have to ring Glenkilhone Rural Transport office first and they will put you in touch with the first available driver.'

'Oh but Manus,' says Bessie, 'I only want you.'

'Bessie, don't be talkin' dirty to me, I might get excited and drive in over the ditch.'

'Manus, you're an awful man. Hopefully I'll see you Tuesday. Bye, bye.'

'Begod Manus,' says I, 'you have the older folk wrapped around your finger.'

'That's right,' he agreed, 'they're the important ones to get. The grey vote is vital for any politician.'

It might be time to send Manus back to his mother.

'WHO LOVES YA, BABY?'

The Mother nearly fainted when I came down for the breakfast yesterday mornin'. I forgot that my attempts at keepin' the peace in the parish had resulted in my appearance bein' seriously altered, at least temporarily.

Let me explain. The war that erupted between two hairdressers in the parish namely; Nancy Spain and Angela Purcell left the population badly divided.

It became deadly serious as the two strong, well-connected women in question showed no signs of backin' down. Angela is married to Tim Purcell who's related to an electoral quota, his mother is Ryan from Borrisnangoul and they have connections in every townland in the region. Angela herself is well-known and popular: she played camogie for the county, was a finalist in the Queen of the Orchard and by all accounts is a nifty hand-baller. As you know, herself and Tim built a big house outside the village where she opened a new hair salon, much to the annoyance of Nancy Spain.

On the other side, Nancy has been doin' hair in this area since 1958. In fact some people claim she started years before when she plucked turkeys for her mother. She built up a loyal customer base down through the years and wasn't about to wave the white flag when Angela put her name over her door. You'll remember how Nancy's nephew sabotaged Angela's big openin' with a load of fresh slurry that he spread in the adjoinin' field. Since then Nancy adopted a different approach. She developed a range of special offers such as two perms for the price of one on Mondays; a free blue rinse for the grandmother when the granddaughter got highlights and inclusion in a free draw for a trip to Lourdes for all clients.

Meanwhile, Angela expanded her services. She went down the road of full beauty treatment offerin' massages, facials, and all kinds of alternative rubs and pokes. She employed this fella to do massages who by all accounts was a 'hunk' that had the ladies queuin' up to get a rub off him.

Between rinses, perms, mud-baths, dyes and body lotions, the parish was becomin' a chemical accident waitin' to happen. 'Tis a good job we all received the emergency booklet from the government recently; for a while it looked as if Killdicken would have need of it.

Last week things started gettin' out of hand with vicious rumours and gossip. First there was the story that Nancy's hair dye was of poor quality and was givin' people the itch. This was followed by a rumour that the Vatican wasn't too happy with the goin's on at Angela's beauty parlour. For a finish, no one at all was goin' to Angela's or Nancy's in case they'd get the itch, a bad reputation or both. Some local women were travellin' to Clonmel to get the hair done while others had taken to wearin' scarves to cover their wild heads until the war was over.

I decided to intervene and see if the two women would agree to work within the ordinary rules of healthy competition. I went to see Nancy and before I had time to get down to business she had me perched on her chair where she did a job on the little bit of hair I had around the headland. She agreed the row was doin' nothin' for her business or for Angela's and 'twas time to cool things down. Meanwhile after she brushed me off she put my name in the hat for the Lourdes draw.

Manus drove me to Angela's who greeted me with an enquiry as to where I got the haircut: I couldn't lie and to keep the channels of communication open I asked her to finish the job with a razor. As she was busy turnin' me into Killdicken's own Kojak she agreed to abide by the normal rules of commerce.

I left Angela's with the bones of an agreement in my head but without a rib of hair on my skull. The things a councillor has to do for his constituents, but at least there was some consolation: I won Nancy's trip to Lourdes.

HICKEY IS FECKED!

If you don't mind the pun, the row between the hairdressers in the parish has receded. However, the disappearance of the last remnants of hair from my head has caused all kinds of talk.

You'll remember that in the course of negotiatin' an end to hostilities between the warrin' salons I had a haircut in both establishments with the result that I'm as bald as an egg. The locals didn't realise that in the interests of peace in the parish I sacrificed the last of my long follicles and so the story has gone around that I'm terrible sick and the treatment made me bald.

I hadn't a notion that people were talkin' about me but in the pub I began to notice that I was bein' treated differently. The Four Horsemen of the Apocalypse; Cantwell, Cantillon, Quirke and Tom Walshe didn't mention a word about my skull or the state of it. Normally they'd get hours of entertainment out of my misfortunes so I was completely puzzled as to why they didn't say a thing about my bald head. Along with that they always refer to me as 'Hickey', or 'the Councillor', however, in the last week or so, 'twas all 'Maurice' with them. They stood up to offer me a stool as soon as I came through the door and before I had time to put a hand in my pocket they had my pint called and paid for. I didn't know what was goin' on.

Tinky Ryan the undertaker took a great interest in me altogether. At Batt Comerford's funeral in Bally the other day I spotted him out of the corner of my eye walkin' around and sizin' me up like a jobber examinin' a beast at a cattle mart. What's more, everyone who sympathised with the grievin' family came and sympathised with me as well. They were grabbin' my hand as if I was a close relative of Batt, a bachelor farmer who was as mean and cantankerous a hoor as you ever met. I was beginnin' to think maybe I was a far out relation and could have a claim on his forty acres.

When I got home I asked the Mother if her people were related to the Comerfords but she informed me that in all likelihood we were more closely related to the Pope. She handed me a bottle and sent me to the church to get a drop of holy water and light a candle for my father whose anniversary is comin' up. As I got to the church gate Nell Regan, Madge McInerney and May Stapleton were passin' in their tracksuits. After gettin' my holy water and lightin' a candle at the front of the altar I turned to find Nell, Madge, and May kneelin' in the back pew with funeral faces on them and they starin' at my bald head.

I couldn't figure out what was happenin'; how could a man's hairstyle have such an effect on the way people treat him? I didn't realise things were so serious until I was in a cubicle in the jacks at the council and overheard three colleagues wonderin' who would take my seat at the local elections. I was about to come out and challenge their political analysis when one of them commented; 'Hickey must be fair sick to say he lost the hair so fast.'

'Oh,' says another, 'it seems he's fecked altogether. Sure all them Hickeys died young; there's some class of an auld weakness in the breedin'.'

I had to sit down and wait till they were gone before I made my way out. While 'twas frightenin' to hear people discussin' my imminent departure from this life, the conversation clarified everything; now I knew why people were treatin' me as they were.

But how was I goin' to handle this? I could play along and keep gettin' gallons of free porter and tons of sympathy ad infinitum; I could make a public statement explainin' that I'm in the best of good health, or I could hit the big time and declare a miracle cure.

Like everythin' in politics, this little mix-up has to be milked for all it's worth. When the time is right I'll put the record straight, but like all my political colleagues, I'll only do this when I have to. In the meantime, I'll enjoy the tay, the sympathy and the porter.

LIFE IS A PITCH

The GAA season should be gettin' into full swing but there's nothin' happenin' in Killdicken. Well, that's not altogether true: there's a lot happenin' in Killdicken GAA circles, but none of it on the pitch. 'Tis a long story. A while back, a huge row split the local club when the then secretary, Brian Cahill, proposed major developments for the club facilities. His plans were totally opposed by Chairman Micksie Dunne who became the victim of a swift coup when himself and his cronies were replaced by a new breed of management led by Cahill.

As soon as the new committee got their plans adopted by the club Micksie launched a campaign of resistance claimin' the proposed new dressin rooms and the all-weather pitch were 'a blueprint for turnin' the tough men of Killdicken into a bunch of cissies.'

He tried to set up a new club but it came to nothin', then he picketed the pitch for a few weeks but as it was the dead of winter only the crows took notice of him. Anyway the whole issue was put on the back-burner after it became clear that plannin' permission and fundraisin' were goin' to take time. Games and trainin' continued on the old pitch as before.

All that changed last week when, for some reason, things started happenin' fierce fast. Plannin' permission came through on Thursday and hot on its heels on Friday mornin' came a letter confirmin' money from the Lotto.

To celebrate the news of the go-ahead, the club unveiled a model of the plans at a special ceremony on Friday night and since then the model has been on display in the Post Office. Most people in the parish are delighted but former chairman, Micksie Dunne is still disgruntled. He's on walkin' sticks after gettin the two hips done and has plenty of time for devilment and skulduggery. Within hours of the model goin' on display he mounted a picket on the street outside the Post Office. He was joined by Dinny Brophy and Lar Culhane, all veterans of the most famous Killdicken team of all time; the 1958 Junior B county finalists. Their claim to fame is not that they won the final but they only lost by two points and finished the game with more than ten men on the field; a record for the parish. You'll hear songs to this day extollin' the virtues of 'the men of '58, loyal, disciplined and true.'

The recent spell of fine weather was great for picketin' so Micksie and the boys got loads of attention. No-one passed them outside the Post Office without stoppin' to have chat and a laugh. In general the protest was very good humoured and the boys got loads of media coverage along with heaps of free ice-cream. If they keep up the protest much longer they'll burst.

Unfortunately, not all is sweetness and light; the longer the protest went on the more controversial the posters and placards became. At the start the slogans were mild enough with messages such as: 'Real Men Don't need Showers', 'Soft times, Soft Men'. But as the week went on things got worse with placards declarin': 'Killdicken GAA Pitch: From Battleground to Playpen', 'Killdicken GAA: a school for Nancy Boys'.

The club committee was gettin' fierce uneasy and complained to Sergeant Miller that the posters were comin' too close to the bone. Sergeant Miller told them he couldn't do anythin' once Micksie and the boys didn't make a public nuisance of themselves. In fact, quite the opposite happened.

On Wednesday there was an attempted raid on the Post Office when two fellas in balaclavas rushed past Micksie, Lar and Dinny shoutin and wavin' guns. As they tried to leave with the proceeds of their crime the robbers found themselves confronted by three ferocious auld men wieldin' walkin sticks and placards; they dropped the money and ran off empty-handed.

Micksie, Lar and Dinny are heroes in the village and have become untouchable. Their opposition to the new pitch has become a very popular cause all of a sudden. Killdicken GAA might yet spend this season hurlin' on the ditch.

A MUSICAL INTERLUDE

The Teerawadra Musical Society is known far and wide for its gala productions of big musicals. While tradin' under the name of Teerawadra, the society is home to would-be singers and performers from all over these parts. In fact, it is home to a heap of individuals who think they should be on stage in the West End and not wastin' their sweetness on the thin air of South Tipperary.

At any rate, come the end of each season they have a party for the cast in one of the local pubs. This year they chose my local, Tom Walshe's, and descended on the place last Friday night after a big feed in the Duck's Quack, a fancy new restaurant in Shronefodda.

The few regulars in Walshe's were yawnin' their way through the *Late Late* when the door burst open and in fell the Teerawadra thespians, full of wine and their own importance, among them Councillors Moll Gleeson and Percy Pipplemoth Davis. The women were drippin' in jewellery while the men were decked out in the uniform of men with notions; blazer, dickie bow and cravat. They called a round of gin and tonics and various other concoctions that caused Tom Walshe to break out in a sweat for the first time in years.

Anyway, once the gathered artistes had topped up their fuel tanks the commander-in chief, George Grace, called order and asked May Lenihan from Cossatrasna for a song.

'Come on now, May,' says he in his finest accent. 'Give us the usual for a start; we'll come back to you for something more adventurous a little later.'

That sounded promisin'.

May prepared herself like an Olympic athlete warmin' up to attempt the hop, skip and jump. She took such deep breaths I was afraid she'd suck the oxygen out of the entire bar and as her chest expanded the buttons of her blouse came under severe strain. A fella would be well advised to stay out of range. Just as she was about to launch into whatever she was about to launch into she stopped and turned to George; 'Should I take it in F or F sharp? I don't want to strain myself this early in the night.'

'Stick with the F, my dear,' advised George.

'Or a B flat well pumped,' suggested our resident musical expert, Tom Cantwell. The assembled show-folk turned and glared at him as if he had committed blasphemy.

May straightened herself, did a major throat clearin' job, yelped her way up and down the scales and eventually got started:

I dreamt I dwelt in marble halls with vassals and serfs at my side,

Cantwell delivered a runnin' commentary; 'Typical of the feckin' Lenihans, full of auld bigness; vassals and serfs at your side did you say? Ye didn't even have a pair of feckin' shoes for yer feet.'

'Order now, please,' demanded George, 'show some respect for the singer.'

'Twas too late, May had made a dramatic dash for the loo followed by a crowd of concerned women anxious to comfort her. George complained loudly and bitterly to Tom Walshe who assured him he'd rein in his 'unsophisticated regulars'.

To calm matters George nominated himself for a song and launched into a version of 'O Solo Mio'. You could see he loves his own sound as he held on to every note for two days longer than necessary with his voice shudderin' as if he was sittin' on a badly balanced spin-dryer.

Moll Gleeson turned to me and whispered, 'I love George's natural vibrato.'

'Jaysus, Moll,' says I, 'and I thought you were a happily married woman.'

I got a thump.

George was makin' slow progress through 'O Solo Mio' when Cantwell decided to join him in the chorus singin' 'Just one cornetto'. The destruction was total.

George attacked Cantwell for his bad manners, Cantwell responded tellin' him he sounded like an ass brayin' into an empty tankard.

The musical society finished their drinks and left in silence.

'Well,' says Cantwell, 'That was a typical Teerawadra Musical Society performance; high melodrama and dreadful singin'.'

WHO ARE YOU AND WHY AM I HERE?

Thanks be to God I have only another month left as Mayor. I'm fed up of speeches and tired of tellin' people I'm delighted, honoured, privileged and humbled to open whatever I'm openin' or launchin'.

Sometimes I have so many things on my schedule I forget where I am and what the event is about. Manus has been vital in keepin' me out of trouble. He's one step ahead of the posse and always has a few words typed out for me but, like the best of plans, things can go badly wrong.

For instance when I was speakin' at the Turf-cutters Annual Dinner Manus handed me the speech he had prepared for the Green Glen Environmental group AGM the followin' night. 'Twas a wonder I got out of the place with my life; I waxed lyrical about the need to stop burnin' fossil fuels, get into our geo-thermals and replace the skylights with solar panels. I was halfway through my script when the audience got into fits of coughin' and splutterin' and chokin'. Concludin' my few words they couldn't believe their ears when I declared that, 'One of the most urgent tasks facin' the people of rural Ireland is to work to save our raised bogs from disappearin' up our chimneys.' I had it said before I realised 'twas the wrongest thing to say in the wrongest place.

I sat down to the sound of stony silence. Chairman, Vinny Treacy rose to his feet shakin' with temper. Through gritted teeth he thanked me for showin' his members what they were up against as they tried to defend their traditional livelihood.

'Down through the centuries,' he continued, 'we have stood firm and fought off invader after invader; from the redcoat to the turncoat we beat them back to the Pale with sword and pike and slane. We'll do the same to the likes of you, Councillor Hickey.'

I left while the goin' was good, ready to string Manus up by the side-locks. When I got to the car I threw the speech at him and he went pale when he realised his mistake.

The worst of all befell me last week. Manus got an urgent phone call to know if I'd open the South Tipperary Annual Poultry Festival at the Langtry Hotel. I agreed and he prepared a wide-rangin' speech dealin' with the importance of poultry in rural life and the place of the humble hen in the history of the state. When I arrived at the hotel I was amazed I didn't see a sign of a hen, an egg or an egg van. I thought I might at least see some sign of the Cock Ryan, a poultry farmer from Cossatrasna who never fails to give me an earful about how the potholed roads of South Tipp are scramblin' his eggs.

To add to my confusion I was greeted by Margaret Hanley Hayes, a woman who wouldn't know a bantam cock from a Rhode Island Red. The said lady is a stickler for time and wanted to get 'proceedings under way immediately.' She ushered me into the drawin' room and was introducin' me as she pushed me up the aisle. 'Ladies and Gentlemen,' she announced, 'put your hands together for our Mayor, Councillor Maurice Hickey who will open our festival with a very, very short speech.'

In response to this instructive introduction I put my prepared speech to one side and spoke off the cuff about my own memories of poultry. I reminisced about a time when hens and chickens and ducks and geese were part of everyday life and suggested that with all the talk of food scares and food scarcity it's time to do away with the gazebo in the garden and replace it with a hen run.

I sat down to a feeble round of applause from a bewildered lookin' audience. The mystery of the Cock Ryan's absence from the event was solved when Ms Hanley Hayes thanked me for my most unique speech to mark the openin' of the Fiftieth South Tipperary Annual *Poetry* Festival. I felt a right turkey as she introduced the next speaker, Seamus Heaney.

BELIEVE IT OR BELIEVE IT NOT

I feckin' hate cats; they give me the creeps. Lately, the Quirkes got a big tiger of a tom-cat with a pair of green eyes that'd burn holes in you. Every time I see him he gets a runnin' riser up in the tailend, but the hoor keeps comin' back to stare at me with his evil eyes. He's the worst article I've come across, he haunts the place.

Talkin about hauntin' and ghosts, the lads in the pub are full of that kind of stuff recently. I was tellin' them how much I'm enjoyin' the fine weather and my stroll down to the pub late in the evenin' and the stroll home afterwards; 'tis lovely.

Cantwell asked me was I frightened passin' Carthy's gate, 'On the contrary,' I answered, 'I often stop there to answer a call of nature on the way home. There's no better place to relieve yourself than through a five bar gate under a summer night sky.'

Cantwell warned me to be careful of what I expose at Carthy's gate or I could find myself deprived of my faculties. He went on to tell me it's the most haunted place in the three parishes.

'You see,' he explained, 'it all goes back to auld Bill Carthy, a kind of a healer who lived in a bohawn inside where the gate is now. Originally from the far side of Shronefodda he had some fallin' out at home and told them he was goin' to England. He got as far as Killdicken and never moved another perch. That all happened in about 1955.'

'When he first arrived,' continued Cantwell, 'he got work jobbin' for farmers. Never a fella for the pub he didn't drink or smoke, however, he'd spend a few hours every day in the church but rarely went to Mass, whether all that was roguery or not no one knows. As time went by he got a reputation as a bit of a healer and when the rumour spread he was the seventh son of the seventh son he began to do a steady trade. It seems many people came to him late at night with sick animals and their own ailments, but while some had great faith in him, others regarded him as a total quack.'

'Of course he came a-foul of the clergy,' whispered Cantwell as if the Pope had the place bugged, 'the PP at that time, one Fr Pius Higgins, decided to close him down and read him from the altar. For ten solid weeks on the trot Bill came to every Mass and stood straight in front of the altar starin' at Fr Higgins for the whole ceremony. Eventually, the local schoolteacher brokered a deal whereby Bill agreed he wouldn't come to the church durin' Mass and the priest promised he wouldn't mention Bill's name from the altar again.'

'Whatever became of him?' asked Cantillon.

'Oh,' says Cantwell, 'The Quirke's had cows at that time and they got some kind of a sickness or other. Auld Quirke came to Bill by night and whatever Bill did the cows ended up with red-water and the entire herd was wiped out. Mrs Quirke was very bitter and gave Bill a taste of the medicine he gave the priest: she stood outside his bothawn starin' in at him for ten days.

Sometime durin' her vigil Bill disappeared and was never seen or heard from again. No one knows what happened to him but they say he haunts his auld bothawn at Carthy's gate to this very day.'

Goin' home that night I decided I'd be brave and stop at the famous gate. As I stood there I thought I saw a pair of eyes starin' at me through the bushes, 'Get lost, ya divil,' I shouted and with that a huge hoor of a cat jumped at me out of the bushes and knocked me on the flat of my back.'

When I got home I hardly slept a wink. The followin' mornin' one of Quirke's young daughters appeared at the door.

'Hello, Maurice,' says she as she peeped in, 'Did you see any sign of Bill?'

'Bill?' Bill? I gulped, 'Bill who?'

'Our new cat,' she answered

I think I fainted.

WELL, 'YES' AND 'NO'

Thanks be to God this blasted Lisbon Treaty is behind us. I steered clear of the whole issue in case I'd further confuse the people. To tell you the truth, I couldn't make head nor tail of it and neither could any other councillor I know. None of them canvassed a vote for the yoke. In fact, one particular council colleague quietly admitted to me that for months he thought the Lisbon Treaty was an ice-cream. Easily known 'twould get the boot when your regular parish pump politico couldn't tell the difference between an EU treaty and somethin' you'd find in an ice box between the Wibbly Wobbly Wonders and the Loop the Loops. Of course I would have understood the lot if I'd had the time to read it but then again, I'm the Mayor.

There was fierce confusion. On the Monday before pollin' day Madge McInerney cornered me in the Post Office and asked me if I was 'for or again this Lisbon Treaty?'

'Madge,' I answered, 'I'm confused myself. There's a bit of me says we should be in there with the rest of them but I also think we should stand back and come at it from a different angle.'

'Well, Maurice,' she continued, 'Don't get me wrong, I'm not a lisbon myself, but if this Treaty lets them girls get married I think 'twould be powerful. What's more, 'tis neither your business nor my business what angle they come at it from, they've the same rights as you or me.'

I was goggle-eyed: Madge McInerney believes in same-sex marriages and thinks the Lisbon Treaty is the answer. What next?

Up to the last week of the campaign the very mention of Lisbon was enough to have a fella thrown out of the pub and barred for life but as pollin' day approached people began to get into a ferocious flap. They gave up watchin' telly or listenin' to the radio because all they got was one blazin' row after another. They didn't bother askin' their local politicians because they couldn't get a straight answer, so they reverted to all manner and method of tryin' to divine how they should vote.

The night before pollin', a crowd of fellas in the pub in Teerawadra gathered around the pool table and divided themselves into teams of 'Yes's' and 'No's'. It was agreed to play for Lisbon; if the 'Yes's' won they'd all vote 'yes' and if the No's won they'd all vote 'no!' A novel way of to decide the future of a continent.

Anyway, Jose Manuel Barroso will be relieved to hear that Europe's destiny didn't hinge on a game of pool in a rural pub in the back arse of the country; a row broke out before the game finished and, like the Treaty itself, the whole thing was abandoned.

Pa Cantillon and the family were equally confused so they decided to consult a woman with close connections to Brussels. Beatrice, their prize Belgian Blue cow was due to calve on pollin' day and they agreed that if she produced a bull calf they'd vote 'yes' and if 'twas a heifer they'd vote 'no.' Beatrice delivered a typical EU fudge when to everyone's surprise she gave birth to twins, a bull and a heifer.

On the evenin' of the votin' I discovered that confusion reigned under my own roof. I went home to collect my pollin' card and found the Mother sittin' at the kitchen table with a 'Yes' and a 'No' leaflet in front of her and she whisperin', 'eenie, meanie miney mo.'

Up to the last minute I myself wasn't sure what I was goin' to do. As I approached the pollin' station I took out a 2 Euro coin and decided twould be heads for 'yes' and tails for 'no.' I tossed it in the air but as it came down the feckin' thing hopped off the back of my hand and rolled into a drain.

I'm not tellin' ye what way I slanted my pen but I hope the Europeans realise what a sophisticated electorate they're dealin' with.

THE LONG GOODBYE

I'm ready for a holiday. In fact I've never been more ready for it in my life. This year of Mayoralty has me worn out. I hand over the chain of office on

30 June and I'll be fairly delighted to see the end of it. However, I'll miss some of the perks of the job. Bein' treated like royalty was great, the extra few quid in allowances has been most welcome, but, on the downside, I'm as big as a house from eatin' sticky buns, sponge cake, tart and vol-au-vents. Still, I'll miss the grub.

I'll miss Manus. He's been with me for most of the year and he's been my constant companion, always on the road with me, always there with a word, a glance, a smart comment or a dirty look whenever I made a bags of things. We had huge rows, but he was great to fight with because he'd never fall out with you.

I'll miss his auld suped up car with the big fin at the back and the go faster stripes down the side. 'Twas a hoor of a thing to get into and a b**"^rd to get out of, especially after a big feed. Anyway I shouldn't be givin' out; Manus was always great, as reliable as an auld clock and as faithful as a sheepdog. In fact his attention to duty and detail drove me mad occasionally; he was a hoor for bein' on time and of course we'd be half way to a function when I'd realise I'd forgotten the feckin' chain of office and we'd have to wheel around and go back.

Many's the time we'd arrive at an openin' or a launch and the committee of the great and the good would be standin' out in the street lookin' up and down to know if there was any sign of the Mayor. When we'd pull up 'twould take me about five minutes to extract myself from the car. Invariably the welcomin' committee would attempt to give me a hand by pullin' me out backwards like a sack of spuds. Tom Gleeson in Honetyne claims he put his back out tryin' to get me out when I arrived late for the openin' of the annual carnival.

Of course Manus would be furious at such a spectacle and as soon as the locals had successfully extracted me from his vehicle he'd speed off in a huff. More than once he sped off with one of my shoes stuck under the passenger seat: it would have come off as I was bein' taken from the vehicle. On one occasion we arrived to open the Rathgubbin dog show and of course we were late. We were halfway there when I realised I had left the back door open and the Mother was away. Manus was like a briar. He did a hand-brake turn and we bombed it back to Killdicken only to find I had locked the door after all. He was like a lunatic altogether at that stage. We arrived outside the hall in Rathgubbin to the sound of yelpin' dogs and the stares of cross lookin' dog handlers.

As I tried to get out of the car the committee rushed to my assistance but when they pulled me out, true to form, one of my shoes stayed behind. Manus hadn't driven a hundred yards when he spotted the shoe, reversed back, fired it out the window and it hit one of May Noonan's prize poodles and sent him howlin' down the street. May was furious and picked up the shoe and fired it after Manus's car but it landed in the middle of the street where 'twas flattened by the Clonmel bus. I fulfilled my duties at the dog show on one shoe.

Anyway, all that is nearly over. Soon there will be no more chain of office, no more Manus, no more big speeches, no more sticky buns and a smaller cheque at the end of the month. I feel a bout of post-traumatic stress comin' on. Amn't I entitled to it?

TAKE THIS CHAIN FROM MY HEART AND SET ME FREE

My last few hours as Mayor were as dramatic as the mayorality itself. That cursed chain of office made one final attempt to strangle me: it might yet succeed if the local Super has his way.

The passin' of the mayorality from me should have been a quiet affair, but the whole thing exploded into an episode worthy of *Hill Street Blues*.

Meself and Manus arrived at County Hall in plenty of time for the handover of power. As we parked he handed me the box with the chain of office and wished me luck sayin' he'd be in the public gallery to see me out. My first port of call was a private meetin' with the County Manager. As we were chattin' he asked me if he could have a look at the chain; the Heritage Officer asked him to check out the stamp on the back of one of the medallions.

I gave him the box, but when he opened it 'twas empty. 'Oh Jaysus,' says I, and I remembered how the Mother took the chain out the night before to polish it and obviously forgot to put it back. What was I goin' to do; she was gone to Waterford for the day. I phoned Manus on his mobile and sent him out to Killdicken for the blasted thing. After fifteen minutes he phoned to say he was at the house but had no key to get in, he asked me if there was a spare key under a pot somewhere. 'No there is not,' I barked. 'Go around to the back door and break the glass panel, there's always a key on the inside of the backdoor.'

A half an hour passed and there was no sign of him. I phoned his mobile every few minutes but there was no answer. An hour and a half went by and as the councillors gathered in the chamber panic set in. I used the Manager's phone to phone Manus's mobile for the umpteenth time and thank God 'twas answered, not by Manus but by a smart-mouthed guard in the barrack in Clonmel. He told me the phone belonged to a youngfella in custody who was caught breakin' and enterin' Councillor Maurice Hickey's house in Killdicken.

Normally I've great time for the forces of law and order but I'm afraid this time I blew up, 'This is Councillor Maurice Hickey here,' I shouted into the phone, 'and the man you have in custody happens to be my driver who was sent to my house with instructions to break and enter to get my chain of office so that I can hand it over to the new Mayor when she's elected this afternoon. I'll tell you wan thing,' I continued, 'when Moll Gleeson becomes mayor and discovers that, thanks to the Clonmel guards, she has no chain of office to drape over her ample bosoms, you and every other guard in that station will find yerselves mindin' sheep in Connemara. Now, be a good guard and put that youngfella into a squad car and get him back to Killdicken. I don't care if ye have to call in the army to blast yer way into my feckin' house; just be here at County Hall in ten minutes with the chain of office and my driver, in that order.'

I slammed down the phone and turned to the County Manager who was shocked at my attack on the forces of the law. 'By God, Councillor Hickey,' he remarked, 'that's one guard who hopes you'll never be Minister for Justice.'

'Listen,' says I, 'you can never find one of them fellas when you need one but they're sure to turn up when they're not wanted.' With that the Manager's phone rang, he looked very serious and hardly said a word as he listened intently to a very agitated caller. When the call ended he turned to me, 'That was the Superintendent,' he said, 'lodgin' an official complaint about an abusive phone call from an elected representative to one of his officers stationed in the barrack in Clonmel.'

Just then a squad car with the siren wailin' screeched to a halt outside County Hall. The back door flew open and Manus was fired out clutchin' the chain of office before the squad car roared off in the direction of Clonmel. 'Come on,' says I to the Manager, 'we have the chain back, Moll Gleeson can smooth things out with the Super.'

BRIGHT SPELLS AND SCATTERED SHOWERS

I'm finished with the mayorality and don't miss it one bit. In fact I feel as relieved as an accused man who's been acquitted after a long trial. Manus is gone back to Kilkenny and we were all sorry to see him go, but he had no more business here now that my mayorality is over; the allowances of an ordinary councillor aren't enough to keep a driver. He's comin' back next week for a bit of a party to celebrate the end of my term of office and then he's off to America for two months.

Anyway, it's great to able to get back to talkin' about important things like the weather. And there's a lot to talk about: it's been ferocious these past few weeks; the same story as last year, a great start to the summer and then it went down the drain in a deluge. If there's one thing this kind of weather brings out it's a plethora of local weather experts. These characters ply their trade in every parish on bar stools, at church gates and in empty slatted sheds where idle silage men look out in desperation at grey skies and flooded boreens.

The worse the weather gets the more people turn on the official forecasters and blame them for it. Every night durin' bad summers poor

Evelyn Cusack is cursed into the pits of hell by farmers with hay down. As she smiles her way through predictions of downpours, flash floods and thundery showers it's a wonder the woman doesn't explode into flames with all the curses that are rained down on her. She'd be better off to give her forecast from under an umbrella in a flooded meadow with the mascara runnin' down her face and she holdin' a half empty bottle of gin in a soppin' brown paper bag.

It is said that in times of prolonged drought, flood or pestilence people turn from the experts and seek comfort in any quack that'll tell them what they want to hear. There is no shortage of such quacks when it comes to predictin' the weather, especially when Evelyn Cusack and the Met Office fail to deliver long periods of 'settled conditions' for June, July and August.

This locality has no shortage of alternatives to Met Eireann. One of the more celebrated forecasters is a woman who keeps geese on soft ground down near Borrisnangoul. She claims that whenever her gander spends more than three days on one leg 'tis a sure sign the weather is goin' to pick up: he knows when the ground is goin' to dry out so he likes to have one dry leg ready to greet it.

Dan Behan in Crookdeedy has a huge reputation for weather forecastin' even though he has failed to save a dry sop of hay in twenty years. He claims to be able to tell the weather from the matin' habits of the mountain goat. 'If the ram is busy early in the season 'tis sure to be a good year,' claims Dan, 'the she goats will want the kids born in a fine year. If the ram is more interested in fightin' than lovin' then its goin' to be a bad year, he's obviously not gettin' enough TLC from the harem so he takes out his frustrations on anythin' that gets in his way.' Dan is wrong nine times out of ten, in fact he knows as much about weather forecastin' as he does about reproduction havin' failed miserably in both departments.

Fishermen always fancy themselves as predictors of the weather but I'm afraid they are as dependable as Dan Behan's ram. In fact if a fisherman around here told me he caught a whale in the Dribble and also told me we were in for a great summer I'd be inclined to believe the whale story first.

When it comes to the weather we should forget about predictions and just put up with it.

Not uNdEr My Roof!

A lively and lengthy conversation took place recently in my local pub on foot of a letter published in the problem page of the local paper. The letter in question came from a woman who was in fierce bother about the sleepin' arrangements she'd be expected to provide for her American niece and the niece's boyfriend who were arrivin' for a visit. The Aunt was worried sick that the visitin' lovebirds would expect to share not only a bedroom, but also a bed. If she agreed to this how would she explain it to her teenage children? She'd be accused of double standards: one law for the Yanks and another for her own. The next thing her nestlings would want to bring their lovers home for a 'sleep-over'.

This is a common problem. Young people nowadays forget that in their parents' youth, gettin' into the scratcher with a member of the opposite sex without a full licence was the most serious of all mortal sins. Even a provisional licence in the form of an engagement ring didn't provide sufficient cover, and indeed it made matters worse if the offendin' couple were accompanied by someone with a full licence; the ancient Romans were hoors for that sort of carry on.

What to do when hostin' young couples who are accustomed to sharin' a scratcher without a licence is a dilemma faced by many a household. Cantwell told us that his sister in Tipp town has three or four youngsters in college and until she took action her heart was broken dealin' with this dilemma. She had a steady stream of 'Jasons and Sandras', friends of her own crew, arrivin' for weekends expectin' to share the one scratcher. The sister put her foot down and told all visitors that the very thought of premarital sex was not permitted under her roof, in her garden, on her garden furniture, in the bushes or in any of the out offices. However, she discovered that durin' the night, the drives and juices of her young guests inevitably got the better of them resultin' in all kinds of shufflin' in and out through creakin' doors.

She decided the only way to fortify the moral fibre of her house when mixed company came to visit was for her to sleep in the corridor. Part of the welcomin' ceremony for any visitin' 'Jason and Sandra' took the form of a lecture on what was and was not permitted in her house. She warned them that she herself would be sleepin' in a sleepin' bag in the corridor and if they wanted to circumvent her rules they would first have to circumvent her. 'Look at me,' she'd say, 'I'm the biggest feckin' contraceptive device in Tipperary.' Accordin' to Cantwell, she's a woman of substantial frame who carries a fair bit of condition; as they might say in Coolmore, she wouldn't go well on soft ground.

Continuin' on the same subject Pa Quirke told us of incident that took place in his own house some years previously. His daughter who was studyin' in Germany phoned to say that two friends of hers would be stoppin' by for a visit while on a trip to Ireland. Quirke's missus was in a flap as to what sort of sleepin' arrangements she'd put in place for them as she had only one spare room, Grandad's old bedroom, God rest him. It was furnished with a double bed. When the pair arrived she was mightily relieved to discover that Hans and Achim were two fine strappin' lads in their twenties travellin' by motor bike and happy to pitch their two-man tent in a field. However, Mrs Quirke would have none of it and insisted they avail of the comforts of Grandad's bedroom, God rest him.

They stayed three or four days with Mrs Quirke waitin' on them hand and foot, feedin' them like thrushes, washin' their clothes and tellin' them what sights to see durin' their sojourn. On the mornin' they were leavin' they thanked her profusely for her hospitality sayin' they couldn't have picked a better place on the planet to spend their honeymoon. Poor Grandad, God rest him.

ON YER BIKE

Recently, our local eco-councillor, Percy Pipplemoth Davis organised a Parish Bike Festival to encourage people to get back on two wheels and away from the car. As an opposin' councillor I couldn't be seen to ignore the event so I took part in everything. My backside will never forgive me.

On Saturday afternoon there was a cycle to the Borrisnangoul Hall for evenin' tay and a 'Ballroom of Romance Dance'. Not to be outdone by Pipplemoth I decided to cycle out to the event so I called my high Nellie out of her retirement home in the rafters of the shed and Cantillon gave me a hand to get her ready for road.

I was accompanied to Borrisnangoul by Superquinn who had rented a ten speed mountain bike for the weekend. As we headed for the Ballroom of Romance I was killed tryin' to keep up with her; I hadn't cycled in years and had forgotten how many hills had to be climbed before a fella got from Killdicken to Borrisnangoul. She was pedallin' like a youngster while I was gruntin' like a small cow tryin' to calve an elephant. By the time I got to the hall I badly needed a massage and a cold shower.

Despite the stiff muscles and sweaty clothes I jived and waltzed the night away as Pee Hogan and the Blue Boys pumped out all the hits of the sixties. 'Twas like goin' back in time with cloakroom tickets, spot prizes and a mineral bar run by the ICA servin' lemonade, fizzy orange, tay and spotted dog. At times the whole affair was too authentic for comfort; while dancin' with May Ronan she told me the pong of BO and strong porter from me reminded her of the dances years ago, I got kinda nervous when she said the smell made her as randy as a mountain goat. 'Twas definitely time to run when she told me there was a free seat beside her on the bus if I didn't feel like cyclin' back to Killdicken.

On the way home Superquinn challenged me to a race, but I lost her at Morrisson's bend when my high Nellie went into a speed wobble and I ended up in a clump of briars. By the time I got to my house I could hardly walk but I didn't care; I was transported back to my youth and it didn't matter how sick and sore I was as long as I had a good night out.

On Sunday mornin' I could hardly move, I had pains in the quarest of places and gettin' through Mass was like climbin' Calvary. By the afternoon I had thawed out a bit and in a fit of over-confidence I decided to participate in a treasure-hunt that involved cyclin' out to Honetyne, up Crookdeedy and on to Shronefodda for a 'Grand Pedal Cycle Ball'. I wanted the people to see that I was as good as Pipplemoth any day.

I teamed up with Superquinn and Pa Quirke, two of the most competitive people on the planet who decided after ten minutes that I was a no-hoper. They took off leavin' me groanin' in agony as the saddle of my high Nellie treated my tailend to a first-hand experience of what it must be like to slide naked down a sheet of super-grade sandpaper. By the time I got to the first refreshment station I had to give up, the Civil Defence wanted to call Doc Doherty to surgically remove the bike from my person.

As I write I'm sittin' in an armchair on a mountain of pillows and cursin' Pipplemoth and his notions into the pits of hell. My high Nellie is bound for the recyclin' centre and if the oil ever runs out you won't find me in the saddle: I'll invest in a good pair of shoes.

WASTE NOT...

Before the arrival of the throw-away society in Ireland people bought little and threw away less. They believed not only in recyclin', but in re-incarnation: anythin' that could have a second life would find itself reborn for a completely different purpose. For instance, when I was a youngfella people bought flour in big four-stone bags produced by Ranks of Limerick or Odlums. When these bags finished life as flour carriers they were washed, scrubbed and sewn together to make bed-sheets. Many a decent hardworkin' man and woman rested their weary bones between sheets provided by Ranks, Odlums and the handy needlework of the woman of the house.

Another item that regularly found itself put to other uses was the fertiliser bag. Nowadays these are sent for recyclin' but years ago they performed many a useful function after their lives as fertiliser carriers ended. They were particularly popular in providin' makeshift cabs for tractors at a time when very few tractors were fitted with such luxurious extras. Owners of the famous Ferguson 35 had every reason to be grateful to Gouldings and Net Nitrate for protectin' them from the elements. In fact, the cab made from fertiliser bags had distinct advantages over its more permanent cousin. If the weather got too hot and the bit of air-conditionin' was called for all you had to do was roll up the bag or drive your fist through it and you got all the air you wanted. Another advantage of this cab was its usefulness in huntin' cattle; the farmer could stay in the tractor and shout instructions at his dog or the cattle, confident he would be heard. However, the man trapped in the permanent cab could be shoutin' his head off and neither the livestock nor Shep would hear a word. As a result, he would be forced to abandon his fancy vehicle and continue his task on shank's mare.

Another popular re-incarnation of the fertiliser bag saw it appear as a windscreen on Honda 50 motor bikes. These motorbikes were as popular as the Ferguson 35 and came fitted with a perspex windscreen. Unfortunately the screens cracked easily and when they did a fertiliser bag would be stuck on to what remained of the original. However, the manure bag wasn't as clear as the perspex and many a 'Hondista' found himself in ditch and dyke as a result of poor visibility.

Be that as it may, Tom Lanigan of Teerawadra is a man who has reason to be grateful to this form of traditional recyclin'. He was a true blue Honda man and like every other rural Hondista the fertiliser bag was his first line of defence from the elements. On his way home from the Drippin' Tap one summer evenin' his judgement wasn't what it should be, a fact complicated by a fertiliser bag windscreen that had endured a hard winter frontin' his machine. As he approached Hogan's bend a combination of these factors along with some freshly deposited cow-shite saw him lose control of his vehicle and career through Mag Hogan's gate. As he neared the haybarn the bike hit a pot-hole and parted company with Tom who became airborne but luckily landed softly and harmlessly in the reek of hay. The bike wasn't as fortunate; it proceeded to slide into the innards of an abandoned Morris Minor that was home to Mag's hens. Of course its sudden arrival created mayhem and Mag, thinkin' a fox was puttin' paid to her fowl rushed to the Morris Minor and emptied the two barrels of her shotgun into the splutterin' Honda. That was the last time the bike needed a windscreen.

But the story doesn't end there. Tom compensated Mag for the loss of two hens and a cock by givin' her the remnants of the bike. The engine became a pump for a power washer and the wheels ended up under Mag's donkey cart, a cart that carried her to the church six months later where she, who had been a widow, married Tom, a widower. The two spent many happy days farmin' her few acres and many a pleasant night of entanglement between her flour bag sheets. That's what I call recyclin'.

WE'RE ALL GOIN' ON A ...

The last council meetin' before the holidays was everythin' you'd expect from the silly season. For a long time now Moll Gleeson, our new Mayor, has been pushin' the notion of twinnin' our council area with some place in Tuscany. It's no coincidence that Moll's sister has a holiday home in the same region and as sure as night follows day she will organise things so that she can combine official visits to our Italian twins with private holidays paid for by the council. Moll is as tight as a camel's tail-end in a sandstorm, and while she enjoys the finer things in life she expects everyone else to foot the bill.

The council meetin' on Monday had a number of

important decisions to make, but Moll's mind was on Tuscany. The sunglasses were perched on top of the head and I'd go so far as to say she had the bikini on under the clothes.

Three minutes before proceedin's were due to start Moll was clangin' the bell and callin' the meetin' to order. As she bombed her way through the agenda it was plain to see she was makin' a bee line for item number seven, 'Proposed Tuscany Twinning'. Councillors on all sides of the chamber became hell bent on frustratin' Moll's plans to get agreement on the Tuscany business in time for her holidays.

The first item of the agenda was a review of the housin' lists that had been published the previous week. This had the councillors hoppin' up and down like lame cuckoos demandin' to know why some people were included on the list and others excluded. Moll suggested that we wait for the September meetin' to get a full report from the housin' officer.

'What report do we need?' I demanded, 'Don't we know who got houses and who didn't, the housin' officer is here in the chamber and let him answer for himself. With all due respect to you Madam Mayoress, you're kickin' for touch because you have the buckets and shovels packed and you are half way to the beach while the rest of us are tryin' to do the business we were elected for.'

Moll saw red and banged the gavel on the counter demandin' I withdraw my remarks, I refused and she suspended business. As we resumed after a five minute break her husband arrived in the visitors' gallery in a flowery shirt that would cause the citizens of Hawaii to blush. He looked straight at his Mayoress wife and pointed to his watch; it was obvious that Moll was on her way to the airport the minute the meetin' was over.

She went through torture for the rest of the meetin' as we snailed our way through the agenda. There was a queue of councillors demandin' all kinds of clarification and points of information from the manager and the officials. Her husband looked as if he would burst a blood vessel with frustration. When we eventually got to the item on the Tuscany twinnin' Moll announced she was departin' immediately after the meetin' for a short holiday (three weeks) in that very region and would gladly make some preliminary contacts on the council's behalf and would report back on her return.

I decided the best way to scupper her free holiday scheme was to kill it with kindness. I suggested that since our hardworkin' Mayoress was clearly under severe pressure to get to a plane we should suspend all discussion of twinnin' arrangements until she returned from her well-earned holiday. Peter Treacy seconded my suggestion and despite Moll's repeated offers to go above and beyond the call of duty while in Tuscany the councillors insisted that she take her holiday and that she bring the meetin' to an immediate close.

She was livid; her little scheme was demolished by her fellow councillors who smiled in her face as they cut the bottom from under her handbag. There will be no high livin' in Tuscany unless Moll dusts off the credit card and pays own her way. Oh, the joys of the democratic process.

HOW TO SQUEEZE A SPONGER

That specimen of human being known as the 'mane hoor' is as common as the magpie. You know the creature yourself: the fella who can spend a day at the Listowel Races, the Munster Final and the Ploughin' without ever puttin' a hand in his pockets except to scratch himself.

One who comes to mind immediately is Din Riordan from Honetyne. He is highly schooled in the art of tightness and widely regarded as a classic mane hoor. He was brought up by very frugal parents and got a university education thanks to an aunt who thought she'd make a priest of him. But there was no priest in Din; the man was too concerned with the cost of earthly goods to think of anythin' beyond a price tag.

He got a degree in economics, but never got a job because he was too mane to buy a decent suit of clothes for an interview. When his parents died he inherited the few acres in Honetyne along with a huge fortune that's still sittin' in the bank in Clonmel.

Tight and all as he is, Din developed a taste for porter, good grub and horse racin', but failed to develop the habit of puttin' his hand in his pocket. He has a posh, horsey accent that gives a veneer of respectability to his spongin'. When he goes to the races he'll bum a lift askin' people if they 'would be so awfully kind as to give him a spin'. At the track he'll poke around until picks up a programme for nothin' and when it comes his turn to buy a round he'll get a call of nature to a jacks at the furthest end of the pavillion.

He places the odd bet on long-odds nags usin' coins and coppers that he carries in a sock.

Those of us who know him grew immune to his tightness, but he went a step too far about two years ago when he bummed a lift with Cantwell, Cantillon, Quirke and myself to the Curragh; he broke our hearts, our patience and our pockets. Not as much as a lollipop did he buy all day and yet he ate and drank as much as any of us. We were livid when we found out a few days later that he had won €120 on a no-hoper. Tom Cantwell decided 'twas time to teach Din a lesson.

Cantwell fed him the story that counterfeit notes had been circulatin' at the races the previous week and all winners were asked to bring their tote winnin's to the track to have them checked. Din went pale and admitted to Cantwell that he had won the €120 and produced the notes. Cantwell told him there was nothin' for it but to bring them to the racetrack. As luck would have it we were all goin' the followin' day and he was welcome to join us. Once we got to the Curragh he wanted to check the money immediately, but Cantwell took the €120 and told him he'd have it checked it after we had a bite to eat.

We went straight to the restaurant and ordered a major feed that included starters, soup, steak, cheese-cake and tay, all washed down with pints of porter. Before we finished Cantwell gave us a signal and left to get the money checked. One by one we all followed leavin' Din to pay the piper. We watched from a distance as the waiter arrived with the bill and poor Din went from bright red to ashen grey. Just as things were gettin' hot and heavy between himself and the waiter Cantwell arrived back wavin' the €120 in the air shoutin' 'winner alright, winner alright'. The waiter snatched the money and gave Din back €5 in change.

The poor misfortune took a weakness and asked to be taken to the car where he stayed for the duration of the races. Not a word passed his lips all the way home meanwhile the rest of us waxed lyrical about the grand steaks and the great porter he bought for us. As he got out of the car in Honetyne he turned and declared, 'Gentlemen, I'm afraid I shan't be available to accompany you to the races for the foreseeable future. Good night.' Good night yourself, you mane hoor.

NEVER TURF OUT YOUR POSTERS

Given the time of year that's in it I was hopin' for a few days peace and quiet. I had no big holiday plans except to hang around, drink a few pints and discuss matters of great indifference with anyone who was willin' to listen. Even those basic plans fell apart when, last Tuesday, I came home to find three loads of turf piled like the feckin' Himalayas at the back of the house.

I went straight into the sittin' room where the Mother was watchin' the telly.

'Where did the turf come from?' I demanded to know.

'From the bog,' came the reply.

'A quare place to find turf,' I countered, 'and pray tell, what's it doin' in our backyard?'

'Waitin' for someone with plenty of time and a great need of exercise to move it into the shed,' she answered.

'And who might that someone be?' I asked, 'given that this house is inhabited by only two people: one a woman who is busy runnin' the world and the other a local councillor with the weight of that same world on his shoulders?'

'The weight being carried by the aforementioned councillor,' she shot back, 'is nothing but fat and lard accumulated from decades spent swallowin' porter and devourin' the contents of every deep fat fryer in south Tipp. Listen, Maurice Hickey,' she continued 'this current break from the uselessness of political life gives you a great opportunity to do somethin' healthy and useful for a change. There's a wheelbarrow and a beet fork in the shed and at cockcrow tomorrow I'll expect to hear the sound of hard work resoundin' around that backyard.'

Desperation set in as I watched my few days of rest and recreation disappear in a haze of sweat, windgall and turf-mould. I made one final assault.

'What possessed you to buy turf?' I demanded, 'we haven't had turf these thirty years because you never stopped givin' out about the dirt of it.'

'Have you not heard of global warmin', the oil crisis and the instability of global energy supplies?' she asked, 'There's no such danger to the supply of turf.'

'It would be in great danger if I had my way,' says I, 'I'd ban it, not for any environmental reason, but because of the misery it brings.' After that exchange I decided 'twas time to shut up and do what I was told.

The followin' mornin', at the ungodly hour of half ten, I opened the back door to survey the task ahead. A quick look at the sky told me I had about an hour before it spilt yet another few million gallons of summer rain on us. With one eye on the loomin' clouds and the other on the Himalayan turf mountain I began the godforsaken task of wheelbarrowin' the stuff into the shed.

As the first drops of the deluge began to spatter on the yard I wondered how I might keep the blasted turf dry while I waited for a dry spell. The solution came to me when I spotted my collection of election posters: I have a ton of these yokes because after every campaign there's an unwritten understandin' that if you find a stray pole poster belongin' to friend or foe you take it down and dispose of it.

These things are waterproof and as the rain poured down on meself and the Mother we employed the smilin' faces of

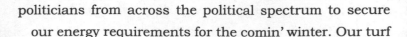

politicians from across the political spectrum to secure our energy requirements for the comin' winter. Our turf was saved thanks to a broad based 'coalition of the willing' that included local luminaries such as Percy Pipplemoth Davis, Moll Gleeson and Peter Treacy. Among a smatterin' of national figures to feature on our turf mound was the famous Bertie Ahern whose posters did a great job; indeed, if he had covered his tracks half as well as he covered our turf he'd still be Taoiseach.

As she watched the rain hoppin' off the posters the Mother declared that she could die happy havin' at last discovered a useful function for politics and politicians. I'll die of exhaustion if I don't get this feckin' turf into the shed soon.

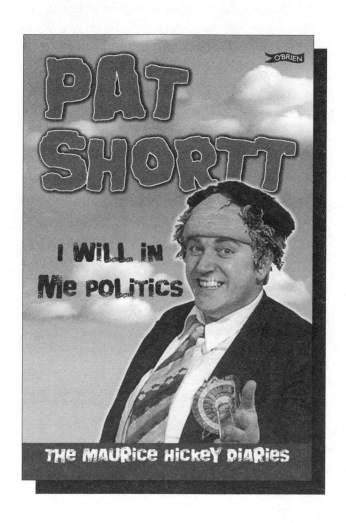

PADDY'S PANDEMONIUM

Now, I'm no fan of the St Patrick's Day parade. However, in an election year, an independent local councillor would be committin' an act of political self-mutilation if he didn't participate in the local festivities.

I became involved in preparations from an early stage this year. I attended all the meetin's and made sure I wasn't landed with any job aside from reviewin' the parade. However, with two days to go, disaster struck. Mick Slattery and the boys on the FÁS scheme were busy puttin' up the scaffoldin' when Tom Walshe, our local publican and chairman of the community council, got a letter from County Hall tellin' him we had no plannin' permission for the reviewin' stand.

There was pandemonium. An emergency meetin' of the community council was called and we racked our brains to find a way round our dilemma. A brilliant solution came from the bould Breda Quinn, or 'Superquinn'. She suggested that we have a mobile reviewin' stand. 'If we put it on a trailer and have it towed up one side of the street while the parade is comin' down the other, they can't say a word to us,' declared a triumphant Breda. Everyone was delighted with the suggestion. Pa Cantillon said that the FÁS lads could build the stand on his silage trailer and he would tow it with his tractor.

On the day, everythin' started wonderfully. The parade was gatherin' at the Bally end of the village while the dignitaries mounted the trailer at the Honetyne end. At the first screech from Paddy McDonnell's auld bagpipes the parade and the reviewin' stand were to start movin'. It was from that moment things started to go wrong.

Cantillon had been on the beer all night and was asleep at the wheel of the tractor. Moll Gleeson, the local FG councillor, shouted at Pa to wake up and drive on. When she hit the roll-over bar a belt of her umbrella, Pa woke up of a sudden and started to move off at a snail's pace, as instructed. Unfortunately, he was goin' so slow he fell asleep again, and crossed over to the wrong side of the street. Meanwhile the parade, comin' down against him, had no option but cross to the other side.

What a disaster. There we were, on the reviewin' stand, lookin' in Mag Ryan's upstairs bedroom window while the Patrick's Day parade passed behind us. That wouldn't be too bad but Mag was actually in the bedroom, cuttin' her toenails. Little did she know that she had the 'great and the good' of Killdicken reviewin' her progress. When she looked up and saw the line of faces starin' in her top window, she screamed and fainted. The scream woke Pa and the tractor jerked forward, comin' to a complete stop outside Moss Kelly's upper floor. Poor auld Moss had been unwell of late and was perched on the throne in the upstairs loo when the reviewin' stand parked itself outside. Far from bein' perturbed by this very public invasion of his privacy, Moss, not havin' been out for a while, was delighted to see so many neighbours. 'How are ye all? 'Tis a great day for it,' says he, without flinchin'. 'At least 'tis dry,' says Moll Gleeson. 'Which is more than I can say for myself,' says Moss, roarin' with laughter. While we waited for Pa to get the tractor goin', Moss caught up with the news of three parishes. When we eventually got started he wished us all a happy St Patrick's Day and told us how delighted he was to see so many neighbours at one sittin'. At least there was one happy man in Killdicken at the end of Patrick's Day. Never again.

I Will in Me Politics by Pat Shortt ISBN: 978-1-84717-084-2